Amorous Accident:
A Dog's Eye View of Murder

Jean C. Keating

Best Wishes
Jean C. Keating
and
Puff

Astra Publishers
Williamsburg, Virginia

Library of Congress Catalog Card Number: 99-95575
ISBN # 0-9674016-0-7

Brown Eyes, the poem used in this book, copyrighted by and used with the permission of Becky Rauvola-Kemp

Astra logo by Beverly Abbott, For Arts Sake

Web design and hosting by Virginia Networks: rdennis@richmond.net

Copies available from the publisher:
Astra Publications
209 Matoaka Court
Williamsburg, VA 23185
(757) 220-3385
www.astrapublishers.com

ACKNOWLEDGMENTS

Many people deserve credit and thanks for help with this book.

In the beginning, it was a poem by a very special lady named Becky Rauvola-Kemp that fired my imagination and moved me to try a work of fiction. She penned the powerfully moving poem entitled **Brown Eyes** and graciously gave me permission to use it in this book.

Three friends, Dot Bryant, Evan Davies and Barbara McDuffie, have read and reread the manuscript for logic and reasonableness, preventing me [I hope] from staging outdoor meals in rain storms, and leaving dangling clues that go unexplained.

John Atkinson and Rick Bailey of the Chesapeake Bay Writers' Critique Group offered the positive encouragement without which no writer can continue to create. Dave Carr introduced me to the Group and heightened my attention to characters' points of view

Marjorie Nicholson devoted many hours to editing the manuscript. Somewhere along the line, she progressed from editor to friend and supporter.

To them all, I extend my gracious thanks for making this book a reality.

Jean C. Keating

Special thanks to Jean who saw beyond the words and continued the fight.

Becky Rauvola-Kemp

About the Author

The author holds degrees in Physics, Mathematics and Information Systems. As an aeronautical engineer with NASA and later Research Coordinator for Virginia's higher education coordinating board, she has authored more than 50 scientific and data management reports and studies. This is her first work of fiction. Now retired, she lives in Williamsburg, Virginia with 15 Papillons and two cats.

Dedicated

to two dogs

who inspired the novel

Brown Eyes

.....whose gentle, loving soul inspired Becky to take a stand and write the powerful, moving verse that appears in this book as a poem by the same name.......and

Astra's Mischief Maaca
January 9, 1983 - June 9, 1999

.....my shadow and foot-warmer, the role model for the Papillon Sky in this novel. He lived long enough to insure I finished his first story. He will live in my heart through all of my days on earth.

Amorous Accident:

A Dog's Eye View of Murder

Chapter 1

Personnel and equipment engaged in recording and evaluating the homicide scene filled the medical research lab. The buzz of human voices augmented the soft cries of several guinea pigs in a cage against the left wall and whines from two dogs in slightly larger cages on the floor in front of the portly figure directing the operations.

Kevin Andrews, his protruding stomach straining the buttons on his shirt, was glad that the body had been covered. Even to the seasoned lieutenant of detectives, the corpse had been stomach-turning. At fifty-seven, Lt. Andrews thought he had seen everything, but the sight of a tall, elegantly and expensively suited male, secured in some sort of metal rack used for animal experiments was new to him.

Unfortunately, disruptions to his plans by a homicide investigation were anything but new. In deference to his Captain's urgent call a short time earlier, Andrews had quickly altered his plans for a Friday off. His anticipated leisurely morning, as well as his planned three-day visit with his godson, had been hastily canceled because of the murder here at the prestigious Commonwealth Cancer Institute.

Trying to simultaneously redress and explain the necessity for the change of plans to his godson was responsible for an additional aggravation. The white dress shirt he'd hastily chosen from his dresser was uncomfortably snug. No amount of re-tying of his tie would hide the strain placed on the buttons to hold the shirt front closed. It reminded him unpleasantly that he was supposed to be on a new diet to reduce his increasing bulk.

His momentary indulgence in personal problems was quickly arrested. A darkly handsome figure stepped over several scattered boxes on the floor and approached Andrews, notebook in hand.

Andrews relaxed slightly at the sight of the handsome face with its high forehead and full head of near-black hair. If he had to be saddled with a tricky case like this one, he could have asked for no stronger backup than this young sergeant.

Bart Foster's full eyebrows arched perfectly over large, intelligent eyes framed by long, curled lashes. Women found the eyes disarming, sometimes a convenient tool in ticklish homicide investigations. Foster's manner was professional and crisp. He wasted no time with preliminaries now.

"Death seems to have taken place between ten last night and two this morning," Foster relayed. "Doc should be able to tighten the time a bit as soon as he finishes the liver temperature test. The body wasn't discovered until this morning at eight-thirty. The victim's secretary has a key to the lab, usually opens things up when she arrives." He might have been describing a bus schedule for all the emotion he allowed his voice to show.

"Identity of the victim?" Andrews queried.

"Michael Porter, Chief of Research here at the Institute, according to preliminary identification by his secretary, Ms. Piper Morgan."

"The one who discovered the body?" asked Andrews.

"Yes. Ms. Morgan had the presence of mind to call the Institute's administrator, Dr. Harold Ketterholt. Ketterholt says he took one look into this room, then ordered the door locked again until the police could respond," Foster said.

"So any prints on the door would have been obliterated by either Ketterholt or Morgan." Andrews hand reached up to scratch his left ear, a routine with which Foster was very familiar. It indicated Andrews' annoyance at the destruction of possible evidence.

"Well, I guess we can be thankful that someone showed the presence of mind to seal the room and wait for our arrival," Andrews said.

"Ms. Morgan was badly shaken by the discovery of the body. I've instructed her not to talk to anyone until you've had a chance to question her. She's in an office across the hall drinking a cup of tea at the moment," continued Foster. "Dr. Ketterholt has returned to his office, but will be available whenever you need him. He said he would notify the victim's wife personally. I took the liberty of requesting he contact the head of security for the Institute and have him standing by. I also asked that he furnish us with a list of names and addresses of staff occupying offices in this building."

"Efficient, as usual, Foster," acknowledged his superior. "See if any of that crowd in the hall outside may have heard or seen anything unusual. I want to talk with Twill for a bit, then I'd like for you to sit in with me while I question the secretary and the hospital administrator."

With something that sounded like a 'yes, sir', Foster turned to the door of the lab to carry out Andrews' request. The pudgy lieutenant of detectives allowed his light hazel eyes to wander lazily over the littered scene of the murder once more. He slouched rather than stood, and his lethargic look fooled many who met him for the first time.

A bent figure replaced the sheet over the head of the corpse and straightened to reveal a tall stick of a man. His rumpled suit seem to float around the thin body. The walking skeleton's head was as bare of hair as his body was void of flesh. A slight fringe of grey hair partially encircled the head on sides and back, and left the shining bald top sparkling in the overhead ceiling lights of the lab. Behind thick lens in horn-rimmed glasses, small brown eyes turned to focus on the detective lieutenant. At a slight nod from Andrews, Dr. Paul Twill, police surgeon for the City of Richmond, picked his way between police personnel and litter to reach the lieutenant's side.

"Well, this one is a mess," Twill began. "Glad they put you in charge. Someone didn't like this fellow—didn't like him a lot!"

"What can you tell me about the cause of death, possible description of murder weapon, and time?" Andrews prodded.

"Well, we'll have to wait for an autopsy for the official findings, but if you want my best guess ..." Twill's attempt at humor was interrupted by a grumpy response from Andrews.

"Give me what you've got, and in plain English too. Not all this mumbo-jumbo you spout in court," Andrews injected.

"Based on the liver temperature test, he died somewhere between 10:15 pm and 10:35 pm last night. He was rendered unconscious by a blow to the head. Something dull. It left a large bump but didn't break the skin. After the blow, and probably while he was still unconscious, he was trussed up like you saw, arms and legs bound behind him with tape. He was secured in that cubic metal frame over there, his head rigidly held by medal rods and a leather harness. A tube was inserted down his throat and secured by a generous amount of tape. Then some type of acid was poured down his throat."

"Acid? Damn! Any idea what kind?"

"Again, you'll have to wait for the autopsy for that. But something very corrosive," said Twill. "Like I said before, someone didn't like this guy! He regained consciousness early on, possibly lived four or five minutes after the acid was poured down his throat."

"Damn," Andrews repeated, "never heard of this one before. Are you telling me the acid killed him?"

"Well, in one way or another. Shock from the pain, acid spilling onto the internal organs through a hole or holes in the esophagus or stomach..." Twill analyzed.

"Spare me the details," Andrews said emphatically. "Would it have been possible for a woman to have trussed up the victim and secured him in that contraption over there?"

"Well," Twill drawled, taking time to weigh the question before responding. "Yes, if he were unconscious at the time. It would have been difficult for a woman, but possible, I guess. But it's a very brutal way to kill someone. Fairly turns my stomach, and you know there's not much that gets to an old police surgeon. I've seen everything after more than twenty years with the force in this town, but this one gives me chills. I guess I just can't imagine a woman doing this," he reasoned.

"Kipling would disagree," Andrews answered somewhat enigmatically. "More deadly than the male."

Twill's face registered his momentary puzzlement before the meaning of the reference registered. A one-sided smile lightened his thin face.

"Ah, yes! The **Female of the Species**! Still, there has to be a reason for such a brutal method of killing," Twill continued. "Do you think illegal drugs might be involved?"

"We'll dust the area, but it seems unlikely," Andrews responded. "At least, I doubt if drugs would be kept in this guy's personal lab. This being a cancer research and treatment center, certainly there are plenty of drugs around. But I don't see why anyone would be looking for them here. The method of killing certainly rules out an attempt to extract information from the victim."

Both homicide officials gazed at the covered figure. Andrews asked, "You're comfortable with your estimate of the time of death?"

"Yep!" Twill assured him. "You're fortunate there. The temperature control in this room makes it easier to estimate. I'd say death occurred somewhere between 10:15 pm and 10:30 pm, maybe as late as 10:35 pm but that would be stretching it."

Andrews mumbled something that passed for thanks.

"OK. I'll take the body now and get the autopsy process started unless you need me further here," Twill concluded.

5

"Go ahead," said Andrews, already turning his attention to the progress of the team dusting for prints and clues.

"Any idea how much longer you'll be?" Andrews remarks were addressed to a tall, fair-skinned youngster who was busy dusting a nearby lab bench for physical evidence. Long, red hair was pulled back in a pony-tail and light freckles dusted a short, tilted nose. Despite the trim look of a three-piece camel suit, the young officer looked even younger than her twenty-four years.

Andrews remarks startled the young woman, but she recovered promptly and replied, "Probably another hour at least. I've never seen so many prints, hairs, and other stuff at a scene before. I guess it's the animals, but it certainly looks like a lot of people have been in and out of here since the last time this place was given a good cleaning."

"All right. Make it as quick as you can. Then seal this place off until further notice," Andrews instructed.

"What about the lab animals, sir?" The eyes of the young officer looked worried.

The cries of the guinea pigs continued. The two dogs had ceased to whine, but both sat expectantly in front of the doors of their cages, soft liquid eyes following the movements of the officers and Andrews.

"Aha, yes! The probable eye-witnesses!" Andrews walked over to stand in front of the guinea pigs' cage. The black-and-white one was making all the noise, he decided. Now he saw why. The fur was gone from the back of the little animal. Strips of raw, inflamed skin were oozing moisture and causing the tiny creature great pain. Little wonder that he continually cried. The other five guinea pigs seemed uninjured but very fearful.

He crossed to the larger cages on the floor holding the two dogs. The larger one resembled a black Shepherd Andrews had owned as a child. She stared at him with soft, expectant eyes but did not retreat when he approached. The smaller one resembled a shaggy mop, wolf-grey hair matted and dirty, one ear flopped almost over its right eye. The smaller dog plainly expressed anxiety at Andrew's approach. He retreated as far as the back of his cage would allow, but made no outcry.

"Now if you could only talk," Andrews muttered aloud, "what you might be able to tell me." He would not admit that the sight of these animals in cages and obviously destined for experimentation touched him deeply. A tough lieutenant of detectives had to maintain an image, especially in front of members of his team.

"We'll see," said Andrews. "Obviously, the animals have to be cared for, but we can't return them to the institute just yet. Not until we're through with the room. Keep the room secured until I tell you different."

"I'll be in the administrator's office or questioning witnesses," he announced. Anything to get away from the pleading eyes of the two dogs.

The little guinea pig was still crying softly as Andrews left the room.

Chapter 2

A uniformed officer stood across the hall from the door of the crime scene holding back a crowd of curious spectators. White lab coats dominated the dress of the group clustered beyond a yellow taped marker. Several of the crowd tried to catch Andrews' attention. One spectator, white coat covering a perfectly fitting pink, silk shirt, was more aggressive in his attempts to get attention. Long, abundant teeth flashed in a face flushed by frustration.

"See here, officer, you can't mean to interfere with the research efforts at this Institute," the mouthful of teeth argued.

Andrews ignored them all.

In answer to the detective's unspoken question, the uniformed officer nodded toward the far right end of the hallway. There Andrews found Foster talking with an elderly lady in a wheelchair. At Andrews' approach, Foster turned his attention to his superior and smiled.

"Lt. Kevin Andrews, this is Mrs. Elizabeth Weir," Foster said by way of introduction. "She's an out-patient here and comes back frequently to cheer her fellow patients." Foster summarized rapidly. If he were hoping to spare his superior the time-consuming task of hearing the story at a much slower pace from the curious patient, his ploy was only partially successful.

Elizabeth Weir interrupted him. "I'm never around at night. The guards won't let us volunteers in after six. So I can't say what went on here last night. But one of the nurses told me Dr. Porter was killed." Before Andrews could cut her off, she injected her opinion of the victim. "He had the bedside manner of a barracuda, you know. Maybe one of his patients finally got even."

Brown eyes, deep set in a puffy face, confronted Andrews with open and unabashed curiosity. A loosely fitted navy dress covered the large, bloated frame which filled the wheelchair, and accentuated the pallor of the woman's complexion. The honey-brown wig which covered the elderly woman's head betrayed its purpose with a too-straight hair line unbroken by any natural hair and contrasted unnaturally with narrow, greying eyebrows. Despite the ravages of the disease, the stout woman was alert and curious.

Andrews' face relaxed slightly though his mouth could hardly have been described as smiling. "Yes, well, we're on our way to talk with the Institute's administrator."

"Oh, Dr. Ketterholt's office is just behind me," the gregarious woman added, quite unnecessarily, since the door directly behind the three announced in big, black letters, "Administration".

Foster took his superior's hint and excused himself politely. Two levels of secretaries later, the two detectives were seated across the desk from Harold Ketterholt.

The chair in which Andrews found himself was wide enough to accommodate his abundant frame comfortably. Foster perched rather than sat in the twin of the Andrew's chair, his back barely touching the back of it, his pen poised over his ever-present notebook.

Harold Ketterholt, the hospital administrator, faced the two detectives across the polished expanse of his desk. Dark hair, heavily-mixed with grey, was trimmed short to minimize the contrast with the bald crown, and his square face was set in a mask of polite concern. For all his elegant attire and studied composure, Ketterholt was obviously nervous. Beneath a high forehead and full, arched eyebrows, his gray, watchful eyes flitted between Foster's notebook and Andrews' tie.

Even Andrews experienced a few moments of self-consciousness. He shifted the shoe with its off-color shoelace behind his leg and straightened slightly to ease the pull on his snug shirtfront before mentally reminding himself he was in charge here. Then he launched into a brief description of the murder investigation and an outline of the cooperation required of the Institute. Ketterholt listened quietly, nodding his head occasionally.

"We appreciate your informing Dr. Porter's wife," Andrews said at last.

"Mrs. Porter was very broken up by the news, but she said she would be available to talk with you at your convenience this afternoon," Ketterholt responded. "I suggested 1:00 pm to give her time to compose herself, but you may call and change that if the time is not satisfactory for you."

Selecting a sheet of paper from his in-box, he passed it across the desk to Lt. Andrews. "My secretary has noted Dr. Porter's address and telephone number here for you. Also, the names, addresses and phone numbers of all other staff who are officed in this building."

Finally raising his eyes to focus on Andrew's chin, he continued, "Such a shocking thing, Lieutenant, I cannot imagine this happening to a man of Dr. Porter's reputation. Why, we must be dealing with a madman!"

"That's what we're here to find out," Andrews acknowledged automatically. He glanced briefly at the paper Ketterholt handed him before passing it to Foster. "Now if you would begin by telling us what you saw this morning," Andrews coached.

"Very little, Lieutenant." Ketterholt, who seemed more relaxed and in control now, looked Andrews directly in the eyes. "I'd just arrived when Ms. Morgan came rushing into my office, screaming about something. Frankly, I couldn't make out what she was trying to say, but she was gesturing back toward Dr. Porter's office, so I followed her."

He paused and glanced briefly at Foster before returning his attention to Andrews. Confronted by only expectant expressions from both detectives, Ketterholt continued calmly. "There was nothing amiss in Ms.

Morgan's office or in Dr. Porter's so I glanced into the lab. One look was enough to tell me the matter was one for the police. So I ordered the suite closed, had Ms. Morgan wait in my secretary's office while a call was placed to the authorities."

"Did you enter the lab at all?" Andrews injected.

"Oh, no! I could see all I needed to from Porter's office."

"Did anything else strike you about the crime scene?" Andrews prompted.

"What do you mean?" Ketterholt eyes narrowed in puzzlement at the question.

"Did you notice anything out of the ordinary? Something that was the least bit different about the area where the victim was found," Andrews clarified.

"Well, Ms. Morgan's eye makeup was smudged, but she was crying so that wouldn't mean anything. And I slipped on the hall floor, but the cleaning crew had freshly waxed the area the night before, so I don't think that can be what you mean either. I'm afraid I didn't see anything that would help you with the case."

Whatever had caused his agitation earlier, Andrews decided, wasn't the gruesome sight of his colleague's body. A doctor saw too much of death to be bothered overmuch by it, the detective decided.

Switching to another area of questioning, Andrews continued. "Were you acquainted with Dr. Porter personally as well as professionally?"

"We infrequently saw each other at social functions," Ketterholt said, "but I rarely socialize since my wife died last year."

Despite the direct reply to Andrews' question, Ketterholt seemed slightly ill at ease again, unable to decide what to do with a pair of grey framed glasses, first putting them on and then taking them off again. Andrews' eyes were half closed, deceptively lethargic looking. But the detective quickly noted the tightening of tiny muscles around the eyes and mouth of the Institute's administrator and wondered at the cause.

"Do you know of any reason why someone would want to kill Dr. Porter?" Andrews asked.

"Heavens, no!" Ketterholt responded sharply.

"To your knowledge, could he have owed a lot of money to someone, or been involved in a messy malpractice case?" Andrews continued.

"Hardly," Ketterholt responded. "I'm certain I would have been told of any malpractice problems, and there were none. As to money, his only financial troubles were that he brought in more money that he could possibly spend. His research and private practice in addition to his efforts here at the Institute brought in a tremendous income."

"And you've never heard of anyone who might wish the victim ill?"

"Certainly not. Porter was highly regarded both as a teaching surgeon and as a researcher," Ketterholt said.

"To your knowledge, has he had any arguments or disagreements with any of his colleagues lately, or with members of the staff?" Andrews questions were delivered in a slow easy drawl, his ample figure slouched and loose in the chair.

"The physicians and staff of this institute are dedicated to the saving of lives, Lieutenant Andrews. Whatever disagreements they might have, they would hardly resort to or be capable of such a brutal murder," Ketterholt asserted.

The administrator's mouth hardened with indignation. His earlier anxiety appeared to have been forgotten in his exasperation at the implication of Andrews' question.

"Someone was! Someone who must have hated Porter a great deal judging by the method of killing," Andrews reminded him.

The brutal truth of Andrews' remarks seemed to quell Ketterholt's indignation. "Well, one member of our staff has frequently complained that Porter was copying his own research and stealing—so to speak—his ideas for Porter's personal research projects. I don't think there was much to it, much basis for his ill feelings, I mean."

"Which staff member was this?" Andrews asked.

"Walter Raines, Dr. Walter Raines. Porter secured far more research grants than Raines. Better writer of grant proposals, for one thing," Ketterholt explained. "For some reason Raines seemed to blame Porter for his, Raines, lack of success. I don't know why he felt Porter had anything to do with his own unsuccessful attempts at securing grants."

"To your knowledge, did this Dr. Raines ever threaten the victim?" Foster injected.

Ketterholt turned to look directly at Foster. He did not answer the sergeant's question immediately, and neither detective made any attempt to rush him.

"I don't know that he did. But something happened about two months ago," Ketterholt conceded. "Porter was very upset about something he got in the mail. Dr. Porter could be very secretive at times, and he seemed unwilling to tell me exactly what it was. He just said that certain people were jealous of his success and he was afraid they'd try to delay his completion of a drug test, which he had to finish by this coming week. In fact he was supposed to present a brief summary of the results to the special peer review committee that was due to visit this weekend. I suppose we'll have to postpone that visit in view of the investigation," he observed more to himself that the two detectives seated before him. Then he continued, "But to get back to Dr. Porter. He indicated his intent to keep his office and research lab locked at night until the project was finished."

"Would the office and lab normally be left unlocked?" Foster interrupted his note-taking long enough to request a clarification on this point.

"Well, yes. The building itself is secured. Access is limited to an entrance monitored by security personnel. Normally research notes and logs are secured in locked files in each senior staff member's office, but the labs and offices are routinely left open to allow assistants to check on research animals and the cleaning crew access to clean the areas."

Ketterholt paused and looked briefly at each of the detectives before resuming his previous line of conversation.

"I had no problem with his request to secure his office and lab. I was curious about what might be bothering him, but didn't want to pry. He went away without explaining further."

"Was that the end of it?" Andrews sat up a little straighter in his chair, but his light eyes retained their sleepy look.

"I'm not certain," Ketterholt admitted. "He kept his office and lab locked from that point on. That's why the cleaning crew didn't discover the body last night. But I think he'd gotten several other pieces of mail which angered and upset him. I never had any indication they were threatening his life, however. More that they were insulting his work."

"Did you have any reason to think that Dr. Raines may have sent the mail which upset the victim?" Andrews asked.

"I wasn't certain," Ketterholt answered slowly. "Frankly Raines is more a talker than a doer, if you take my meaning. I wouldn't want to imply that Raines would have threatened Porter's life. He might have threatened to expose some portion of his research as untrue, but I wouldn't say it was Raines' style to threaten Porter's life."

Andrews shifted in his chair, adjusting his slouched body to a more comfortable position.

"Did you suspect someone else at the institute might have been harassing Porter then?" Andrews asked.

"The assistant chief of research is a brash, young man whose ideas were frequently different from Porter's. You have to realize that medicine is a high energy field. Plenty of strong opinions and strong wills. Langston— that's Dr. Matthew Langston—repeatedly had words with Porter, especially over the wisdom of some of his research. Langston accused Porter of selling his credentials to industry. Porter retaliated by accusing Langston of being too squeamish to do any meaningful research." Now that Ketterholt had overcome his earlier nervousness, he seemed to enjoy the spotlight as the authority on hospital happenings.

"Do you have any idea what was behind these accusations?" Andrews asked.

"New and improved drugs are tested on animals to determine the levels of toxicity to consumers. Porter did a lot of that. It brought him a tidy profit," Ketterholt responded candidly. "Langston objected to such tests, arguing that animal models were not suitable for predicting effects on humans."

"And you supported Porter in his line of research?" Andrews asked astutely.

"Well, I didn't discourage it, certainly. The school collected overhead on the grants since our facilities were used for the testing. It added additional funds to our budget to use for other things," Ketterholt admitted.

"I'm surprised that Langston was named the assistant chief, holding such differing views as he did to those of the victim," Andrews injected.

"Langston was highly recommended, but his association with this institution hasn't gone smoothly," Ketterholt admitted. "He won't be associated with us much longer. His contract expires in three months and he's going into private practice."

"Was Porter responsible for the termination of Dr. Langston's contract?" Andrews asked, his voice deceptively soft.

"Perhaps not exactly in the way you mean," Ketterholt answered. "I'm not certain Langston would have remained in any case, but he wouldn't remain with Porter here. The two had vastly different ideas on the correct direction of research. It is unfortunate the two of them could not get along, but Porter was the senior member and Langston was determined to end his association with this institute at the end of his present contract."

"Where would we find Dr. Langston and Dr. Raines?" Foster asked.

15

"My secretary will have their numbers," Ketterholt answered immediately. "Their offices are on the floor above. I don't know their schedules. Their secretaries will be able to give you a time when they can be reached in their offices or a location where they can be reached this morning if need be."

"Fine. Foster and I will talk to them later. Now, you said the cleaning crew didn't discover the body last night because the victim kept his office locked. Does that mean that cleaning people were in the building last night?" Andrews asked.

"I wouldn't know. I believe the cleaning crew usually starts around eight, but I don't know if or who would have been in the building then. The crew was supposed to strip the hall floors and re-wax them in anticipation of a special weekend tour. I know the task would have added additional time to the work schedule last night, but I don't know how long. Frank Hogge is head of security. He'd be able to tell you who was in the building at what time and how to locate them," Ketterholt elaborated.

"Wouldn't someone in the cleaning crew have heard the victim's cries if they'd been in the building?"

"Not likely. The labs are soundproof," Ketterholt said.

"There is one thing more," Andrews continued. "Routinely, we would keep the crime site sealed until we're certain all testing for clues to the crime have been completed. However, the lab in which the murder took place contains a number of animals. One seems to be in a great deal of pain and cries constantly. I'd appreciate your suggestions on how we should handle the animals."

"The animals are probably associated with some drug testing project. Dr. Thomas Berkley worked with Porter on such projects," Ketterholt answered. "If you like, I can ask him if the animal is of any further use. If so, a technician can sever the vocal cords. That will stop the noise."

"That wasn't what I meant, Dr. Ketterholt," Andrews said. His eyes were less hooded now—angry. "I was inquiring for directions on how to alleviate the pain of that little animal in the lab, not make it worse."

It was obvious that Dr. Ketterholt didn't like Andrews' challenge. The administrator's attempt at inscrutability was ruined by the grimace of anger which hardened the muscles around his mouth and eyes. It was equally obvious that he wasn't going to push the point now.

"Unless Dr. Berkley sees a need for their continued usefulness in some test, you may do with them as you please," Ketterholt snorted. "But we will expect word from you very soon as to when the animals will be returned to the staff for use with our research efforts."

Andrews switched topics and resumed his diplomatic approach. "When was the last time you saw Porter?"

It took Ketterholt a moment to quell his annoyance at Andrews' implied criticism, but he answered calmly enough. "Around three yesterday afternoon, I believe."

Without being asked, he elaborated, "He seemed perfectly normal at that time. Said he was leaving a little early, having dinner with his wife. He didn't seem worried or apprehensive."

"And you didn't see or hear from him after three yesterday afternoon?"

For some reason the question seemed to cause the balding administrator some discomfort. The lens of the grey framed glasses, which he picked up and put on before answering in the negative, emphasized the worry lines around his eyes.

"I went to bed early last evening. I wasn't feeling well, and wouldn't have heard the phone if he did call."

"Might he have left a message on your answering machine?" Andrews pressed, hoping to determine a possible cause for the nervousness.

"Don't have one. Hate talking to machines," Ketterholt responded.

"But you were home all evening?"

"I went to bed around 7:30 pm with a terrible headache, as I told you earlier, and was asleep the whole time. Of course, you've only my word for it, I'm afraid. My wife died several years ago, and I live alone now."

Well, I guess that's all for now," Andrews said diplomatically. "Thank you for your time this morning. We will endeavor to keep the investigation from intruding any more than necessary on normal operations of the Institute."

"That would be greatly appreciated. Until later, then," Ketterholt said, rising from behind his desk to offer his hand to the two detectives. Andrews reluctantly rose from his comfortable chair and extended his own hand in farewell.

Andrews and Foster exited the office suite of the hospital administrator to find the hallway outside the crime scene somewhat calmer. But the sight of the yellow ribbon across the door to the victim's lab reminded Andrews of the need to do something about the animals within.

"Before we talk to the victim's secretary, I think I'll try to call my godson and his wife," he advised Foster. "Maybe Genna can suggest some course of action that would utilize the fact that the dogs in the victim's lab saw the homicide and the murderer."

Foster nodded but said nothing.

"At least things are calmer in Williamsburg, and Genna and Jonathan can be thinking about how to use the dogs' knowledge while we deal with other witnesses here."

"Oh, that's right," Foster responded. "You'd planned a long weekend with the Colts, hadn't you? Well, leave it to work to get in the way."

"Before this case is finished, I'm going to wish many times over for the quiet and calm of Williamsburg, I'm sure," Andrews admitted.

Chapter 3

Contrary to Andrews' opinion, the atmosphere at Heron's Rest in Williamsburg, the home of Andrews' extended family, was anything but relaxed on this Friday morning. Andrews' godson, Jonathan Colt was, as usual, trying to write, with *trying* being the operative word. His latest science fiction manuscript was going nowhere.

Dogs were, also as usual, occupying the full attention of Jonathan's wife. Genna Kingsley Colt was, in fact, up to her ear lobes, or, at least elbows, in dog problems, but not of the kind being planned for her by Jonathan's godfather.

A third, much smaller inhabitant of Heron's Rest, paced a hallway off the master bedroom and growled periodically. The tiny dog was agitated by the smell of blood coming from the adjoining room.

Large ears held obliquely on the head of the little red-and-white dynamo flicked forward in interest, fanning long fringes. Dark red hair covering the little dog's head and ears were set off sharply by a white nose band and wide white blaze. The deep red color had prompted the choice of Red Sky at Morning as his name. He was called Sky. A half-mask of black against the red made his eyes seem even larger as he stared at the door barring his way into the room beyond. He could only growl and fuss, while his large ears and trailing fringes fanned back and forth emulating the flight of a butterfly, the distinctive characteristic which had given his breed the name of butterfly dog or Papillon. The motion did not help him with getting over the half door which kept him from his mistress.

In the room beyond, an occasional whimper of anxiety and pain came from another Papillon stretched on an old sofa. The attempts of a soft, human voice to offer comfort and encouragement only intensified Sky's jealousy.

A small-boned woman of medium height bent over the canine stretched on the sofa. Grey eyes banded in green and accented by long, black lashes softened only slightly a square face dominated by the stubborn set of a strong jaw.

"You have to push," Genna vocalized. She knew the small dog she attended could not understand the words, but both needed the reassurance of her voice.

The birth was taking too long and Genna knew it. She was grateful that her young bitch was whelping in early afternoon when her vet was only a fifteen-minute trip away. X-rays taken two days earlier had indicated that Champion Lov-E-Lee's Amber Fire, affectionately know as Amber, was carrying a single, large puppy. The puppy's size and breech position contributed to the difficult time Amber was having in whelping him. The young bitch was exhausted and showing signs of giving up the struggle, and the puppy's shoulders and head were still trapped in the birth canal.

"You can do it, Baby," Genna crooned. "You can do it."

It was too much for the frustrated father in the hallway. With all the force of his five-pound body he hit the half-door, dislodged the latch which was only partially closed, and tumbled into the nursery before righting himself some four feet from mistress and mate. Now that the assertive little bundle had achieved his objective, he exhibited uncertainty as to what to do next. His ears fanned the air in agitation and another low growl rumbled in his tiny throat at the unfamiliar smells confronting him.

"Stop it, Sky." Genna snapped sharply. "We've got enough problems in here without your fussing."

Amber's head came up in response to the sudden intrusion and her weak grumble warned Sky not to come any closer. But the exertion produced the final push needed and the puppy's shoulders and head finally slipped free. Amber made no attempt to reach the puppy to stimulate it or lick it clean however. Not a good sign.

Sky seemed rooted to the floor where his energetic entrance had first propelled him. Having reestablished his normal position as Genna's shadow, he seemed unsure of what to do next. The smell of fresh blood on his mistress and the higher-than-normal temperature in the room seemed to enhance his discomfort. A fretful whine ensued mixed with increasingly heavy panting.

Genna's hands were busy with a surprisingly energetic puppy. Sawing through the tough umbilical cord and tying it off, while trying to hold the slippery puppy, were proving more difficult that she'd anticipated even without the intrusion of Sky into the nursery. She rose quickly from the stool which had supported her at Amber's side during the last hour and activated the intercom button with her elbow.

"Jonathan," she spoke into the grill of the intercom, "please come give me a hand.....or two."

She returned to the stool beside Amber's bed on the sofa, confident that help in the form of her own mate would arrive almost immediately. She placed the squirming puppy on a heated washcloth, still pinching the cut end of the umbilical between two of her fingers.

The tall, sandy-haired figure which came at her call paused just inside the door. Like Sky, Jonathan Colt surveyed the scene facing him, a mixture of concern and reluctance plain to read in his face.

"I can't tie off the umbilical and hold this little guy at the same time," Genna directed. "Come hold him for me, please."

The large hands attached to the six-foot-plus frame hesitated for the briefest fraction of a second before doing as requested. Long, but gentle fingers, enclosed six-ounces of fussing puppy while Genna successfully secured a knot on the end of the umbilical and then

21

sealed the end with iodine. Then she handed Jonathan a warm, moist washcloth to clean his hands, while she used another to clean the puppy and insure that nose and mouth were free of mucus.

Despite his long and difficult birth, the little male squirmed vigorously and began to whimper with renewed volume. Genna placed him near a nipple and left him to push his way to food while she cleaned and settled Amber.

Left out of things, Sky danced in place on the floor and chortled at the lack of attention to his own person.

Jonathan reached down and scooped the toy terror up in his arms, and stepped back out of the nursery to give Genna some relief from Sky's fussing. Pulling the bottom part of the half door closed again, he rested his arms with Sky cradled in them on the top of the door. So positioned, the canine could see but not interfere with the nursery events.

The gentle pushing of the puppy seemed to give Amber new energy. She curled her head over him in a protective way and added her tongue to stimulate his progress toward a feeding station and the protective colostrum so vital to his survival.

Genna wiped up her own hands and tossed soiled linens into a laundry basket set beside the sofa for that purpose. Then she sat back quietly on her stool and surveyed dam and pup.

After long minutes of frantic activity, the room was suddenly hushed of sound. In the stillness only the soft mewing of the new life could be heard.

Sky swirled his head between short looks at the tall man who held him and longer looks at his mistress , mate and new son, but remained quiet for once.

Jonathan surveyed the scene and his own mate, a mixture of smug satisfaction and pride showing on his face.

The architect who designed Heron's Rest had created the room as an exercise room, locating it between the master bath and the bonus room over the garage. With its independent heating and cooling systems to accommodate expected increased activity levels, it had become the room of choice for maintaining a higher than normal temperature for the expected birth of Amber's puppy.

A smug, satisfied and silly grin softened Genna's face as she gazed affectionately at the nursery's first occupants. Jonathan smiled at the sight.

The soft cream walls, woodwork and floor were softened by the faded blue of the sofa cover and the soft blue throw rugs on the floor. One wall was covered with framed prints of Papillons, some red and white like Sky, others the darker tri's such as Amber and still other prints of the striking black-and-whites of the breed.

The opposing wall was dominated by a large painting of a younger Genna holding her first Papillon, a beautiful, nearly white dog with brilliant red markings, eyes framed by large ears trailing red and black fringes. The brass plaque at the base of the painting read simply, **Bright Star, Beloved Friend**. Sky had come to Genna as a puppy after the untimely death of Genna's beloved Star. While Genna obviously adored Sky, the misty look in her eyes now, as she momentarily glanced at the large portrait of Star, showed plainly that a piece of her heart belonged, would always belong, with the magnificent canine in the painting.

Jonathan's face softened. Genna noted his attempt to come to her side, swiftly aborted when he glanced down at the tiny dog he curtailed in his arms.

He whispered softly, "I love you."

"Me too," Genna affirmed. Then turning her eyes back to the portrait she'd observed him viewing she said, "and I still love him too."

Both swallowed hard to clear the lumps in their throats. "I've been thinking," Genna began again in a shaky voice, "about a kennel prefix for our new family."

"A what?" Jonathan seemed confused at first, but then continued, "Oh, the beginning part of the name you mean?"

The tall man's eyes focused noticeably on a framed photo of Sky on the side wall. The brass plaque beneath was hard to read, but desperation breeds results. He made out the long title for the fur-ball in his arms: Champion Wing's Red Sky at Morning, CDX.

"Well what's wrong with 'Wing's' or 'Lov-E-Lee's' ? "he asked, coming up with the correct prefixes to Sky's and Amber's names.

"But we didn't breed Sky and Amber," Genna explained patiently. "This little fellow is the beginning of an entirely new kennel, so he has to have a new prefix to indicate he was bred by us."

Jonathan looked totally confused by Genna's conversation.

Genna continued, "What would you think of Astra as a kennel prefix? I don't ever want to forget Star. Astra is French for star, and it would keep his name and memory alive through all the generations of dogs to come."

Sky fidgeted and repositioned himself in the nest made by Jonathan's arms. Jonathan momentarily frowned at the phrase, generations of dogs, but Genna did not notice.

"So what are you thinking of naming the little one then?" Jonathan asked.

"How about Amorous Accident. Astra's Amorous Accident." Genna nodded and continued, more to Amber than the two males in the doorway, "I think that will be great, don't you Amber? And from the lighter coloring on the top of his skull, I'd say he's going to have a light-tan overlay to his dark-red color, so we'll call him Rusty."

The phone began to ring, and Jonathan excused himself to answer it, taking Sky with him.

Genna sat for a time enjoying the pushing and pulling of the tiny head against Amber's underside. Blind and deaf, with eyes and ears sealed shut, the tiny mite worked energetically at nursing. Only when the newly named puppy dropped away from his dam and curled in sleep, did Genna move him to a heated basket, offer food and drink to his reviving dam, and carry Amber downstairs to the yard to stretch and relieve herself.

When dam and mistress returned to the upstairs nursery, Amber rushed to the puppy's basket, all earlier signs of disinterest gone. Genna cleared the soiled bedding from the sofa and placed a softly padded sleeping box on the floor for dam and puppy to use. When she transferred the sleeping puppy from the warmed basket to the fresh sleeping box, Amber climbed in beside her baby and carefully curled around his tiny form.

Jonathan returned, Sky a good ten feet ahead of him. The five-pound dynamo was already leaping to achieve a view over the re-closed half door before Jonathan could catch up with him. Jonathan scooped up the energetic little bundle and returned him to the cradle of his arms before sharing the phone call with Genna.

"That was Uncle Kevin. A doctor at the Cancer Institute was found murdered this morning. Uncle Kevin's boss has canceled his day off and dumped the case in Uncle Kevin's lap. He said to tell you he was sorry about lunch and the weekend, that he'd call when he knew something more definite about his schedule."

"Oh, drats! And I so wanted to show him the addition to our family," Genna said.

Little did she know that this murder case and Andrews' next call would bring even more additions to her little family.

Chapter 4

The office of the victim's secretary was small and cramped, but it afforded Andrews and Foster the privacy they needed for questioning Piper Morgan. They were recharging with a cup of coffee before sending for Ms. Morgan.

"Did Genna have any suggestions about how to make use of the dogs from the crime scene?" Foster asked.

"I didn't call her after all," Andrews responded. "Didn't really know how to phrase a question without seeming silly. Besides, getting Genna involved would probably be a mistake. Given her feelings about animal welfare issues, she'd be more interested in protecting the dogs than in finding the killer."

Foster chuckled softly under his breath. "I thought you'd be worried about her getting her nose into the case and bugging you with questions."

"Well, that too," Andrews admitted.

Andrews twisted his bulk around trying to get comfortable on a small sofa without either popping the shirt buttons that were already straining to contain his overstuffed middle or spilling the strong, black coffee he was holding. Finally he redirected the topic of conversation.

"What did you think of our first witness?"

Foster paused for a second to collect his thoughts. His response, when it came, was succinct and confident.

"A real cold fish, I think. Didn't care about the little animal's pain. Makes one wonder if he'd be that cold

26

about a man's suffering. Didn't like questions about Mrs. Porter, though. It'll be interesting to find out what that was all about, and whether it has any bearing on the homicide. He certainly didn't mind putting the shaft to Raines and Langston. Seemed to enjoy it, in fact."

The senior detective paused to sip his coffee before continuing. "Twill said the victim was killed by having acid poured down his throat, a rather brutal method wouldn't you think?" he asked rhetorically. "Porter was awake and aware for a considerable time, about four or five very long minutes maybe. There were numerous ways to kill Porter without resorting to torture, if ending his life was the only objective. He was knocked unconscious first with a blunt instrument. He was helpless. Then he was trussed up in that metal rack for some reason and acid was forced down his throat."

Gruesome topics never bothered Andrews' stomach—his brain maybe, but not his stomach. He paused in his verbal review of the case to take a few more swallows of his cooling coffee. Foster sat attentively in his color-matched chair sipping on his own mixture of coffee, sugar and cream. From experience both detectives knew it would be a long day with many turns and twists in a trail of words that might lead anywhere but so often led down blind alleys.

"We seem to be dealing with a sadistic killer," Andrews mused. "Killing Porter wasn't sufficient. The killer wanted to see him suffer. What type of individual is so pitiless or depraved that he or she would want to pour acid down the victim's throat?"

Foster nodded in agreement. Both men sat quietly for a few minutes, wrapped in their own thoughts. The only sounds to be heard were soft slurps as the two sipped the last of their coffees.

"Ketterholt wasn't at all concerned that the animal in the lab was suffering," Foster said finally.

"So you noted before," Andrews acknowledged.

Foster reached out and took Andrews' empty cup, thrust it inside his own. He stood, walked over to the waste basket and tossed both empty cups disgustedly into the trash.

"Want me to ask Ms. Morgan to come in now?" he asked flatly.

"Might as well."

Several months ago Foster had worked with Andrews to solve a brutal child murder. Andrews knew the younger man abhorred cruelty in any form. Throughout the entire period of their investigations, Foster's cheeks had been flushed with suppressed anger which he kept otherwise in rigid check. They were flushed now, giving his olive complexion a rosy glow.

"I'll get her," Foster said, as he exited the office.

He returned shortly with a dainty woman in her late twenties. Her short, curly hair was fashionably cut. The light blue tweed suit had cost plenty, Andrews decided, and he didn't doubt, given the quality of the clothing and the careful makeup, that the flashy ring on her hand was real. The red eyes and copious tears didn't seem to fit the fashionably dressed woman. Finding a human corpse had affected her strongly it seemed.

Foster introduced her to his superior as Piper Morgan, the secretary of the victim and the one who had found the body. She took the seat previously vacated by Foster in the black saucer chair. Foster drew the desk chair around to form a small circle among the three of them and Andrews began his questioning with soft consoling words.

With the skill of long experience, the senior detective walked her through finding the body and reporting the problem to Ketterholt. A routine question regarding possible enemies of the victim brought a fresh round of tears. Between sobs the petite secretary praised her former boss as a humanitarian and dedicated doctor, and protested that one would "have to be crazy" to want to harm him.

Under Andrews' soothing handling, the tears gradually dried and the voice answering his questions became steadier and easier to hear. Dropping his normal direct approach, the experienced investigator addressed the issue of the victim's work habits from the angle of office routine.

"Now, Ms. Morgan," Andrews continued in his softest voice, "am I to understand that the normal event each morning would be for a secretary to open the office and lab for the doctor for whom she worked?"

"Well, not exactly. Most of the offices are left open, since the office building is secured by the security desk out front," Piper Morgan responded. She had regained her composure. Except for the red eyes she looked the part of a poised, efficient young professional.

Andrews assured her that he knew about the locked lab and office from Ketterholt's information and the reasons for the situation.

"To your knowledge, who besides yourself or Dr. Porter would have keys to these two offices and Dr. Porter's laboratory?"

"Well the security people and cleaning crews have keys. But they didn't use them—the cleaning crew I mean. Dr. Porter asked them not to. You see, Mic—Dr. Porter—started to get some awful mail about two months ago. Someone was very jealous of his success, you see. They kept sending him awful notes. He was very upset. He said that whoever was doing it wanted to stop his research and he wouldn't allow that. He was a dedicated doctor and a wonderful person, you know." She sat up straighter in her chair. Her eyes shone with a follower's zeal for a prophet.

"He was very brave about the threats," Morgan continued. "Said he had gone to Dr. Ketterholt and arranged to secure the lab from tampering. He wouldn't let anyone but his student assistant and Dr. Berkley—that's his partner on the project—into the lab since that time. He wouldn't let the regular cleaning crew in to clean it, said it could wait till he finished his research project. Why, the only time he'd let anyone in his office to clean it was during the day, and I had to be here to watch them when it was cleaned. It was terrible. Maintenance fussed at the extra effort and time for the cleaning people. But he said he didn't know who to trust, that someone was trying to ruin his work."

Foster's pen was busy on his note pad trying to keep up with the pace of Piper Morgan's comments. Andrews settled back further on the plaid loveseat, partly to give his witness a chance to calm herself and partly to give Foster a chance to catch up with the conversation.

"You're doing fine, Ms. Morgan," Andrews said soothingly. After some thought as to phrasing the question, he finally settled for, "Now who would normally open the mail in this office—you or Dr. Porter?"

"I always opened the mail and stamped it with the date received before putting it on Dr. Porter's desk," was the prompt reply.

"Good. Would you be able to describe the threatening notes he received?"

Andrews' voice was so soft it barely carried to the two people sitting in the small conversational circle with him. The question caused Piper Morgan to sit up straighter in her chair and her chin quivered as though she might be going into another fit of tears, but she collected herself under the soft, soothing voice of the senior detective.

"I know this is asking a lot of you, Ms. Morgan," Andrews continued, "but it would help immensely if we could learn more about these notes and determine who was sending them."

"Oh, I do hope you can. Such an awful person. And the notes upset Dr. Porter and disturbed his work," the young woman gushed.

Foster sat poised on the edge of his chair. Andrews reclined further into the back of the couch. Both detectives waited quietly for their witness to continue.

"Well," Morgan said finally, "about two months ago, Dr. Porter got a letter complaining about excessive costs and unsuccessful treatments from some child's parent. It was long and rambling, and I didn't read it all. I remember the look of the letter more than its contents. It wasn't signed, and there was no address or name on the envelope. That was most unusual and I commented on it when I took the mail into Dr. Porter. Oh....and it was handwritten. That was unusual, too. Most people send typed or computer-generated letters. Anyway it was hard to read and long, so I just took it in to Dr. Porter and left it on his desk."

Piper Morgan stopped for breath, leaned back in her chair and looked first at Andrews and then at Foster. Apparently deciding that she needed encouragement, Andrews asked, "What happened to the letter? Do you remember where you filed it?"

"Well, no. Later in the day I asked Dr. Porter if he wanted me to file the letter and he said, 'no'. He said something about 'ignorant laymen blaming everyone but themselves for their troubles' and something else that I didn't catch. When I asked him what he meant he said, 'never mind' and 'forget it'. But he didn't forget it. In fact, he seemed very upset by the letter. A few days later, he went to Ketterholt and started locking the lab at night. He had me put a sign on the door that the cleaning crew was not to enter."

"Did you save the envelope?" Andrews asked.

"No. I throw those away when I open the mail unless they contain an address that is not on the letterhead," Morgan answered promptly. "But the envelope containing the rambling, handwritten letter didn't have a return address." After a few minutes thought, she added, "But I remember that the post mark was local. Does that help?"

"No matter," Andrews said. "What about the other letters?"

"What other letters?" the young woman asked. The brown eyes held only surprise at the question.

Ketterholt had mentioned multiple incidences of hate mail, but Andrews wanted an independent confirmation. He kept his voice low and gentle.

"I thought you said earlier that someone sent him 'awful notes'. I thought you meant more than one."

"Oh. I'm sorry.....I wasn't exactly accurate, you see. The other curious pieces of mail weren't letters. They weren't notes either. They were, well, just drawings, pictures," she dithered. Without prodding she continued, "Strange pictures. Just lines and a circle. There were four of the drawings -- no five. And something else about them really bothered Dr. Porter. They came in interdepartmental mail folders and not through the regular mail. That's why Dr. Porter said he didn't know whom to trust."

"Lines and a circle?" Andrews face looked frozen, as he fought to keep the frustration out of his voice. "What was there about lines and circles on a page or pages to make Dr. Porter regard them as threatening to him or his work? Did he think they were a coded message?"

"I don't know. Well....I'm sure he had his reasons....but they were just drawings to me."

"No words or symbols? Just lines and a circle? Nothing else?"

"Yes. Or do I mean, no! The circle was colored brown. But nothing else," Morgan said, somewhat confused by trying to answer three questions with one word.

Andrews paused to digest what the young woman had just told them. Foster took advantage of the pause to ask a question of his own.

"What makes you think the victim regarded the pictures as threatening?"

"He said so," Morgan responded.

Andrews and Foster exchanged knowing looks but said no more. Piper Morgan glanced first at Andrews and then at Foster for a cue on how to proceed. Finally Andrews cleared his throat and continued, "That seems to cover the hate mail issue. Now would you please tell us when you last saw Dr. Porter alive."

At first it appeared that this question too might produce another round of tears, but the woman managed to retain her composure. With very little pause she answered, "I left work a little early yesterday. I guess it was around four-fifteen. Dr. Porter was still at his desk answering some correspondence, I think. I stuck my head in the door to tell him I was leaving......" Her voice trailed off at that point but she did not cry.

"Would you know if he had any late appointments or meetings scheduled for last night?" Andrews asked.

"I believe he was going out to dinner with his wife," she responded flatly.

"Did he mention anything else about his plans last evening?" Andrews pressed further for some indication of the victim's plans for the night of the murder, while his mental processes tried to assess the change in tone at the mention of the wife.

"No. Just that he'd be leaving shortly."

"Did he express any intent to return here after dinner or to meet anyone besides his wife?" Andrews continued.

"No, he didn't mention anything else about his plans for the evening," Morgan said emphatically.

"Just for our records, would you tell us where you were last night ," Andrews asked.

The question appeared to cause no undue strain on the diminutive woman, and she responded instantly. "My next door neighbor came over last night and we watched a video and ate a light snack. She left around 9:00 pm. Then I went to bed."

"You live alone, then?"

"Yes. I guess that means I don't have an alibi, doesn't it?"

Andrews smiled indulgently but did not answer except to thank her for her time.

"Please let me know if I can do anything to help," Morgan concluded. "I do hope you find the person quickly who did this. Such a terrible thing, Lieutenant. Dr. Porter was such a wonderful person. If only you could have known him! So brilliant and yet so modest."

Chapter 5

The two detectives separated after their interview with the victim's secretary. Foster went to question Frank Hogge, the head of security for the medical school. Andrews returned alone to the victim's lab. Most of the investigative team had finished and left. A uniformed officer was stationed at the door between the victim's office and his secretary's to insure that no unauthorized persons passed the bright yellow ribbon barrier. Within the lab itself only the young pony-tailed officer and a black sergeant remained. Andrews noted that the bolt was secured on the lab door leading out into the hospital corridor.

"Anything new turn up?"

Andrews addressed his questions to the senior of the two, a towering block of a man whose lined face reflected every one of his fifty-three years. A good man to have on your side in a tight spot, as Andrews well knew. Long ago the two of them had gone down an alley together after a suspect in a bank robbery. Andrews owed his life to the quick instincts of this uniformed officer and the push that got him out of the way of a bullet. He was relieved to see this man, Sergeant William (Billy) Brown assigned to help with this investigation, knowing it would be a tricky case even before he'd heard Ms. Morgan's story.

Billy wasn't the most articulate of officers, a fact which had kept him in the uniformed ranks. His speech was generally cryptic; his written communication efforts amounted to unreadable code except to a select few. But

Brown's powers of observation were unsurpassed, his interpersonal gifts with people of all walks of life were unbeatable. It would be a tricky case at best. Now it seemed personal as well as professional jealousies would be present, a situation guaranteed to anger and frustrate an excitable and officious police officer. Brown would handle it all with calm, caution, and courtesy.

Brown crossed the lab now to stand close to Andrews. Formalities were not observed between these two old work horses, but Brown kept his voice low just the same. Andrews noted his friend's careful avoidance of giving the young officer the wrong idea about the proper respect due a detective lieutenant.

"White dude.....about five-ten or eleven and one-eighty. Pale eyes, light hair, mouth full of teeth. Slick dresser ....pink silk shirt, fancy suit." Brown briskly sketched in the subject for Andrews. "Tried to push his way into the lab here. Not happy when I wouldn't let him. Little dog went crazy when he heard the altercation. Howled. Cut his paws trying to dig his way through the back of that metal cage. Black one retreated to the back of his own cage. Yipped like he was being stuck with something."

"Did this dude have a name?" Andrews asked dryly.

He didn't have to ask if the intruder had succeeded in entering the lab with anything more substantive than his angry voice. Brown was still standing and nothing and no one would have been allowed by that police barrier while he was.

"Yeah. Name of Berkley. Doctor Berkley if you please. Real important. Least wise, according to him. Says we have no right to keep him from entering the lab." Brown went on sketching the scene with swift and vivid, verbal strokes.

"Interesting," Andrews observed.

His half-closed eyes traveled slowly over the cages holding the two dogs, both of whom were cowered now in the back of their respective enclosures.

"I suppose the two dogs were definitely in here when the murder took place." Andrews already knew the answer, but a career habit of seeking corrobaration made him ask.

"Hair and debris all over the floor. Not under the cages. Moved 'em to check. Weren't moved for a long time before that. Or cleaned," Brown said emphatically.

The black-and white guinea pig still cried softly. The remainder of the little animals were curled into the smallest possible balls, trying to hide in the back corner of the small cage. The wire mesh floor of their cage did not afford a comfortable or secure rest and the mass of little bodies was constantly reshuffling itself as tiny feet slipped off the wire and into a void.

"Was Berkley concerned with feeding the animals?" Andrews queried.

"Didn't say he was. Said he wanted the research notes. Said we were interfering with an important project," Brown answered in his abridged fashion.

"Research notes, is it? Now that's very interesting!" Andrews' visual scan covered the room and came to rest once more on the two dogs. "The victim would have made a lot of noise before he died. I guess there's not any question that these two would have been unwilling witnesses to Porter's death?"

"Nope," Brown replied promptly. "They'd remember the noise and terror, maybe? Associate that with the person who killed Porter?" Brown's quickness wasn't limited to vivid descriptions of a suspect. "Think maybe the dogs 're telling ya Berkley was here last night when the victim was killed? That's what upset 'em so?"

"Maybe," Andrews agreed. "And maybe not. Maybe I'll just have a talk with Berkley before paying a visit to the victim's wife."

"What do you want done with things here?"

"Call and get someone from Bunko division down here. Have them examine the research notes, letters, all the papers Porter kept in his private office. I want to know why someone was sending him hate mail. And I want to see any letters and drawings and anything else they find that might be threatening."

"Want me to bundle up all of the papers, ship 'em down to headquarters?"

"Not just now. It may not be anything. Have Pepper —if he's the one Fraud Division assigns to the case— use the victim's office. Assign officers to secure the area until Fraud can review the victim's papers."

Andrews stood for a few seconds more, his eyes hooded and staring at nothing in particular. Finally he said, almost to himself, "Strange. Someone wanted to brutalize, punish. The killer couldn't have been seeking to extract information or why render it impossible for the victim to speak by inserting a tube into his mouth and down his throat!"

One of the dogs whined softly. That and the soft cries of the guinea pig reminded Andrews that something had to be done about the live evidence from this murder scene.

"While I'm talking to Berkley, get a Dr. Matthew Langston down here. According to Ketterholt, the hospital administrator, he's the deputy chief of research here at the institute. See what he wants to do about the animals. He's supposedly had words with the victim on various occasions. See how the dogs act when he comes into the lab. Don't let him silence the dogs or carry off anything. And don't let him cut any vocal cords," Andrews instructed, a look of disgust evident on his craggy face. "Otherwise just see what he does."

"Understood," Brown responded with brevity.

"Maybe I'll just call in my own personal expert while I'm about it," Andrews commented more to himself than to Brown. Returning to the victim's office, he used the phone to dial his godson's home.

Genna was stretched on the floor of the nursery, her chin resting on crossed arms elevated by a pillow from the sofa. She had moved little in the last hour, fascinated by the sight of Amber and the tiny mite she'd named Rusty. The puppy was now some four hours old, and was resting from his latest stint of nursing. Jonathan had returned to his writing, taking a reluctant Sky with him to his study. Genna was fascinated by the tiny puppy. Rusty slept soundly except for occasional twitches which jerked his body, nature's way of developing and strengthening muscles while he slept. The ringing of the phone disturbed Amber less than Genna's movement to answer it.

"Oh, Hi, Uncle Kevin. We're so sorry that you couldn't make it down today." She paused to listen and then added, "Of course we understand, just wish you could have had some time off."

Amber had raised her head at the disturbance when Genna moved to retrieve the cordless phone from its base. Now she settled more snugly around her sleeping puppy as Genna stood for a long time listening to Andrews' sketch of the problems facing him with the two dogs in the victim's office.

"Well, of course, it's likely that the dogs will react to the killer. If you need somewhere safe to keep them, you can always bring them down here."

She listened fretfully while Andrews explained something from his end, then continued, "I won't allow them upstairs because Amber's puppy is here. It's a big boy and we've named him Rusty. But there's no danger that the two dogs you have there could bring anything into the house that would hurt the puppy. The nursery is on a secure ventilation system."

There was another long pause before Genna concluded the conversation with an invitation to Andrews to spend the night in Williamsburg. "Come whenever you can this evening. We'll care for the dogs, feed you dinner, and put you up for the night if we can persuade you to stay. And you can meet your new great-godson." She hung up on the sputtering detective as he protested that he was no great-godfather to a dog!

In spite of his protests, there was something approaching a smile on Andrews' face as he returned the phone to its base. He waved at Brown, and went to find his next witness, turning in the direction of the security entrance in search of Berkley's office.

His stomach chose that moment to enter an audible complaint regarding the scarcity of food offerings. He rationalized that it was better to eat something in order to have quiet and comfort during the questioning of the next witness. So he was very disappointed to find the office suite of Dr. Thomas Berkley before locating any vending or drink machines.

Chapter 6

"Surely you can understand the importance of these research efforts to you, your family, and all mankind. Aren't you concerned for the millions who die each year from cancer? From leukemia? Where would diabetics be without the insulin we've developed to combat that disease?"

Thomas Berkley's large, well-nourished body perched on the edge of his plush desk chair, his arms resting on the edge of the desk. Pale eyes of some shifting color between blue and grey flashed his exasperation at his inability—so far at least—in convincing Andrews to release the victim's research notes.

"I've seen no evidence so far that your particular research is involved in any of those areas. Perhaps if you stuck to the subject we would get further," Andrews said.

When Andrews first came to Berkley's office, the victim's partner had flashed a bright smile full of long, substantial teeth. Perhaps sizing up the detective as dull and easily maneuvered, he had ignored the lieutenant's opening questions. Instead, he had expressed horror and dismay at the homicide, respect for his colleague's business sense and expertise in gaining and holding grants, and a determination to continue the work in his memory. Toward that end, he insisted he must gain access to the research notes from the victim's office as soon as possible. Nothing else was as important as continuing the research effort for the good of mankind.

To Berkley's consternation, the ample figure in the overstuffed shirt did not respond pliantly or respectfully to this approach. Scare tactics and attempts to arouse guilt were equally ineffective. Berkley's thin, reddish-brown hair was a bit ruffled now, and his insincere smile had been replaced by a scowl. The scowl showed just as many of the long, bulky teeth.

"No one will be permitted to remove any of the victim's papers until police investigators can examine them for some clue as to who might have killed Dr. Porter," Andrews repeated slowly and steadily. "The sooner we can complete our initial investigation, the sooner you can get the papers you seek. Now, let me repeat my last question. When did you last see the victim alive?"

"Very well, Lieutenant. I went into Michael's office yesterday afternoon around four to talk with him about the final tests for the Rappa project."

"Did everything appear to be normal when you talked to the victim at that time?"

"Well.....yes. We talked about the tests. They were progressing well. He asked me to write up preliminary results today, suggested we try to get together tomorrow morning and review my draft. There's a blue ribbon group due in Monday to review the Institute's funding as a whole, and Michael wanted to present positive progress with this one, if not announce that it was near completion. He said he'd be glad to get this particular project finished and behind him. He'd been bothered by someone.....he didn't know whom......harassing him about the research."

"What was the purpose of this research project?" Andrews injected.

"I'd rather not say. It is confidential."

"I'm not attempting to judge the quality or advisability of your research. I'm attempting to determine a motive for a very brutal murder in order to apprehend the person who committed that crime," Andrews affirmed.

Berkley adjusted the cuff of his lab coat and his pink silk shirt cuff, straightened the name tag on his left pocket, and cleared his throat before answering. "We were testing the toxicity levels of a new topical drug for skin cancer."

"This experimental drug would be manufactured by the Rappa Corporation?" Andrews asked.

"A right to patent is held by Rappa Pharmaceutical. Whether or not the company decides to produce the drug will be decided by the results of our research," Berkley acknowledged.

"Would the victim have been engaged in this research project some two months ago also?" Andrews asked.

"He was involved with many important research efforts," Berkley began, but apparently decided the detective was not going to be denied a direct answer. Finally, he said, "Yes, we've been working on this for about three months."

"I understand that the victim received a letter about two months ago which upset him greatly. So far we've heard only vague references to this letter...that it threatened his research or his life or both. As a result of this letter, the victim began locking his office and laboratory to anyone other than yourself and his assistant. Is that correct?"

"Well, essentially correct, yes. Michael was angered by the letter. I didn't think it actually threatened his life," Berkley said.

"Then he discussed such a letter with you?"

"Yes, he did." The victim's partner straightened in his chair and rested his arms on the corner of his desk once more while he continued his response to Andrews' question. "In fact, he showed it to me the day he received it."

"Can you describe it?" Andrews asked.

"Well.....blue or black pen on cheap white paper, I would say. I never saw an envelope....I think Michael said it came through the U.S. mail, and was mailed locally....had a Richmond cancellation stamp. Other than that, the letter had no address except Michael's and the Institute's. It was handwritten and the handwriting was large, bold and hard to read," Berkley continued carefully.

Either the letter had impressed Berkley far more than he admitted, or he had excellent powers of recall. He continued, "It appeared to have been written by an angry and aggrieved parent who complained about the high cost of treatments given a child. Apparently the child died despite the efforts of this Institute and Dr. Porter."

Andrews nodded. The description augmented and did not disagree with that given by the victim's secretary.

"Why would your partner had regarded such a complaint as a threat to his research?"

"Because the letter said so. I'm not sure I remember exactly how it was said...but something about his greed for money having robbed the child of any will to live, just as his experiments were heartless and designed only to bring him money."

"Any idea what the writer meant by Porter's experiments robbing the child of the will to live?" Andrews injected.

"I've no idea," Berkley responded. "The only thing I can tell you is that the writer said the child had died and that Michael's life and research should be constrained and controlled."

"Did he happen to give you a copy of this letter?" Andrews asked. It was a very long shot, but since Berkley seemed to have a far greater knowledge of the threatening letter's content than heretofore revealed, it was worth inquiring.

"No, but Michael may have kept the original in his personal files."

"Then hopefully we'll find it among his papers," Andrews acknowledged. "Did either of you have any idea who might have written the letter?"

"No," Berkley responded, "and Michael didn't want to say much or stir things up at first. In fact, he would have completely ignored it had he not begun receiving other notes through our internal mail."

43

"Did you see these other notes?" Andrews asked.

"No. Michael never showed any of the other odd bits of mail to me, but he told me about them. They weren't all notes. He said he got a poem with a note that said something like 'How does it feel to learn your callous ways destroyed a child's will to live?' That showed that the sender of the poem and the note was someone within his inner circle, you see."

"A poem? What kind of a poem?" Andrews pressed for more information on this new piece of evidence.

"A poem about an animal used in a drug experiment. And a few days after the note and poem, he started getting drawings. Odd bits of lines really, intersecting half circles about a closed circle, the way Michael explained them. The descriptions he gave of the drawings didn't make a whole lot of sense, but when I tried to ask about them he'd get upset and say to forget it. I think the thing that got to him was that the note and drawings and the poem came through the internal mail. I think that's what began to unnerve Michael. It seemed to point to someone close to him, someone on the staff here at the institute, you see."

"Did he think the sender of the threatening letter and the sender of the note and drawings were the same individual?" Andrews asked.

"I don't know. I think, though, that he did. He became very interested in signatures by staff members on other internal correspondence, attempting to determine similarities between staff's signatures and the writing on the threatening letter."

"Were the second note and poem in the same handwriting of the original letter?"

"I don't know. I don't recall Dr. Porter ever saying anything about that. And he never showed me a copy of the later mail," Berkley said thoughtfully.

"But you think he did not request help from the administration or from security about this hate mail?" Andrews asked.

"No, at least not directly. He went to Ketterholt...he's the hospital administrator...and arranged to keep his lab and office locked until we could complete this research project. He notified maintenance and security that he was securing the lab, but just to inform them to keep out, not to seek help with identifying the writer."

"Do you know of anyone who would have wanted to kill your partner?" Andrews asked, a hint of embarrassment in his voice. His stomach was complaining more audibly now. The cup of black coffee sent down an hour or so earlier was calling for company.

Berkley appeared oblivious of Andrews' digestive problems. He shuddered visibly at the question. Andrews had briefly described the killing at the beginning of their conversation, saying that the victim had been secured in a metal rack and some corrosive material poured down his throat.

"God! Not like that!"

Andrews waited quietly while he let Berkley think about the crime and decide what he wanted to say. Finally, the victim's partner continued, "What I mean, Lieutenant, is that Dr. Porter was the type of individual who made a lot of enemies. But not the kind of enemies who'd want to do such a terrible thing."

"Why don't you tell me what type of enemies you do mean," Andrews injected skillfully.

Berkley brought his hands together and rested his chin on his joined hands. Making eye contact with the slouched figure in the chair opposite him he continued, "Michael was the first doctor in his family. Making it big was very important to him. He was a tireless worker, and inclined to be impatient with help and colleagues alike. Professionally, he was respected by most but not liked. He married a lovely bit of fluff who spent money as fast as he could make it. I had the feeling during the last few months that there might have been trouble between him and Danielle—that's his wife—but I can't be certain."

"Do you know of any person or persons that might have wished him dead?" Andrews repeated.

Berkley's scowl lines shifted slightly. An almost-smile briefly flickered and was as quickly suppressed. He broke eye contact with his questioner and reached for a water pitcher. He busied himself with filling two water glasses and offering one to Andrews before replying to the question.

Finally, as though reluctant to respond, he continued, "Ordinarily I wouldn't discuss internal problems with an outsider, but since this is a murder investigation, I guess I really have no choice."

Andrews sat patiently and in silence. He had wondered at the sudden shift in tactics by this man earlier, suspicious when Berkley became open and direct in his answers after trying to circumvent questioning at the beginning of their conversation. Now, finally, he might learn what it was Berkley had wanted to plant in his mind. He wasn't going to give Berkley an inch, however. Let him feel guilt if such an emotion was possible for him. Andrews somehow doubted that it was. So he just waited.

The victim's partner took a final sip of water before replacing the glass on the desk and making eye contact with the detective lieutenant again. No reassuring words of support for the necessity of his information was provided by Andrews, and Berkley finally proceeded in his most confiding tone.

"The assistant chief of research is a brash, young surgeon named Langston, Dr. Matthew Langston. His appointment was a big mistake, and neither the staff here at the institute nor Langston has been happy. He and Dr. Porter disagreed about many things, but Langston was especially vocal about the research Dr. Porter and I have been doing in recent months." Berkley paused to see what effect his words would have on the fleshy figure across from him.

Andrews' determination to let Berkley stew was weakened by the growing insistence of his stomach that lunch time was long past. Finally deciding that satisfying his personal prejudices was less important than satisfying his stomach, the slouched figure yielded to the necessity of quickening the pace of Berkley's tale.

"Did you ever hear Dr. Langston threaten the victim?"

46

The long teeth flashed briefly as Berkley's mouth reacted in pleasure at Andrews' interest. "Yes, I'm afraid I did. Not that I'm suggesting he would have murdered Dr. Porter, you realize."

Berkley paused, but the lax figure facing him just gazed back and said nothing. Perhaps realizing that no further encouragement would be given, Berkley rushed on with the information he'd intended to surprise Andrews with from the start of their conversation.

"Anyway, about six weeks ago, Langston rushed into Dr. Porter's lab to argue with him about some assistant's problem and interrupted Dr. Porter and me in the middle of an experiment. We were .....well, speculating on the response of a test subject to a particular strength of an experimental drug, discussing the physiological changes resulting from its ingestion of the chemical. Langston became enraged, said we were sadistic jerks to be gambling on how long it would take the dog to die. He stormed out of Porter's lab after saying he hoped one day that Porter died slowly and painfully....that when that happened, he would find a reason for laughter. But until that day, he said he could only despair that Porter was as cold and heartless as he found him to be."

Andrews shifted his considerable bulk to a more comfortable position in the chair while he extracted a small notebook from his coat. It was more in the nature of a prop than anything else. His memory was vast and totally dependable. At the end of the day he would be able to accurately and completely document all the conversations, observations and conclusions—if there were any—arising out of his activities. But the act of writing things often lent importance to those points in the eyes of individuals being questioned.

He didn't like Thomas Berkley, Andrews decided. He wouldn't like him even if he weren't hungry.....which he was. But he was a professional, and he couldn't let his personal reactions to a witness interfere with facts relating to a case. He didn't like the manipulative manner in which Berkley had sought to control the conversation earlier. And he disliked the surreptitious attempt to slander the present occupant of a position Berkley probably coveted. But it did not change the fact that what Berkley was relating might be important to the case.

So Andrews controlled his dislike. He indicated he would make a note of the incident and follow up on the information.

"What was the problem with the assistant? The one which prompted Langston to interrupt the victim and you in the victim's lab?"

"Dr. Porter's assistant, Mark McBroon? She—Mark is short for Markley—got upset with Michael, went down the hall crying, and bumped into Langston in the hall. Langston took it upon himself to confront Michael with the charge that he was callous and insensitive." Berkley's hand brushed the air in a sign of dismissal of the worth of the incident.

Andrews was getting more than a little impatient. Berkley's evasiveness did nothing to quell the rising acid levels in his stomach. But he managed to keep his aggravation out of his voice. "What upset Ms. McBroon?"

Berkley looked pained. "Oh, she said we were betting on the dog's reaction. That we were awful. It was just a silly, woman's thing."

"Langston seems to have responded the same way," Andrews pointed out. He suppressed the temptation to add that Langston wasn't a woman and see what Berkley's next excuse would be. Instead he added, "We'll look into it."

"And just for the record," Andrews continued smoothly, "where were you between ten and ten-forty last night?"

The tightening of lines around Berkley's mouth and eyes betrayed a slight nervousness with this last question, but he answered without any delay. "I'm afraid you'll have to look elsewhere for a suspect, Lt. Andrews. I was at home with my wife last evening, all evening. We'd planned to go out with friends to dinner, but Mrs. Berkley wasn't feeling well, so we spent a quiet evening at home together."

Andrews made a mental note to check that with Mrs. Berkley. For now, he thanked the victim's partner for his information, collected his bulk to stand and shake hands with the obviously relieved doctor and departed to find Foster and satisfy the growing demands of his appetite for food. .

Chapter 7

The spring afternoon was cool and a brisk breeze made the car comfortable for sitting. Andrews and Foster had settled on a drive-in for lunch as the only option which would allow them to eat quickly and talk in private while they ate. The remote corner of a shopping mall gave the two detectives the privacy they sought.

A car had its limitations, however, as a dining area to Andrews' way of thinking. In fact, so far Andrews had spent more time wiping salad dressing off his shirt than talking. Moreover, sitting next to Foster while the slim sergeant savored a roast beef sandwich and fries was not likely to put any dieter in a settled frame of mind. It did even less for a large, beefy lieutenant of detectives who had been very hungry to begin with, and who had tried—really tried—to stick to the rabbit food and diet salad dressing allowed on his latest diet.

In a futile attempt to ignore the enticing aroma of hot fries, Andrews busied himself with briefing his partner on his earlier conversation with Thomas Berkley.

"Already I don't like this crazy case," Andrews glowered. "Poems and funny drawings were seemingly taken by the victim as threats. Hardly dangerous sounding to most people, but his murder was certainly real and brutal."

Foster ate slowly and appreciatively. To Andrews' continued discomfort his slim partner was still eating when the brief review of the annoying interview with the victim's partner was concluded.

"Now if you ever finish stuffing your face, maybe you can fill me in on what information you obtained from the security people," Andrews grumbled finally.

Beautiful white teeth flashed brightly against Foster's olive complexion as the younger detective smiled at his partner's complaint. "This new diet getting on your nerves already?"

"Of course not! The salad was very filling," Andrews lied. "We've got a busy afternoon ahead of us, and I'd like to hear what you learned about activities at the Institute last night before we talk with the victim's wife," he snapped.

Foster chuckled and took a last sip of his cola. "OK, just let me get my notes," he said.

He calmly secured the empty cup and wrappers in the empty paper bag and put the trash in the plastic litter container on the door handle before reaching for his notebook. Andrews glared impatiently but said nothing else.

Notebook in hand at last, Foster began his briefing on the interview he'd held earlier with Frank Hogge, the chief of security for the Institute. With his characteristic efficiency he described the surroundings of the crime first.

"According to records, the official name for the building where the body was found is the South Complex of the Commonwealth Cancer Institute. It's an eight-storied affair, roughly shaped like a 'T' and computer controlled," Foster began.

"What the hell does the computer control?" Andrews interrupted.

"Temperature, humidity, amount of fresh air," Foster responded. "No windows or openings except through secured doors."

"Well, why didn't you say so in the first place!"

Foster continued with his briefing as though he had not heard Andrews' grumbling. "The building houses the offices of the administrator and office suites for the senior staff of the Institute. The South Complex is connected to clinic and hospital laboratories by a long corridor on the ground floor."

Foster paused, apparently waiting for another complaint from Andrews, but none came. The portly figure next to him was seemingly engrossed in straightening his shirt to ease the pressure on that garment's buttons.

"There are only two ways in or out of the building. A back door leads from the foyer of the freight elevator to the back alley. This door is secured except for deliveries or arranged loading of supplies from the building. The door cannot be opened without a key."

"What about from the inside?" Andrews injected.

"Even from the inside the door requires a key to open, and a guard is always present when it is opened," Foster continued. "Security procedures require the guard to note time and identity of individuals entering the building through this door. It was opened yesterday afternoon at 3:22 pm for a delivery of equipment. A guard was present to record and supervise the delivery. The door was secured afterwards. Another guard accompanied the delivery-man to his destination on the fifth floor, remained with him while the equipment was received and signed for, and escorted him out again through the back door at 3:52 pm. Hogge himself opened the door at 7:12 pm to allow the cleaning crew to bring in equipment and supplies, locked it behind them. And Hogge was the one who opened the back door at 12:26 am to let the cleaning crew leave with the trash and equipment."

"Rather tight security, isn't it?" Andrews injected.

His frame had adopted its more normal slouch in the car seat. After much effort he seemed to have successfully diverted his attention from a comparison of the lunch he'd eaten with the one he'd wanted to eat.

"Not really. A rather common security procedure given the amount of expensive equipment housed in the building."

"So in Hogge's opinion the murderer didn't enter through the rear door?"

52

"No way, according to Hogge."

"Maybe he's right. And maybe he's not willing to consider everyone," Andrews evaluated aloud. "Who has keys to this back entrance?"

"Hogge, of course. He has a master key. And Ketterholt," Foster said.

"Ah," Andrews grunted, squirming in his seat to redistribute his bulk while he searched his pants pockets for something.

The senior detective finally located a roll of lifesavers and pulled them from his pocket, opened the package absentmindedly and was about to pop one into his mouth when he remembered his manners. Belatedly he offered one to Foster.

"I could ask if those candies are allowed on your diet, but I think I'd prefer spending the afternoon with a slightly satisfied backslider than with a diet martyr," Foster chuckled. "No, thank you. I'll pass on one for myself."

Foster ignored the glare he got from his partner for those remarks and continued with his description of the building in which the murder had been discovered.

His token acknowledgment of social manners satisfied, Andrews wasted no time in popping a small piece of candy in his mouth.

"So that leaves the entrance covered by a security desk as the point of entrance for most of the staff," Andrews summarized. Crunching sounds issued from his jaw as he happily added a lemon lifesaver to his sugar level.

"Don't tell me that we're lucky enough to have an itemized record of the comings and goings of the people of interest in this case! I couldn't stand the luck!"

"Unfortunately, it isn't that easy," Foster replied. "The security desk isn't manned constantly during the day. The entrance into the security hallway is accessible by staff members with a card key between 7:30 am and 6:00 pm. The idea is to keep unauthorized individuals out, but not to create excessive difficulty for the staff to go and come," Foster explained.

"How would people like the victim's assistant get in?" Without waiting for an answer to that one, Andrews added, "And how did your latest lady friend, the garrulous old gossip in the wheel chair get in this morning?"

Foster smiled at the mention of Elizabeth Weir. "She certainly can talk the ears off the donkey! Seems she's known by all the guards as well as the rest of the staff. Still, I'm not certain they'd let her in after hours. This morning she was passed through the security doors by the guard to check in with the Volunteers Office which is in the Administrative wing. She seems to be affectionately regarded as a harmless soul, whose outgoing personality seems to bring cheer to the other patients around the Institute. As staff, assistants have access keys."

Without waiting for a response from his senior partner, Foster continued with his summary of the security procedures around the crime scene. "Between the hours of 7:30 am and 6:00 pm, no record would be kept of staff traffic. After 6:00 pm, entrance through the security entrance into the building is very restricted. The card keys don't work; a guard must open the door to allow entrance or exit, only staff are allowed in the building during the night hours, and staff are required to sign in and sign out."

"Well, that should give us something to go on," Andrews observed.

"Not as much as you might think. Records of entrance and exit by staff after hours consist of sheets which are filled in by the individuals themselves, and most times these entries are not watched carefully by the guards," Foster cautioned. "For example, there's no record of when Porter left yesterday afternoon. We can only surmise that he did so before 6:00 pm when the doors were secured to card key use. According to the records, he signed back in at 9:45 pm. There's no record of his signing out again."

"Didn't that concern the guard?" Andrews asked pointedly.

"Not really. The doctors often forgot to sign out. If a guard returned from his rounds and found a doctor standing at the door to be let out, the guard wouldn't question him or her. Nor would the guard delay letting the doctor out while he checked to insure the individual signed the security log. Not if the doctor was a well known member of the staff," Foster related.

"So why keep a log at all if no one paid it any attention?" Andrews asked disgustedly.

"In case of an emergency like a fire, the guard would certainly seek to find an individual shown by the log as still in the building. But under normal conditions, it would be assumed that the individual had left and forgotten to sign out on the security log," Foster responded soothingly.

"What about the other key individuals in this case?" Andrews asked.

"Dr. Matthew Langston left the building around 8:10 pm according to the log sheet and returned at 9:45 pm. There's no record that he left the building after that; he didn't sign out again."

"Maybe he didn't leave," Andrews injected. After much fiddling with the roll of lifesavers, he'd finally weakened and popped another one in his mouth.

"I spoke to the guard who was on duty at the security desk last evening. He remembers saying goodnight to Dr. Langston twice, so is certain he did leave, but he doesn't remember when. He thinks it was after midnight, but he's not certain."

"So you're telling me that the records of comings and goings might be useless," Andrews said sourly.

"Maybe not useless. Certainly less than totally reliable." Foster continued his brisk recount of the security situation. "The system would catch entries by other than staff and personnel, but would certainly allow any number of unrecorded entries and exits by personnel of the Institute. For example, Dr. Harold Ketterholt was gone by 6:30 pm when Hogge patrolled the administrative suite. No return is recorded. But he has a key to the door from the back alley to the freight elevator;

he could have entered through there and avoided being seen by the guard station."

"Well, we wouldn't want to make it too easy for us, now would we?" Andrews sounded disgusted.

Thanks to the increase to his sugar level provided by several candies, he was beginning to settle back into his relaxed slouch. It didn't imply his mind was any less active in the area of the investigation. It signified a victory —temporary though it might be—over his hungry inclination to chuck his present diet and go back to that drive-in for an order of fries.

Foster continued with his briefing. "Dr. Thomas Berkley never signed in or out yesterday."

"He said he left early yesterday, around 4:15 pm or so. Claims to have canceled a dinner engagement because his wife wasn't feeling well and that the two spent the evening together," Andrews summarized. "Very convenient"

"Well, if he came in during regular hours and left when he said, there'd be no reason he'd show up on the security logs," Foster continued. "Have you talked with Dr. Walter Raines?"

"No. According to his office, he left Wednesday afternoon for a medical conference in D.C. We'll have to confirm that. Even so, he's only two to three hours driving time away, so we can't cross him off our list. "

"I sent word to Dr. Langston," Andrews continued, " that I'd like to talk to him this afternoon after we'd had a chance to talk with Porter's wife. The secretary, Ms. Morgan, said Porter planned to have dinner with his wife last night. I want to know whether that was true, and if so, if he told her he was going back to the Institute last night and why," Andrews mumbled.

"Anything else about activities at the Institute last night that I should know about before we talk to Langston?" Andrews asked.

"Hard to say," Foster admitted. "The guard on duty last night referred to 'an unusual amount of coming and going by the professional staff' but he hadn't mentioned anything unusual until he learned of the murder. Until we compare last night's after hours traffic with other nights in the last two weeks I couldn't say whether last night was different.

"So Langston could have been in the building at the time Twill estimates the murder took place. Ketterholt could have let himself in the service entrance without being seen by the guard. Raines would appear to be out as a suspect if he was attending meetings in D.C. at the time of the murder. Berkley didn't sign in or out last night. Too bad. That one is hiding something. It may not have anything to do with the murder, but Berkley certainly is fearful that we'll find out something he doesn't want known." Andrews reached for another sugar fix, popped an orange bit of hard candy in his mouth before continuing. "What about the victim's assistant, McBroon? Was she in the building after hours last night?"

"I'll have to check. Hogge gave me a copy of the security log sheets for last night, and I can check it quickly if you want to wait," Foster responded.

"Check it later," the senior officer directed between crunches on his lifesaver. "Tell me about the cleaning crew that was in the building last night."

"The cleaning crew consisted of a supervisor, Will Chambles, and four assistants. Hogge let them in through the freight entrance at 7:12 pm last evening according to his signed log. Hogge let these same five people along with their equipment and trash out of the same freight entrance at 12:26 am Friday morning."

"Except for Chambles, none of the crew has worked for the Institute very long. That's not unusual. The job pays very little, gives no benefits, and relies on what basically are short term employees. Two of the crew have been with the Institute between seven and eight months, one has been working at the job for about a month, and one was new last night," Foster relayed succinctly. "I've got their names and addresses. Would you like to question them yourself, or shall I arrange to talk with them?"

Andrews busied himself with unwrapping another lifesaver and popping it into his mouth before responding. When he did, it was to explore an entirely different thought without answering his junior partner's question.

"What about stairs? There would have to be stairs in case of emergencies," Andrews queried.

"The stairs are in the center of the building, running beside and behind the elevator bank. The stairs end in the security corridor behind the security desk on the main floor. No additional entrance is involved," Foster replied. He waited patiently while Andrews shifted candy from left to right sides of his mouth, past experience telling the junior officer that a second query about questioning the cleaning crew was unnecessary.

"I'll leave the questioning of the cleaning crew to you," Andrews said finally. "After we question Mrs. Porter, I need to get back to the Institute and talk with Langston for certain, and do something about the animals. We can't close off Porter's office suite and leave the animals in there without providing for their care."

Frown lines deepened between the beefy detective's eyebrows. His jaw tightened against more than the hard candy he'd been chewing. "The Captain will think I've lost my mind, if I go rattling on about crediting dogs' reactions for fingering a murder suspect!" Andrews muttered to himself. He was regretting admitting to his partner at the beginning of their lunch that he'd contacted Genna and planned to arrange to take the dogs to Williamsburg.

After a moment he added, "So one of the cleaning crew was new the night of the murder! Wonder if that means anything important to this case. Was this one added because of the extra work with readying the place for that special meeting Ketterholt mentioned? Or was this a replacement? What happened to the member of the cleaning crew he or she replaced? See what you come up with on that angle."

"I'll get on it first thing after we talk with Mrs. Porter," Foster promised.

Several more candy-crunching noises later, Andrews added, "What did the new cleaning crew member look like?"

"Well," Foster began, one side of his mouth curled upward in the beginnings of a smile, "according to Hogge the new guy was big, beefy and towered over both Hogge and the supervisor, Will Chambles. But that could have meant anything, since Hogge is around 5' 8" and weighs around 155 to 160 pounds. When I pushed Hogge for specifics, he estimated this Drew Roalf to be 5' 11" to six feet and 240 pounds of flab, brown eyes. He wore a cap, and Hogge didn't remember his hair color."

The last lifesaver followed its predecessors into Andrews mouth as he digested this latest information. Apparently satisfied for the moment, he directed, "OK, you can follow up on that later, while I'm talking to Langston. Let's get the nasty work of talking to the victim's widow over with."

Chapter 8

Like many spring days in Virginia, this one had turned grey and threatening by the time the two detectives made their way up the long drive of the Porters' home. Well manicured beds of azaleas lined the flagstone drive, and a sprinkler rotated gently on the nearby lawn, arguing the homeowner's lack of faith in the gathering clouds or preoccupation with a homicide. The deep green leaves and abundant azalea blossoms of pink, lavender and white provided a Technicolor path to the double-doored entrance of a large two-storied brick home.

Foster's pressure on the bell was answered by a rotund woman with short, stiff hair resembling nothing so much as dried straw. Andrews introduced himself and his partner. In a voice that was penetrating rather than comforting, the woman informed them that she was a friend who had come to help her neighbor. What more she might have said was interrupted by the arrival of a second woman.

This one moved with a fluid, athletic stride, her slender figure set off to perfection by a black silk shirtwaist dress which accented a slim waist and lovely curves.

"Thank you, Martha. I was expecting these gentlemen."

The voice was soft and smooth like its owner. An oval face framed by shoulder length blond hair turned toward Andrews. The soft black of her dress accentuated the clear, translucent complexion and the brows and lashes darkened by more than nature.

"I'm Danielle Porter," the figure in black continued.

After Andrews repeated his introduction of himself and Foster, Danielle Porter continued. "Martha and another neighbor are helping to organize things in the kitchen for friends who may call later today. I believe we will be able to talk more comfortably in the study behind you," Danielle directed, a long-nailed hand motioning to the door behind them which led into a small room lined with bookcases.

"Martha, I'll be in the study with the gentlemen for some time. Should anyone call, it is most important that I not be disturbed. I trust your judgment to handle anything while I talk with these detectives."

With a parting touch of her hand on the thick upper arm of her friend, Danielle followed the two police officials into the study and closed the door.

A large desk and comfortable chair took up most of the floor space in the room to which Danielle Porter directed the two. An emerald green rug and two large potted schraffleras softened the dark walnut furnishings. Floor-to-ceiling bookcases lined one wall of the narrow, long room, but a quick glance by Andrews at the titles of the books which filled those shelves convinced the senior officer that the contents held little interest for ordinary individuals. The slender wife of the victim directed the two to small chairs surrounding a round table in the far end of the room.

The two detectives waited for the blond beauty to settle herself in one of the chairs before seating themselves. Andrews did his best to fit his ample proportions into the chair, but ended up with the feeling that he was perching rather than sitting. Foster was forced to sit far back in his own chair to allow his note taking to be shielded from the view of their hostess.

Acknowledgments of her shock and pain at the news of her husband's death along with reassurances of the necessity for talking with her flowed automatically from Andrew's lips. Behind the automatic drivel of words reserved for families of victims, Andrew's mind was busy assessing the lady herself.

Despite the careful makeup, it was obvious that she had been crying. Large smoky-green eyes were red-rimmed and puffed, and a slight squint argued that corrective glasses or contact lenses were normally worn to correct her eyesight. The tenseness of her jaw bespoke the control she exerted to keep her emotions under control, a tenseness that accentuated the age lines visible around her mouth and eyes. But her voice was soft and steady in responding to Andrews' queries.

"I appreciate your need for information regarding my husband's activities last evening. I told Harry....Dr. Harold Ketterholt ....when he called that I would give you all the information I could. Harry said Mike was brutally killed in his own lab." Here Danielle Porter's chin quivered in sympathetic vibrations with her voice, but she caught herself quickly and continued.

"I'm sorry. It just seems so unreal. I find myself wondering if this can really be happening to me. But I want to help in any way I can."

Before Andrews felt compelled to say anything more, this poised, newly created widow of the city's most recent violent crime continued. "Suppose I just describe our activities last night...Mike's and mine... and give you a little background on what we talked about at dinner. I don't know how much will be relevant to what has happened...Mike's death, I mean. You'll have to forgive me if I babble. I haven't had any experience with this sort of thing before."

Her tight control slipped a little remembering the reason for this meeting, but the slim blond recovered her composure and continued. "It seems to me I should just tell you straight out all I can think of that has been bothering me, what Mike and I have talked about during the last few months, and what went on last night, and let you, the experts, sort it out. Decide whether it means anything or nothing with regard to his death."

Andrews was poised to commend her on her common sense, but decided that it was inappropriate to use the word common when referring to anything about Danielle Porter. Before he could decide how to rephrase his comment, she went on without waiting for a response from either of the two policemen.

"Mike has...had... always worked long hours, but in the last two months he was rarely home. He'd made excuses of a critical deadline on some research project, but I didn't believe that explained his tenseness or his obsession with finishing this particular project. Something else seemed to be wrong. I became suspicious that another woman might have been involved. I'm not proud of it, but I began to scrutinize his check book and found that he bought several small presents that he wouldn't explain. Four weeks ago I discovered that one of those presents, a bottle of expensive perfume, was delivered to his secretary's apartment. I tried to talk to him about Piper Morgan, but he brushed me off, saying I was getting upset over nothing, that he'd have the project finished soon and I'd see that there was nothing between him and Ms. Morgan but a professional relationship. But something about the way he looked when he said that didn't strike me as truthful."

A slight raggedness crept into the smooth tone of Danielle's voice, but she continued with only a slight indication of the stress she felt. "I wasn't satisfied with his answers, and continued to press him about the situation between him and his secretary. Last night at dinner, he gave me a different explanation, but maybe I should explain other events first." The beautiful widow looked to Andrews for directions on how to proceed with her information.

Andrews had certainly not expected such directness nor such succinctness from the source, especially after the difficulties encountered earlier in the day in questioning professional colleagues of the victim. He was reluctant to exert any control over the conversation while the information appeared to flow so freely. Foster's pen was busy recording this unexpected flow of information into his notebook.

Seeing that Mrs. Porter obviously needed encouragement on her choice of structure to the testimony, Andrews finally said, "Certainly tell us in any manner you judge best." When she still paused as though uncertain for the first time how to proceed, Andrews asked, "Did your husband seem to be worried or afraid of anyone?"

"I never had any reason to think so, at least not until last night," the slim woman responded, enigmatically. "I don't think he was afraid, but he was worried about work. Months ago he received an anonymous letter from a grieving parent who seemed to blame Mike for the child's death. I don't think the parent's response bothered Mike as much as the idea that someone in the medical college might have been encouraging the ill will. He was upset about the letter, but cancer strikes all age groups and parents tend to blame the doctor when a child is lost. But then a few days after the angry letter, he received a poem in the internal mail with a note attached that said something about 'How does it feel to know your greed for money has robbed a child of his will to live?' The original letter hadn't mentioned the sex of the child. The note did, so Mike figured that someone in the medical college might be behind the ploy to encourage ill will against him and his research."

"This poem," Andrews injected. "Was it threatening to your husband?"

"Well, no. It was just a poem about the thoughts of an animal used in research. Mike became very angry. Said he was tired of all the bleeding hearts that refused to accept the necessity for research but were ready enough to profit from the results," Danielle Porter responded.

"But Dr. Porter thought it came from someone on the staff?"

"He was certain it did. It came in an internal mail envelope rather than through the U.S. Mail. So did the drawings," Mrs. Porter added.

"Tell me about the drawings. Did your husband describe them or say why they were upsetting to him?"

64

"The drawings were crude attempts to represent the eye. The poem had been entitled **Brown Eyes**, you see. Mike thought the drawings were meant to remind him of the letter and the poem, and to keep him stirred up so that he couldn't concentrate on his project. He said he was afraid that the instigator might progress from words to attempts to destroy his research. So he arranged to keep his office and lab locked at night."

"Did he mention anything else, any name or suspicion of who might be behind these harassments?" Andrews queried.

"He was certain it was either the deputy chief of research, Matt Langston, or another member of the staff, Walter Raines. Raines was always hanging around trying to prove that Mike had copied his ideas for research projects. Matt Langston was opposed to outside research, disdainful of the money it brought into the school's budget, and repeatedly accused Mike of abusing animals," Danielle Porter continued.

"Did your husband ever express fear of either of these two individuals, or indicate that either had threatened him?" Andrews wanted to know.

"He was mostly contemptuous of Walter Raines. Said he was a fumbling, has-been. But Matt Langston worried him, made Mike very angry. I think that the problem was Dr. Langston's position—as deputy chief—and his strong beliefs that animal models were useful only in avoiding legal suits. Langston believes that discoveries touted as medical advances, when discovered with animal models, rarely, if ever, work the same on human subjects."

"I never felt that Mike was physically afraid of either of them, or of anyone else for that matter." Remembering perhaps the reason behind this meeting and conversation, the new widow's chin quivered with emotion. "Oh, God! Neither of us thought his life was in danger."

With some effort, Danielle Porter managed to control her facial features and her voice. "He was just angry and frustrated at what he considered impediments to his research efforts."

"What about Langston's concern that animals were being abused?" Foster injected with an apologetic nod to his superior for interrupting.

Shoulder length blond hair swung attractively as the beautiful oval face turned toward the younger police official briefly before replying. "I tried not to think too much about that. Mike used cats and dogs obtained from the local pounds. He said they would have been killed anyway, and might as well serve some useful purpose by their deaths. But Langston shouted at Mike at a party several months ago about betting on how many times a dog would wag its tail after being given a lethal dose of a new drug. I was so upset by their argument that I left the party early. Mike was furious at Langston, said he was just jealous of the money Mike made from his outside research," the victim's wife recounted. Her cheeks were slightly flushed as though remembering the conversation still caused her discomfort.

"Langston accused my husband of encouraging students and support staff to be callous and cold, insensitive to causing pain and suffering in animals and in people. He said they'd all become insensitive, money-grubbing souls who would be void of any compassion and feeling," Danielle Porter related, her voice shaking now at the memory.

"It was very embarrassing. Everyone at the party ceased what they were doing and turned toward the confrontation between Langston and my husband."

The soft voice of the victim's wife wound down. Andrews remained silent for a long minute to allow Foster to catch up with his writing and Danielle Porter to recover her composure. He was at a loss, despite years of experience in police work, to decide whether her remembered pain was for the implications of the conversation between her late husband and his deputy chief or embarrassment at appearing in an uncomplimentary position among her social set.

"That generally describes the way things have gone in our lives during the last months. Mike continued to work late hours, and I couldn't rid myself of the feeling that there was something more than he was saying between him and his secretary, Ms. Morgan. Finally, I couldn't stand the thought that he was making a fool of me. I told him I wanted a separation and suggested he get an apartment and move out." This admission seemed to break through the beautiful woman's control and tears stood in her large green eyes, threatening to overflow.

Andrews and Foster waited quietly for her to recover her composure and go on with her narrative. Andrews considered asking her if he could call Martha and have something brought in, but decided that the loud, abrasive voice of Ms. Moss was exactly what was not needed.

"Sorry," she said at last. "I feel so very bad that I was suspicious and driven by petty jealousy, when all along Mike was in need of my help. Last night he came home early to take me out for a romantic dinner. We did more talking than eating, and got a lot of things out in the open if not settled. He finally admitted that he'd given several small presents to his secretary, but he said it was in appreciation for her support and encouragement in the face of the upsetting mail campaign over the past two months. I'm afraid I didn't find his explanations totally acceptable, but we did agree to put the separation on hold until he could finish his latest research project."

"Did he mention any other worries other than the hate mail you've described?" Andrews inquired.

"Well, he did mention that he suspected that his assistant might be working against him. He said he'd found his research notes reordered and suspected that someone had been borrowing them and perhaps copying them."

"Anything else?"

"No. Not that I can think of at the moment. He said he needed to finish the project and get his money, but that when he finished, we'd take some time together, maybe go on a cruise if I'd like," the slim beauty confided. "He brought me home about 10:00 pm, and said he would return to the lab and get a little more work done."

Her voice broke then and the tears, which had only threatened to flow earlier, began to make shimmering streaks down her cheeks. Her voice was so low that only the small diameter of the table at which the three sat allowed Andrews and Foster to hear her final comment. "And that was the last time I saw Mike."

Andrews gave her little time to dwell on her grief, knowing from too many years of experience that to do so was to invite even more crying. In a tone that was soft and soothing, he commended her for her concise briefing of events surrounding her husband's work, thanked her for her courage and asked her to be indulgent with him and his partner long enough to answer a few more questions.

"What time did you and your husband actually have dinner and where?" Andrews probed, hoping the inclusion of place and herself in the question would soften the obvious reason behind the question.

Despite his adroit handling of the situation, Danielle Porter seemed to sense the relationship of this question to the coming autopsy. Her chin quivered as she pinpointed dinner at 7:00 pm in one of Richmond's most exclusive and expensive restaurants.

"And your husband brought you back home before 10:00 pm? Can you remember how much before 10:00 pm that was?" Andrews' voice was smooth but firm.

For a moment, Andrews thought the beautiful woman might give in to the stress with tears, but she collected herself with some effort and responded. "Well, actually, I probably said it wrong. He brought me home around 9:00 pm; but it was nearly 10:00 pm when I finally went up to bed and looked at a clock."

The time correction was consistent with a thirty-five to forty minute trip back to the victim's office and the 9:45 pm sign-in at his office that night. Still, Andrews had a troubling feeling that there was something here the woman before him was not saying. If so, it would come out in the ensuing investigation, he was certain.

Aloud, he responded smoothly, "Just one more question, if I may, Mrs. Porter. Would you say your husband was an accurate judge of people's feelings, attitudes?"

Additional tears appeared to be arrested while Danielle Porter's mind focused on this latest and obviously unexpected question. "After what I've just related to you about my jealousy over Ms. Morgan I would appear to be a poor judge myself. But, you know, I don't think Mike was a very good judge of people's feelings. You'd have to know his background maybe to understand, but he thought everything could be solved with money. And the more he made, the more he thought he had to make. Of course, many of the adverse reactions he roused in others may have been based on greed, but I don't think all of them were. And he could never see any other motives."

"Would it matter?" she asked lamely.

"I just wondered," Andrews responded noncommittally.

By now the grey clouds had fulfilled their promise of rain, and Andrews and Foster took their leave of the late Dr. Porter's beautiful widow amid rumbles of thunder. Their brief walk to their car was hastened by the growing intensity of the rain which fell on them. The lawn sprinkler still sprayed water to and fro in total disregard to the watering job being done by nature.

Chapter 9

After some discussion, the two sleuths decided to double their efforts by splitting up responsibilities for talking with witnesses. Andrews dropped Foster off at headquarters to get his car and take a break before talking with the cleaning crew that evening. Andrews returned to the Institute alone to continue gathering information there.

By the time Andrews had gotten back to the murder scene it was slightly past four on a rainy Friday afternoon. The salad and black coffee which had served the beefy detective as lunch had long since been reduced to an empty pit centered somewhere in his upper chest. The lifesavers had furnished only momentary satisfaction. He was hungry and wet. Moreover, the air-conditioning in the administrative wing of the Institute was working overtime, and he was cold. So he was not in an amicable mood when he returned to the scene of the crime.

Piper Morgan's office was empty except for the uniformed officer who guarded the door between the secretarial office and the victim's office. Andrews waved the man back to his seat, opened the door to Porter's office, and closed it behind him after entering.

A slight man with thinning blond hair and wire-rimmed glasses looked up briefly from a pile of papers on the victim's desk. His round face and pale skin were dotted with freckles, a sight which somewhere in his past had given rise to his nickname of Pepper. Few who met him ever knew his real name of Peter Rogers.

"Hi, Lieutenant," the slight man greeted Andrews. "Hope your afternoon has been more productive than mine. Wouldn't mind telling me what I'm looking for, would you?"

"If I knew, I wouldn't need Fraud's best sleuth," Andrews replied sourly. "All I know is that the victim's partner is trying to get the victim's papers and the two dogs in the lab, perhaps for legit reasons, his secretary thinks he's a saint, his wife thinks he's cheating on her with his secretary, he admitted sending his secretary presents, someone had been sending him hate mail, everyone I've talked to is lying about something, and I've got a crime scene that I can't close off properly because of animals. "

Pepper gave no notice that Andrews' snippy remarks were taken personally. With a noticeable appreciation for his task, he returned his attentions to the papers he'd taken from the victim's private files and continued his scrutiny. In what seemed like a brush-off to Andrews, he waved his hand toward the door between the victim's office and lab.

"Billy is in the lab. Said he needed to talk with you when you got back."

Andrews crossed to the lab door, then turned briefly back to Pepper. "Also, the victim was engaged in some sort of research project that he felt pressured to complete, that he felt someone was threatening. If you come across a file with a letter about causing a child's death or some funny drawings or a poem called **Brown Eyes** let me know ASAP."

Without waiting for another smart answer from Pepper, Andrews reentered the victim's lab to find Sergeant Billy Brown trying to get a brown guinea pig to take a piece of lettuce from his hand. The tall police sergeant turned slightly and smiled at his superior.

The first thing Andrews noticed was that the little black-and-white guinea pig no longer whined pitifully. In fact, the little animal was nowhere to be found. The remaining five had been moved to a larger cage. A metal tray filled with shredded paper covered the bottom of their new cage and containers were secured to its wire sides. The containers held what looked to be water in one and small brown pellets in another. Andrews guessed the pellets were what passed for food. Now that the floor of their cage afforded them adequate support, the tiny animals were inclined to move around more seeking water and nourishment. As with most small things, these five helpless creatures seemed to have no fear of the large, black human who stood over their cage with his leafy offering in hand.

"What happened to the other one, the one that was hurt?" Andrews asked in place of a greeting.

"Young Doc said he was dying and in pain. Gave him a shot and put him to sleep. Put his little body in the fridge over there in case we needed it," Brown answered in his condensed fashion. "You said....."

"I remember what I said," Andrews snapped. "Langston?" he queried.

"Yeah. Called him like you said. Told him we needed to talk. He was down in minutes. Took one look at the little creatures and the dogs, said we could talk later, animals needed him first."

Andrews nodded approvingly. Despite his sour mood, the observant detective noted that Brown had no reluctance toward bestowing a medical title on Langston. All things small and helpless had an immediate champion in this rugged officer with his granite face. He obviously approved of Langston as a fellow champion of the defenseless, and away from outside eyes and ears, let his approval of Langston show as plainly now as he had his disapproval of Berkley earlier.

Andrews turned to inspect the cages along the adjacent wall which still housed the two dogs. Old blankets had been folded and placed in the back half of the cages to form a soft bed. The smaller, grey dog lay on its side. It quivered with anxiety when Andrews moved toward the front of its cage for a closer look but did not attempt to rise. The larger, black animal had been resting on its blanket when Andrews had entered the lab earlier, but now sat up to watch Andrews cautiously.

Water and food had been provided for each dog by containers attached to the wire mesh front of each cage. Unless the containers had been refilled, however, the grey dog had not touched the offered food.

Andrews noted the changes with approval. Langston was apparently very abrasive with people but kind-hearted when it came to animals. And he was also very vocal in his criticism of those who were not, if the information provided by his colleagues was to be believed. This was the man that Berkley claimed had wished Porter a slow and painful death? Was it possible that anger over ill treatment of an animal or the proper direction of research could have been sufficient to drive this man to kill a fellow doctor? If so, it would be the first in Andrews' experience for that motive. And if so, why last night?

"I'm tired," Andrews thought to himself. "Too early to go phrasing questions like that." Aloud he asked, "How did the two dogs react when Langston came down to the lab?"

"Little one didn't try to get up. Black one retreated to the back of the crate. Didn't seem any more upset than when you or I go near his crate, though. Young Doc took each out in turn, examined them, put something on the front paws of the little one. They were plenty worried, but not crazy wild like when Mr. Stuffed-Shirt came in. Guess the two are smart enough to know a friend," Brown answered.

The lines on the rough face softened slightly then creased again. "Oh, almost forgot. Langston said the little one's respiration rate was slowed and he was willing himself to die."

Andrews' only reply was a question. "Did you say anything else to Langston?"

"Told him you wanted the animals cared for. That you'd want to talk to him when you got back today. Said he'd be around."

"One more thing....." Brown continued, "before you talk with the young Doc. Pepper wanted a box of computer equipment brought in, so I unbolted 'da door from lab to hall to bring it in that way. While I was carrying the equipment into the office yonder and helping Pepper set up some stuff, an assistant of Mr. Stuffed-Shirt used his key to come in through the door from the hall. When I jumped him, he said he'd been sent by Berkley to get one of the dogs to be used in an experiment. I sent 'im packing with detailed description of what would happen if he crossed a police line again."

Andrews digested this last bit of information with growing concern. He glanced once more at the two dogs. What was so important about these two that Berkley wanted them or one of them out of the hands of the investigating team? If he tried to put the two dogs in protective custody and the Institute complained, his Captain would be unlikely to back him or tolerate the unfavorable publicity that would result. He really couldn't explain to himself why he thought it was important to protect the two. Some instinct born of long experience argued that it was. He'd called Genna earlier about caring for the dogs based on that instinct. Maybe it was just coincidence, but Billy's telling of this latest threat to the dogs heightened Andrews feelings that the dogs were somehow important.

"Probably more that I just don't like Berkley than anything to do with the investigative procedures," Andrews groused. "In addition to wet, cold and hungry, I'm also out of my mind. I guess I'll go talk to Langston now."

Billy Brown appeared not to notice the lack of continuity in Andrews' conversation. He turned to renew his efforts to entice a small, tan-and-white guinea pig to take the remainder of the lettuce from his hand.

Chapter 10

The security desk at the front entrance to the building was well guarded perhaps to keep the curious press away from the scene of the murder. The security officer there directed Andrews to the second floor suite of Dr. Matthew Langston.

At the indicated location, Andrews found a door open between hall and lab through which he saw four men and one woman busily examining slides, notes, and a computer screen. None of the five appeared to pay any attention to him, but no one jumped in surprise either when Andrews said, "I'm looking for Dr. Matthew Langston. Could one of you tell me where I might find him."

One of the five, a slightly built, dark-haired man that looked to be in his mid-thirties raised his head, squinted at Andrews through thick glasses, but did not move from behind a lab table. "I'm Langston. What can I do for you?"

Andrews' identification brought an instant invitation to join Langston in the adjacent office. Langston directed him through the lab and into the adjoining blue carpeted expanse of paper files.

Andrews' traverse of Langston's lab convinced the detective that the reason for the explosion of plastic and paper containers holding most of today's takeout foods was that Langston had cornered the market on glass. The lab was crowded with the four remaining lab workers and jars, bottles, tubes, and mixtures—glass in all shapes and sizes. All that would be needed to make it into a witch's laboratory was a lot less light and a lot more cobwebs. Andrews was relieved to see no small or large animals in cages in the lab, however.

"Have a seat where you can find one," Langston directed after closing the connecting door between office and lab.

Therein lay the problem. Each of the two visitor's chairs, as well as the desk, couch, and much of the floor were covered with papers and books. Apparently, Matthew Langston had diverse and compelling interests which did not include returning things to the proper place unless that proper place was the floor or a chair.

"Just push those off on the floor," Langston said, suiting the actions to his words by removing a pile of bound volumes and a notebook from the nearest chair and depositing them in a convenient spot beside the desk before continuing on around his desk to plop himself into the chair behind it.

Andrews seated himself as directed in the vacated chair, then found that he had to sit very straight in the chair in order to see Langston's face over the pile of papers on the desk.

The slight figure which faced Andrews across his messy desk was hardly what the senior investigating officer had expected. Ketterholt and Berkley had suggested an angry, combative individual whom Andrews had been prepared to find difficult, if not unlikable, at first sight. Instead he found an energetic figure that responded to his intrusion with interest and cooperation, squinting slightly to focus on Andrews' face. Abundant black hair capped a high forehead and fell across the younger man's eyes as rapidly as one short, broad-fingered hand brushed it back.

"Now, the police officer in Porter's lab said you wanted to talk with me about the murder. What would you like to know?" Langston asked while Andrews was still trying to decide how best to sit in the chair and see the young man across the pile of papers on the desk at the same time.

76

"How did you get along with the victim?" Andrews opened, deciding on the direct approach with this forthright individual.

"Not very well," Langston answered candidly. "I thought he was in the profession to make a fortune, not out of any real interest in medicine. He was concerned with making money, didn't care whom he hurt. I was especially critical of his so-called research methods, especially his conclusions and told him so to his face. Since I never cared who overheard my opinions, I imagine you already know that."

Nothing condescending about this young doctor's manner Andrews concluded. He liked Langston's blunt responses and the way the younger man maintained eye contact.

Before Andrews could formulate another question, Langston injected one of his own. "From what I heard, Porter was secured in the rack he'd used for animal experiments, and acid was forced down his throat. Is that correct?"

"Yes," Andrews admitted. "I heard you wished the victim a slow and painful death. Any correlation?"

"I suppose you've been talking to Berkley," Langston said resignedly. "I believe I did mention something like that."

The hazel eyes met Andrews' defiantly. Christie's Inspector Battle always insisted that murderers were cocky. Andrews wished real life was that simple. He decided Langston looked more unmoved than cocky.

"Were you threatening Porter?" Andrews asked.

Langston's steady gaze did not waver from Andrews' face. "I walked in on a test being conducted by Porter and Berkley. A dog was strapped down and dying. Porter reached over to check the dog's breathing and the dog tried to lick his hand in a last desperate appeal for help. The two bastards began to laugh and jeer that the poor little beast didn't have the sense to know friend from foe. Then the two started exchanging bets on how many times the dog would wag its tail before it died. It made me very angry. I probably wished the two of them every

77

bad luck in the world. I'm not sorry and I don't retract a single thing I said. But I didn't personally threaten to take his life, if that was your question," the young doctor said.

Andrews sat silently, but Langston did not add anything more. "Why were you so angry?"

"To kill, to cause pain and suffering, and to laugh and joke about it! You don't find that sufficient reason to get angry, Lieutenant?" Langston's speech fairly exploded from his chest.

Andrews could understand the descriptions given by Ketterholt and Berkley a little better now. The slightly built, near-sighted bundle of energy, which his entrance had first beheld, had become the angry creature he now confronted across a littered desk.

Andrews took his time deciding whether to calm the waters or continue while Langston was visibly agitated. He finally asked, "Are you suggesting that Porter was killed in a manner which replicates the testing he was doing on animals?"

For the first time since Andrews had met Langston, the younger man seem to consider his response before speaking. When he did his eyes still maintained contact with the detective's, but Andrews had the faintest idea that Langston might be forcing himself to do so. "Yes, I am."

Considering the lack of reserve which had characterized Langston's conversation from the beginning, this seemed odd. And a wiry old fox—or at least a fat one—like Andrews knew when to push a witness. He did so now.

"Do you know of anyone who might have wanted to kill Porter?" Andrews asked.

"Not particularly. Money was his god. He didn't care whose toes he stepped on or whom he hurt to increase his wealth. That type of individual makes few friends and a lot of enemies. But the kind who'd be likely to kill him professionally, not physically. Money may buy a lot, but not real friends, Lieutenant."

Deciding that this approach had achieved its purpose, Andrews switched to another line of questions. "When was the last time you saw Dr. Porter?"

"Don't remember exactly. I passed him in the halls in the normal course of the day yesterday, I suppose. But I didn't keep an account."

"You didn't see him last evening then?" Andrews prompted.

The younger man allowed a slight smile to soften his face before replying. "You've done your homework I see, Lieutenant. Well, I worked until a little after eight last night, went out for a bite to eat and came back about 9:30 pm. Worked on a paper I'm presenting at a convention next month until after midnight. If that puts me in the building during the time when Porter was killed, you can make the most of it," he continued.

The young doctor squinted slightly. Andrews decided he was not a good liar at all, but wondered at the cause of the facial changes that signaled tension.

Aloud, Andrews queried, "Porter returned to the hospital around 9:45 pm last night. According to the security log, you signed in at that same time. Are you certain you didn't see him or speak to him last night?"

"No. If I signed in at 9:45 pm last night, then that's what the clock at the door said. I just didn't find it important to remember in any great detail. As to seeing Porter, I didn't. There was a broad body in cap and coveralls pushing some sort of polishing machine up and down the hall outside Porter's office suite. I think I annoyed him by tracking across his wet finish. But I came straight up here to my second-floor hideaway and was too busy working on my paper to notice anyone else. Besides, Porter would have had no reason to come up to this floor. We didn't have the kind of relationship that invited conversation, Lieutenant. If he were here late, it was to work on a research project and I wouldn't have been involved."

"Did you see or hear anything unusual during the time you were in the office last night?" Andrews queried smoothly, ignoring the challenge in Langston's voice.

"Nothing except the usual chatter and clatter of the cleaning crew. One or two individuals interrupted me a couple of times, to ask if they should clean the office and to get the trash... things like that. But there was nothing unusual about that."

"Did you go out of your office for any reason during the time between returning at 9:45 pm and leaving around midnight?"

"No. Sorry to disappoint you, but I didn't leave my office during that time, and didn't hear or see anything except the individuals that I took to be members of the cleaning crew," Langston responded.

"I understand that Porter kept his lab and office locked in the evening, didn't allow the cleaning crew in to clean unless he was present, because he'd believed someone was threatening his research. Did you know anything about that?" Andrews continued.

"He mentioned a letter from a former patient. And some other things. I didn't pay it too much attention."

Andrews would have bet his next paycheck that the slight shift in Langston's tone betrayed knowledge of the situation the young deputy director of research refused to admit.

"Oh! Porter was so upset about what he viewed as threats to his research that he locked his lab, complained to the head of the hospital here, and you didn't pay it too much attention?" Andrews challenged.

"Not really. His only worry was that his research projects would be delayed and he'd get his money late. He didn't give a damn who or what he hurt. So anything that made him uncomfortable was a plus in my book," Langston admitted bluntly.

"You disliked Porter then? Didn't that make it difficult working directly for him?"

If Andrews expected this direct and blunt-spoken witness to be intimidated by the question, he was disappointed.

"Yes. Very much so. In fact, my contract expires in two months and twenty-six days and I'm leaving the Institute." the young doctor answered candidly.

80

"Was Porter responsible for the failure to renew your contract?" Andrews asked pointedly.

Short fingers brushed back the dark hair which had fallen across the younger man's eyes again. Another slight smile softened his face, and his voice echoed a chuckle as he replied, "There you go, Lieutenant, leaping to conclusions. The Institute would gladly have renewed my contract. They would have before this murder. But now that the chief of research is dead, this place would be even happier to keep me. But before you decide that gives me a motive for murder, let me assure you that I'm the one that won't stay. I can't stomach the hypocrisy around here. The professional staff demand respect as saviors of mankind but are motivated only by greed. I didn't become a doctor to exploit people or animals."

"Did you write the letter to Porter accusing him of robbing a child of the will to live?" Andrews injected softly.

The question was delivered so smoothly that it took Langston a moment to focus on this line of questions. The same lock of unruly hair fell down and was again brushed back in what was obviously a near-continuous battle with gravity before Langston answered.

"No, Lieutenant, I didn't."

Andrews' years of experience in detecting minute changes in tone and facial muscle changes screamed that this was not exactly the truth.

"Do you know who did?" Andrews persisted.

Perching on chairs was Foster's specialty, Andrews decided, and not suitable to a fat, old man. His back was beginning to ache from the unaccustomed position and his stomach had long since begun to insist that a salad and pack of lifesavers were too little and too long ago. In the hopes of relieving the ache in his back if not his stomach, Andrews slouched into a more comfortable position in the chair causing his shirt front to gap open. From his more relaxed position his view of the slight, near-sighted face was obstructed by the messy jumble of papers which littered the desk between the two men, but not too obstructed to see the defiant look in

Langston's eyes which looked across the room at nothing in particular and returned to focus on Andrews' face again.

Langston's answer, when it came, was at least truthful this time. "If I did, I'm not sure I'd tell you." .

"I would advise you against attempting to withhold evidence in a murder investigation, Dr. Langston," Andrews cautioned.

"Evidence is one thing, Lieutenant. Suspicion is another. Don't try to tell me the police are interested in unfounded suspicions."

"Semantics, Doctor. In court, lawyers call them hearsay. I just call them leads. Now who do you think might have sent that letter to Dr. Porter?"

Langston shook his head slightly, causing another thick clump of hair to fall down across his eye. "I couldn't say, Lieutenant."

"Or won't. For now I'll let that pass, Doctor," Andrews responded. "What can you tell me about a poem entitled **Brown Eyes**? According to Mrs. Porter, it's about the thoughts of an animal used in research. Dr. Porter received the poem in the internal mail along with a note referring to the threatening letter, according to several witnesses," Andrews explained.

Langston pushed his chair away from his messy desk, stood and walked over to the window. For a short space of time he stood with his back to Andrews, saying nothing. Except for the slight growls coming from the vicinity of Andrews' stomach and the breathing of the two men, the room was silent. Finally, Langston turned back to face Andrews but did not resume his seat across the desk.

"I've got a pretty good idea who sent the poem and the note. And don't give me any of that lead stuff....I'm not going to say anything else until I am certain....except this. If it's the person I think, the individual's intent was to harass Porter but not to threaten him. Like me, the individual would have enjoyed making the bastard uncomfortable, but is far too civilized to actually do physical harm to anyone, even a jerk like Porter."

"You seem to suspect a lot of things which you're not willing to share. Very well, Doctor Langston, I don't have the inclination right now to press you for your ideas. Later I might feel differently."

Clearly Langston had not expected the police detective to give up that easily. He looked somewhat puzzled, as though braced for an argument that hadn't materialized, and returned to his seat behind his desk.

Andrews wasn't particularly concerned for the moment with Langston's suspicions regarding the note's authorship. Pepper would probably locate the threatening letter, notes and drawings, and routine police work would yield the identity of the sender or senders. And, Andrews reasoned, it would give him a reason for questioning Langston later. At the moment, he had other objectives to fulfil.

"Thank you for assisting us in caring for the animals at the crime scene."

If Andrews' sudden shift of topics startled his witness, it didn't show. Langston responded smoothly, "No thanks are necessary. The animals are the Institute's responsibility, anyway."

"You said Porter would have returned last night to work on a research project, one in which you would not have been involved. Do you know what that project was?"

Langston paused for a long time before answering. When he did, it was to respond with another question rather than answering. "You think the research project might be related to the murder?"

"I don't know," Andrews admitted. "I just have to cover all the bases."

"Well, simply stated, he was testing the effects of a new drug for use with skin cancer.

Andrews remembered the raw, open flesh on the back of the little guinea pig he'd seen in the victim's lab this morning. "Was the guinea pig you euthanized involved in that testing?"

"Yes." Langston looked a little pained but did not say anything more.

"Did the little animal have skin cancer?" Andrews's half-closed eyes did not miss the tightening of the muscles around the younger man's mouth. "I would have guessed some type of burn, but then I'm only a layman."

"It was an acid burn, " Langston responded flatly.

"That doesn't seem to have much in common with skin cancer." Andrews observed. He waited to see if Langston would try to pretend he didn't understand the question.

Langston shifted his frame around in his chair and sighed before answering, but when he did it was not to dodge the question. "It would be described as a cancer-like open sore when Porter and Berkley delivered their report, and it would probably go unchallenged. But no, Lieutenant, it most certainly would not, in my professional opinion, have much to do with skin cancer."

So much for useful research results. Andrews secretly agreed with Langston's evaluation of the victim's work if this was a representative sample. But his job was to find a killer, not to dabble into areas which were not his expertise. Another grumble from the general area of his stomach nudged him toward closure of this talk. He was certain it wouldn't be the last anyway.

"A patient stopped me in the hall this morning. Said Porter had the bedside manner of a barracuda and suggested that one of his patients got even," Andrews said by way of transition to the topic he really wanted to address, the continuation of care for the animals while the crime scene was secured. "Do you think that is an angle I should investigate?"

The comment brought a chuckle from the younger man. "A rather rotund lady in a wheelchair, I presume. That would be Mrs. Weir. She's somewhat of a fixture around here, and has an opinion about everything. In fact, if it's opinions and guesses you want, you couldn't go to a better place."

"She said she came back frequently to visit patients here, but didn't admit it was for treatments."

"She combines treatments with visits to other patients, and I think she likes the attention the wheels

84

get her. At her weight, rolling is easier than walking most of the time. She's very opinionated, Lieutenant, but I doubt that Porter's bedside manner has...or rather had...any bearing on the crime," Langston added. "She shouldn't have been passed through to the Volunteer Office this morning, however. I've told the security people to discourage that. Her health isn't good, and this Institute cannot afford to list her as a volunteer."

"I think her interest was in the gossip about the homicide rather than any volunteering," Andrews admitted, remembering the flushed, pale face he'd encountered in the hallway. Then he added, "Did she know Porter well?"

A beautiful smile softened the features of the young doctor. "Well, she's around a good deal. Her daughter and son-in-law run the family decorating and upholstery business now, and Mrs. Weir has a lot of time on her hands. She likes visiting the Institute's personnel and the patients, so she probably would feel she knew Porter at least casually. She'd probably know the recent gossip about him, whatever that might be, more than I. But I wouldn't say the two moved in the same circles, Lieutenant."

"Well, if I need to catch up on the gossip, I'll know who to talk with. Her illness doesn't appear to have stilled her interest in people and living." Andrews observed.

"One more thing and I'll leave you to your work. The victim's office and lab will be sealed as long as necessary to review his papers and office suite for clues. I'm at a loss to know what to do with the animals in the meanwhile. What would you suggest?"

"I'll be glad to arrange for them to be moved," Langston offered.

"I'd rather not lose track of them," Andrews admitted. "I can't say how they might tie in, but until I've reviewed everything, I'd like to keep them secured." Andrews knew the explanation sounded lame.

Langston looked confused, but he tried again to offer his cooperation. "Do you want me to arrange for someone to go into the lab and feed the animals"?

Andrews explained the necessity of keeping people out of the crime area, and finally admitted that he wanted to take the two dogs with him. To Andrews' delight, Langston immediately agreed and offered to bring the guinea pigs into his own office, promising to keep them available.

When Andrews indicated he'd like to make a few phone calls and then leave with the two dogs, Langston responded cooperatively, "I'll arrange with Hogge to let you out through the service entrance with the dogs whenever you like, Lieutenant."

Andrews' relief at getting out with the dogs without difficulty was offset by Langston's next words. "I'm not a vet, but the smaller one looks to be in bad shape to me. I think he's simply given up, lost the will to live. His respiration was depressed, his heart rate was down, and he refused to eat or drink when I was in the lab earlier. If you expect to use the animals in any way later, you'd better have a vet look the little one over soon. It may already be too late to save him."

Chapter 11

Andrews declined Langston's offer of cages for the dogs. Instead, he elected to put the larger one in the back of his station wagon and to place the smaller one on the seat beside him as he drove through the early spring evening to the Colt's home in Williamsburg. The black dog was anxious but obviously delighted to be freed of the cage and the sounds and smells of the medical school. The smaller one appeared not to care, lying impassively on the seat beside Andrews and breathing shallowly. Worry over his four-footed witnesses and indecision over just how much to tell Jonathan and Genna about the case occupied Andrews' mind as he drove.

The afternoon rain had given way to a clear night sky. Andrews gave notice neither to the beauty of the spring evening nor that of the scenic two-lane byway running closest to the James River, which he'd chosen to take on his way to Williamsburg. Long before he reached any conclusions on how much to tell the Colts, he was turning off Route 5 and into the long drive of the Kingsley property called Heron's Rest.

Jonathan Colt opened the front door of the Colt home and walked out to meet his godfather before Andrews completely stopped in the front of the house.

"Hi, Uncle Kevin. Figured you'd need some help with your charges. Want me to take the little one here on the front seat?" Jonathan asked in what served for a greeting.

87

Without waiting for Andrews to answer, the tall host opened the door of the passenger side and gently lifted the inert lump of bones and matted grey fur. With the smaller dog cradled securely in his long arms, he turned back toward the open front door.

"Just leave your car where it is. No one else needs to use the front drive tonight." Jonathan led the way back into the house with his limp burden.

Andrews collected the larger dog from the car and followed his host into the house through the great room and into the huge eat-in kitchen beyond. Genna waited beside a kitchen table that had been draped with a blanket and rubber sheet. With the briefest of waves and a soft hello to Andrews, she turned her attention to the small bundle of misery which her husband deposited on the table.

Grey eyes swimming with tears looked up to face Andrews briefly. "Take the other one out back and let her run around in the fenced enclosure," Genna directed. "Leave me alone with this poor little fellow for awhile."

Tears tracked down the square face and wet a quivering chin, softening only slightly the strong jaw. That jaw was clinched tightly now, Andrews noted, reflecting a mind singularly focused on helping the pitiful bundle of fur on the table before her.

The two men quietly turned to leave the kitchen with the black dog. Andrews noted with approval the gentle fingers which reached to stroke the head of the grey dog on the table, and the soft, throaty voice that promised the animal his troubles were over.

A short time later the two men stood together in the yard enjoying the cool evening and the antics of the black dog, which lost no time in taking advantage of the offer to explore the large, fenced enclosure behind the house.

"I'm not certain Genna and I are doing the little fellow in there any service by encouraging him to live," Jonathan said, a worried frown plain on his face. "On the phone you said you were seizing them from a medical research lab temporarily, didn't you?"

Andrews could only mumble an agreement with his godson's statement. All the way down from Richmond he had debated just how much to tell Jonathan and Genna about the circumstances surrounding the dogs and the related murder investigation.

"It was a foolish thing to do, involving you and Genna in this. But I didn't know what else to do," the portly figure admitted.

"Genna and I would never have forgiven you if you hadn't," Jonathan assured him. "But I presume you are prepared to have Genna fight you all the way about returning them to the lab."

That problem had been Andrews' big worry also, but he tried to suppress discussion of it at this time. The need to protect the dogs until he could learn their importance to key figures in this case was more important.

"I would have thought you had enough dogs around here now," Andrews hedged. "Where are all your 'children-in-fur' as Genna calls them? I haven't heard anything from them since I arrived."

Jonathan and Genna had no children nor did they plan to have any. They were dedicated to their individual and demanding careers. But two dogs, and now one very young puppy plus one much larger cat, called the Colt household home, entertained the couple with their antics, enriched their lives with their devotion, and were referred to by Genna as the Colts' "children". Ordinarily the cat adorned the top of the TV console and the two adult dogs were underfoot, into everything, and swarming around a visitor until they received the amount of attention, praise, and affection which the two presumed their just due. With all the distress and concern for his two canine charges, Andrews had not missed the noise and milling bodies of the resident canines until now.

"Sky is upstairs on our bed pouting," Jonathan admitted, "because Amber is getting most of Genna's attention today. Genna told you about the newest addition, little Rusty, didn't she?"

"Oh, yes. She informed me that I was great-godfather to a dog," Andrews snorted. "Sky's son to boot!"

Sky was Genna's constant shadow but Andrews' nemesis. Spoiled, self-assured, demanding, and in Andrews' mind, disrespectful, Sky not only encouraged, he demanded the attention of even tired, cranky detectives who thought they came to rest and relax at the Colt's home. Sky appeared to reason that any human who entered his domain was fair game as an opponent in a tug-the-toy game, and all visitors were persistently offered the slimy end of a rawhide bone to hold.

Andrews was constantly amazed at the changes in his godson since he'd met and married Genna two years ago. Jonathan's father and Andrews grew up together and decided on a career in law enforcement together. Andrews never married, but had been a frequent visitor in the Colt home when Jonathan and his younger sister were growing up. Jonathan's parents were killed in a car wreck when Jonathan was a senior in college. After that, it seemed only natural that Andrews should continue in his role of "uncle" to his diminished but affectionate extended family.

Jonathan showed early talent at writing, and by his late twenties was an established science fiction novelist. Andrews could never understand the public's interest in the books, however. They were paper sleeping pills for Andrews, try as he might to interest himself in them for Jonathan's sake.

An old cat adopted Jonathan at some point shortly after the beginning of his writing career. Since it required little attention, asking only food and water and a small space upon which to sleep away the hours while Jonathan wrote, it was an equitable arrangement for both the glossy, black short-hair and the young writer. Neither got in the other's way. Jonathan occasionally discussed his plot difficulties with the cat, who never criticized the work, and Jonathan refrained from littering the top of the TV which was Cat's chosen sleeping spot.

When Jonathan's younger sister married, Andrews and Jonathan continued their unbroken routine as bachelors. And then Jonathan met Genna Kingsley.

Old Robert Kingsley, Genna's grandfather, made his fortune by means of a lucky discovery, a little device that was the important part of auto-pilots in aircraft. He'd patented the device and it made him very wealthy.

Genna Kingsley was an engineer like her grandfather and a wealthy woman too, something all too many people coveted. More than two years ago Genna had found herself involved in a murder, cast in the role of chief suspect. Jonathan had met and fallen in love with her then.

Before that time, Jonathan had never had a dog, never been around any animal except Cat, and never indicated any desire to be. Then he met and married a young woman who called Papillons her siblings and adjusted his honeymoon plans three different times so that Genna's dog, Sky, could accompany them on that honeymoon. In spite of it all, Andrews was forced to admit that his godson was happy in his choice of partners. He seemed not only able but content to write in the confusion of two small dogs milling around his office and yapping at each other and at Cat.

Andrews reverie was audibly interrupted by a loud rumbling from the region of his stomach. Before he could apologize, Jonathan laughed out loud.

"I think your body is protesting the late dinner. Genna has something prepared, but the two of us aren't likely to get any attention until she gets the little dog settled. How about some cheese and crackers in the meanwhile? Would you like a beer, some tea, or what?"

Andrews decided to compromise on his diet, again. Cheese and crackers were probably more starch than he was supposed to have, but he was very hungry and besides, he deserved some reward for foregoing a beer, didn't he?

"Tea will be fine. I'm supposed to give up the beer for awhile, until I get some of this girth reduced," he admitted, patting his rotund middle. "Shall we leave the dog out here a while longer?"

Deciding between them not to do so, it took the two men more than a few tries to catch the dog. Once caught, however, the dog reentered the house and accompanied the two as far as the study. Obviously accustomed to being in a house, the dog found a convenient corner, sniffed around a few times, curled herself into a ball and settled down with head on front paws to watch cautiously the goings on of the humans.

Jonathan risked Genna's censure to collect a tray of drinks and food from the kitchen before returning to the study to relax with Andrews over snacks. Unlike other dogs Andrews could name, his canine witness did not feel obligated to share in the humans' food. Deciding that the black dog deserved a name, Jonathan and Andrews christened her Blacky and drank to her health.

"Genna will probably have other ideas," Jonathan acknowledged.

"No doubt," Andrews agreed between bites. "Genna has this thing for alliterations."

Upon meeting Cat, who had been Cat to Jonathan for more than four years, Genna declared that such an uninspired name was unworthy of the elegant gentleman and promptly changed his name to Kit Kat. Cat or Kat still ate out of the same bowl, labeled **CAT**, and slept on the same TV, so Andrews couldn't see that it mattered. But it made Genna happy and was therefore fine with Jonathan.

Andrews wondered how dinner was coming. He wondered how the little grey dog was doing. But he didn't wonder enough to get up and inquire about either. It felt good to relax, nibble on the cheese and crackers and let someone else decide the agenda for a change.

"Rough case?" Jonathan asked.

"Touchy and confusing. Everyone had an opinion about the victim, most of them contradictory. We learned about the murder at eight this morning," Andrews responded grimly, "and Sergeant Foster and I have been rushing around all day talking to people connected with the Institute and the victim's wife."

"By the way, I left this phone number with my office in case Sergeant Foster needs to reach me tonight. I tried to contact Foster before I left Richmond but he'd already left to have dinner. I didn't think you'd mind," Andrews continued.

"Of course not, but Genna and I hope you're planning to spend the night with us," Jonathan said.

Andrews had been undecided when he came, but now that dinner was running so late, he quickly decided that a restful night with the Colts would be just what a tired and confused detective needed. His bag was still in the car, packed last night for his intended weekend visit.....before this latest homicide had interrupted his plans.

There was always his nemesis who was upstairs somewhere, of course. But maybe a little time away from his apartment was worth a bit of tug-of-war. He relaxed a bit more just thinking about not having to drive back to Richmond tonight.

Aloud he said, "Thanks. I'd like to. Foster plans to return to the Institute tonight and talk with the cleaning crew. I talked to him just before leaving Richmond to see how the search of trash from last night was coming. We still haven't located the murder weapon."

"Four members of the cleaning crew and a supervisor were in the building last night during the time of the murder, but it isn't clear whether any of them saw or heard anything related to the murder. Anyway Foster will be questioning them this evening."

"Funny the cleaning crew didn't hear or see anything strange, isn't it?" Jonathan asked. "At least, the news reporter on TV said neither the security nor the cleaning crews had heard anything."

"Oh, well. Foster will earn his pay tonight questioning the cleaning crew, if they've been exposed to the press already. But I'm not certain how much they could contribute. The victim kept his office suite and lab locked and the labs are sound proof, or supposed to be."

"But a cleaning crew would have master keys to get in, wouldn't they?" Jonathan asked.

"Well, in most cases the offices are open. But the victim complained about threats several months ago and kept his locked. The threats were, according to the victim, to his research not his life," Andrews explained. "But he's very dead now."

Andrews' review of the homicide in Richmond was interrupted by Genna. Her face was relaxed and the corners of her mouth turned up slightly in the beginnings of a smile.

"Dinner is served in the dining room, gentlemen," she said brightly, "and in case anyone is interested, Mushie is resting quietly in a bed in the kitchen. I got some water and Karo syrup down him, along with two teaspoons of Nutrical. He won't eat yet, but he's breathing normally."

"Mushie is it! Well, I would have named him Lucky myself. But if you want to call him Mushie, go right ahead. I don't suppose he'll mind," Andrews said agreeably.

The two men expressed their satisfaction at both items of her news, and quickly relocated themselves around the dining room table. Genna nodded briefly to the black dog on the floor of her husband's study, promised the dog her attention after dinner, and went to join her husband and guest.

Chapter 12

Andrews couldn't decide whether the meal was delicious because of its quality or his extreme hunger. At any rate it was enjoyable and extremely satisfying. Even the occasional sounds of Sky's scratching, which filtered through to the dining room from the bedroom on the story above, did not diminish his pleasure at the fresh salad, flaky rolls, crisp vegetables and the shrimp, cheddar cheese and rice dish which was before him. Both men devoted their attentions to piling their plates and ingesting the culinary offerings with gusto. Jonathan paused from time to time to brush the flecks of bread off his navy, knit shirt. Not Andrews. He let crumbs lie where they fell and continued his efforts to provide his jaws with food as fast as he could chew.

Genna ate sparingly and seemed more inclined to conversation. Engrossed with his food and his momentary but singular concern with appeasing his stomach, it took Andrews a few minutes to realize that Genna was continuing the conversation she'd started in the study after calling him and her husband to dinner.

"He won't mind being called Mushie because that is his name. He's wearing a tattoo. I called two national dog registries before I got some information about him. He was stolen from his back yard in Pennsylvania three months ago while his owners were watching the eleven o'clock news. They've been frantic to find him since that time," Genna informed her dinner partners.

"What?" Andrews said, finally focusing on the topic of conversation.

"That little dog in there is stolen property. Why didn't the institute call and try to identify him from his tattoo?" the young woman demanded. "His owners have been frantic."

The grey eyes challenged first Andrews and then Jonathan, as though one of them should answer the question. Andrews was busy with another line of concern.

"I don't know that it was wise to let a dog registry know about the dog," Andrews said. "Both dogs are evidence in a police investigation at the moment. After that situation has been resolved, I'll have to take the issue of his ownership up with Institute personnel...", the beefy man tried to explain and deal with a mouthful of food at the same time. He was hotly interrupted by Genna.

"Police matter, be damned! That dog doesn't belong to the institute and it doesn't belong to you," Genna snapped, her voice several tones higher.

She recovered her control almost immediately, however, and continued on a softer, more reasoning note. "Given Mushie's condition, he's not much good to you as a witness. The next time he meets the jerk who terrorized him, he'll just will himself to die. He's had all he can take of terror and loneliness. And as far as the Institute being entitled to take him back, well we'll just see about that. He's stolen property and he's going back to his rightful owners. Mushie needs his humans as much as they need him. And as soon as the registry can locate them and give them this phone number, I'm going to try to get them together again."

The square jaw was clinched again, and dark eyebrows raised in a challenge of Andrews.

"All Uncle Kevin means, honey..." Jonathan tried to inject.

"I don't care what Uncle Kevin means," the grey eyes flashed at Jonathan. "We agreed that we would live on your earnings, except for the maintenance of my family property, but I never said I wouldn't spend my money any way I chose to help animals. And whatever it takes, I intend to see that Mushie is reunited with his owners," Genna said angrily, but her chin began to quiver and her grey eyes were bright with unshed tears.

Andrews was reminded once again of his role in exposing Genna to the dogs, and his godson's caution earlier of Genna's protective attitude toward them.

"All right, honey. Mushie will go back to his owners as soon as it can be arranged. What's the point of having a police lieutenant in the family if he can't arrange little things like that," Jonathan said soothingly.

Andrews opened his mouth to protest this commitment of his efforts, but the jade eyes in his godson's narrow face silently implored his assent or silence. A nearly imperceptible nod passed between the two men, as Andrews acknowledged that Genna was too emotionally involved to listen to any options at the moment that contrasted with her own plans for the pathetic bundle of grey fur resting quietly in the kitchen.

Andrews silently accepted the responsibility for setting up this emotional outburst. He should have known, he told himself, that it was not wise to involve Jonathan's wife in this case and bring the dogs to her. He cursed himself for acting on impulse in removing the dogs from the lab in the first place. Given Genna's discovery that the smaller animal was tattooed and stolen, maybe it was that fact alone which Berkley and Ketterholt had sought to hide.

Aloud he said, "I can't fault your reasoning, Genna. So if you do locate his owners, just tell them what you wish and we'll work something out about getting...what's his name? Mushie?...getting Mushie back to them. I'm certain I can arrange something with Mathew Langston."

Jonathan's broad hand with its short, well-groomed nails had reached across the tablecloth to hold and squeeze his wife's smaller one. Genna fought back tears.

"While we're waiting to hear from the tattoo registry, maybe Uncle Kevin will fill us in on this case. From the TV news coverage I've heard so far, it promises to be interesting. Who knows, maybe you'll be able to see some logical explanation for this case too." Jonathan cast an imploring look at Andrews.

It was the last thing Andrews wanted to talk about, especially tonight, but he realized that Jonathan was trying desperately to distract Genna from her anger over Mushie's situation. She had shown interest in previous homicide cases, in finding, as she put it, the simplest explanation which fitted all the facts of a case. The only trouble Andrews had was in sifting though the day's events and separating facts from side issues. When Jonathan's green eyes flashed another appeal to him, Andrews reluctantly began to review the events of the day with his godson and Genna without trying to edit out what he might view as nonessentials.

Genna and Jonathan listened attentively to Andrews' recitations of the discovery of the body and the resulting investigations to date. Genna's tears dried and she appeared to focus more objectively on the situation surrounding the murder and to lose some of her earlier agitation over Mushie's situation. Then during a long pause while Andrews was finishing the last bit of food on his plate, Genna interrupted the sated man with a query.

"So a letter from a disgruntled parent was followed by a copy of Rauvola-Kemp's poem and then drawings of eyes to repeatedly remind the victim of lab animals' plights. But Langston wouldn't tell you whom he suspected of sending the drawings and poem to the victim? Do you think Langston could have sent them himself, just hinted he suspected someone else?"

Genna's question caught Andrews with a mouth full of food, and he choked in surprise at the implication hidden in her questions. Gasping for breath and coughing, he managed to whisper, "Whose poem?"

"I asked you a question first," Genna teased.

"Oh, all right!" Andrews conceded. "Langston is cocky enough and brash enough to have done it, but everything I know about him so far indicates an individual who fights openly and verbally. So far, I don't know of any child he has lost to illness or otherwise. Now, whose poem?"

"You said someone sent Porter a poem called **Brown Eyes**, didn't you? I assume you mean the classic anti-vivisection poem written some years ago by Becky L. Rauvola-Kemp," Genna replied.

"I've never heard the name. Do you mean you know of such a poem?" Andrews managed in strained tone. The threat of rice down the windpipe did not improve a man's feeling of well being.

"Sure. A framed copy of the poem is hanging on the wall in my study. Want to see it?"

At an affirming nod from the surprised detective, Genna excused herself and went to get the document.

"Well, I never....." Andrews finally stammered.

"You said Langston was critical of Porter's experiments with animals," Jonathan reminded his godfather. "It looks as though he wasn't the only one, or that he sent the poem and drawings to the victim."

Before Andrews could reply, Genna returned with a small frame containing beautifully calligraphied lines of poetry. A dog's head with pleading eyes was drawn in pen and ink at the bottom. The title of the poem centered at the top read **Brown Eyes**. In the bottom right hand corner, a name appeared: *Becky L. Rauvola-Kemp*. Genna handed the frame to Andrews without comment.

All day various witnesses connected with the case had described the victim's agitations at receiving what turned out to be a poem. Now Andrews saw why as he read the touching and powerful message in the framed lines.

Brown Eyes

Brown eyes—warm and sparkling
With the glow of friendship and life.
Deep pools of compassion reveling a loving soul
Of innocence and trust too freely given.
"Never mind the cage and bars—
Ignore the dark and the loneliness
Just for a touch—a pat
Of the superior being's hand
(Which never comes—but maybe...).
Never mind the fear and uncertainty—

Ignore the pain and suffering
That exist as the experiments are done
Maybe then I will be loved....after.
Just think, for now, of home, of long ago.
My old owners—do they know where I am?
They loved me almost as much as I loved them."
Brown eyes—confused and dulled by drugs.
As a hand reaches for him
A flicker of hope still lights his eyes.
His tail still thumps feebly, and a soft whimper
Breaks the sterility of science.
Another needle punctures his hopes—
And he gasps for breath as the hand records the time.
Brown eyes—clouding and staring.
The last signs of life convulse through his lifeless body.
One last useless whine escapes from his tightening throat.
Followed by his final fight for LIFE.
The hand reaches for his neck to check
For the last pulsation of blood—of life.....
His tongue reaches out to touch the hand
In his last loving gesture of gentleness and forgiveness.
Through all the hell and torture
He still loved, and believed, and hoped.
He still dreamed of his home, the field he once ran in,
The love and happiness he knew, the freedom he had.
Go—find your home now—
Rest in peace at last, Brown Eyes.
The experiment is done.

"While you're reading that I'll clear the dinner plates away and get our dessert," Genna said softly. She was obviously pleased with his attention to the poem.

Andrews was so absorbed with the poem that Genna had to ask twice whether he wanted regular or decaf coffee with his apple pie. "Oh, decaf please," Andrews responded finally.

"Well, what do you think? It says it all beautifully doesn't it? And it certainly seems that someone was trying to raise Porter's conscience about his experiments, don't you think?" Genna prodded as she settled into her seat at the table again.

When Andrews failed to answer immediately, Genna switched the topic back to food. "Hope you like the dessert," she said. "Jonathan said you were on a diet, but I know how you love my apple pie, so I fixed it anyway. You don't have to eat it if you'd rather not."

Andrews was pleased with the unexpected acquisition of the poem.... he knew it had to be the same poem numerous witnesses had described today ...to feel more than a momentary concern for his diet. In the next day or two, routine police investigations would find a copy of this same poem, perhaps among Porter's papers. But he had it tonight. He thought of calling Foster and sharing the find with him. Then he remembered his partner would be at the Institute, questioning the cleaning crew about the previous evening.

"May I keep this to show to my partner tomorrow?" the tubby policeman asked.

"Well, I guess so..." Genna replied. "But take good care of it. I want it back as soon as you can part with it."

"Where did you find a copy of this poem, Genna?" Andrews tried to keep the question low keyed, but his official tone came through.

"Are you adding me to your list of suspects now, Uncle Kevin?" Genna asked with a laugh.

Jonathan had kept quiet through most of their exchange, eating his pie in silence and listening to the verbal tussle between godfather and wife. An audible chuckle indicated his amusement of this latest exchange of wits.

"No. Just trying to determine where someone might have gotten a copy of this poem." Andrews looked briefly at Jonathan for support, but decided the grinning rascal was enjoying his discomfort and was unlikely to help. "It might help to determine who sent the poem," he answered defensively. "Besides, you're more than an hour's drive from the crime scene, you don't have a car phone and I was on the phone with you both at 9:10 last night," he added just to tease her.

"Well, I really can't tell you. My copy was in some handouts obtained at a legislative subcommittee hearing on an animal protection bill some years ago. I'm afraid I don't know who from."

"Ketterholt said the murder was the work of animal rights terrorists. Now if only animal rights activists have a copy of the poem, can you give me a good reason why I shouldn't regard this poem as strengthening that view?"

"Oh, you're really asking for it, Uncle Kevin," Jonathan got in with a laugh before Genna took up the fight.

"Well, for two very good reasons I can think of immediately. First, they wouldn't have left the little guinea pig behind to suffer through the night. Secondly, they wouldn't have made a martyr out of a creep like the victim," Genna reasoned.

Jonathan grinned and went on eating his pie. Andrews enjoyed these verbal battles as much as Genna did. Both found them an enjoyable means of relaxing.

The phone rang and Genna excused herself to take the call on the kitchen extension, leaving a bemused husband and his appreciative godfather to finish their desserts.

When Genna didn't return immediately, Jonathan and Andrews finished their meal with small talk about Jonathan's new book. Andrews' mind was on the case and not the plot Jonathan was outlining, but the visitor didn't feel guilty about the divided attention to his godson's conversation. He'd never understood any of Jonathan's plots even when he tried. Finally, Jonathan suggested that the two men return to the study and more comfortable chairs.

"I'll just clear the table and join you in the study," Jonathan said.

Suiting his action to his words, Jonathan gathered a stack of dirty dishes into the kitchen just in time to hear Genna saying, "Good-bye" and "We'll expect you both sometime tomorrow then" to the phone.

"Who was that?" Jonathan inquired apprehensively.

A smug smile and shining grey eyes were briefly visible as Genna took the dirty dishes from him and turned to put them in the sink. "Mushie's owners," was spoken so softly Jonathan almost missed it.

"They're coming here? Tomorrow?" Jonathan stammered. "But Uncle Kevin hasn't worked that out with the Institute yet."

The determined face which turned to face him held no appreciation of conflicting opinions.

"It made no difference what I think. Or what Uncle Kevin thinks. Or what the Institute thinks," Jonathan prattled.

"I know," Jonathan groaned. "Mushie doesn't belong to Uncle Kevin or to the police or to the Institute! He's stolen property and you'll make an issue out of it if we let you. In your present mood, you'd love a fight with anyone and especially the Institute—as public and as messy as possible. Compromising Uncle Kevin's case doesn't mean a thing."

Genna came to stand in front of her husband and put her arms around his neck. "He was on a wire run inside a fenced back yard. His owners put him out for a few minutes while they were getting ready for bed. When they went to get him, they found the wire cut and him gone. They've been searching for him for over three months. He's their only "child" and both have been sick with worry. Do you really blame me?" Genna asked gently. "Look at Mushie. He knows everything's going to be all right now."

In a quiet corner of the kitchen the object of the controversy lay quietly on a bed composed of the folded rubber sheet and blanket which had covered the kitchen table on his arrival. Mushie's eyes were half closed, but he lay now with head between paws, more responsive than when he'd arrived some two hours before.

Jonathan sighed in resignation. "I should protest your high-handed manner in this, but I guess I really don't have the heart to.

"So, what are you're going to do?" a throaty voice asked.

"What any red-blooded, American husband would do in a situation that he can't win." He pulled his wife to him and kissed the stubborn chin. "Go explain the way of things to Uncle Kevin."

Mushie's half-closed eyes followed Genna's movements around the kitchen as she cleared away the cooking things and loaded the dishwasher. She spoke to him softly, calling his name frequently, but the feeble movement of his tail could hardly be called a wag. Still, he didn't appear frightened when her routine movements took her closer to him or react in fear when she turned on the dishwasher.

"Probably used to the noise," she vocalized. "I bet you watched your folks in Pennsylvania load their dishwasher and know that it won't hurt you."

Genna prattled on about nothing in particular as she set out a small and a medium size metal dish and mixed dry and canned dog food for Sky and the larger black dog in the den. Before leaving the kitchen with the other dogs' dishes of food, she got Mushie to swallow another teaspoon of Nutrical and several tablespoons of water.

Her husband and his godfather were settled into two comfortable chairs in the study when she joined them again. Andrews carefully hid his concerns over the impending arrival of claimants to the grey dog.

The black dog was sitting up and fearfully backed against the corner of the study. Her attitude differed from her pre-dinner stance and Genna's attention was diverted to the new problem.

"Did something happen to the dog to make her upset?" Genna asked.

"Blacky.....Jonathan and I named her Blacky....didn't like being turned over by the two of us to check for another tattoo," Andrews answered gruffly. "I wanted to make certain you wouldn't rob me of my remaining witness."

He kept his head down to hide the slight smile touching the corners of his mouth, and didn't look Genna in the face.

Genna's face softened and she almost laughed."Oh, stop pretending! You're not really upset about Mushie and you know it," she admonished. "You were hoping to find a way to identify Blacky's owners too."

"And really get myself in trouble with my Captain?" Andrews countered. Then he gave up his pretended gruffness and laughed. "All right, so I was. But," he said more seriously, "we've gotten Blacky so upset with turning her on to her back that she doesn't want Jonathan or me to come near her now."

"That's all right. She'll calm down in a minute," Genna comforted. Turning to her husband she said, "Maybe she'd feel safer with another dog to keep her company. Why don't you go upstairs and let Sky out of the bedroom. He'll be delighted to meet another lady friend."

"But will Blacky be delighted to meet Sky?" Andrews gibed.

"Uncle Kevin finds Sky's energy level a little difficult to take after a long day of detecting." Jonathan chuckled as he uncurled his tall, lanky body from the easy chair and started for the upstairs bedroom to get Sky.

"Uncle Kevin finds Sky's energy level hard to take at any time of the day," Andrews corrected.

Genna ignored the two men, crossed the study at a slow pace, and spoke to the fearful dog in soft tones. She gently deposited the larger dish of food in easy reach of the trembling black muzzle. The black dog, which Andrews and his godson had dubbed Blacky, followed the offered food dish with her eyes but did not relax her tensed position or lower her muzzle to sniff the contents.

The sounds of Jonathan's footsteps on the stairs were followed immediately by an explosion of furry energy as Sky bounded into the study. The fluffy bundle was up on the arm and across the back of Andrews' chair the second after the little dog entered the room, kissing the tensed detective's ear on the way.

"Damn," Andrews howled. His abrupt movement to dodge the little dog's energetic greeting proved too much for one of his shirt buttons. All day the button had strained to contain his spreading diaphragm; it finally lost the fight and popped.

After a second lick on the back of Andrews' unprotected neck, Sky was off the chair and on his way across the study to his mistress. His detour up and across Andrews had given Genna a chance to stand and face the tiny dog's greeting. With a leap that would have done a gazelle credit he launched himself straight up and level with her chest so that all she had to do was extend her arms to catch him. Laughingly she did so and managed not to spill the small dish of food she still held.

"I don't guess he'll want any food until he settles a little," Genna observed as she turned to put the dish of food away on the shelf of the bookcase which lined the end of the study.

"Sailors and everyone else should take warning when Sky comes to call," Andrews grumbled.

"Now, Uncle Kevin," Genna said fondly, "he's been waiting patiently upstairs to get a chance to visit with you. Besides, he's been locked out of the nursery all day and I've been paying more attention to Amber and his new son than I have to him. He's a little excited, but he'll calm down in a minute."

"That remains to be seen," Andrews countered as he scrambled around on the floor for his missing button.

The tiny bundle of silken fur flattened himself against his mistress, his pointed muzzle tucked under Genna's chin. A pink tongue darted out to lick the lobe of her right ear. The woman's slender fingers stroked the long, white coat while Sky's flowing tail fanned the air in rapid acknowledgment of his happiness.

"We have a visitor, Sky," Genna told the tiny animal as though he understood every word. "She's very uncertain of her reception, so you need to be gentle and make her welcome."

Turning so that she and the small dog could face Blacky, Genna repositioned Sky so that his attention could focus fully on the visiting canine. As Sky noticed Blacky's presence for the first time, his large ears cupped and flickered back and forth like a butterfly in flight.

"Be nice now, Sky," Jonathan admonished from the doorway. "She's been through a lot of stress and isn't certain she trusts anyone at the moment."

"After being exposed to Sky, Blacky may decide she's safer back at the research lab," Andrews injected sourly. Sky was, after all, not Andrews' favorite dog.

"Blacky will be fine," Genna pronounced. Leaning over, she deposited the tiny bundle of white-and-red hair on the floor several yards in front of the anxious, black dog.

Even Andrews had to smile at Sky's antics as he danced and postured in front of this newly discovered visitor. His long, white coat flashed silvery in the artificial lights of the study as he alternately jumped forward to touch noses with Blacky and jumped back when she pulled back in indecision.

Blacky's coat was dull and unkempt, a visual contrast that underlined the difference in advantages enjoyed by the two animals. But Andrews' training at minute observations noted that between cautious checks on the positions of the three humans, the black dog was beginning to respond to the friendly advances of the tiny terror.

Andrews found his missing button at last and eased his bulk back into the easy chair. Blacky watched his actions closely, but did not cringe against the wall of the study as she had earlier. Jonathan's movement across the study in response to a ringing telephone was awarded the briefest of looks, before Blacky returned her attention to the red-and-white canine dancer in front of her.

"Sure, he's right here," Jonathan said into the phone. He held the phone out toward Andrews saying, "Lt. Brown wants to talk with you. If you'd like privacy there's an extension in the kitchen and another one in our bedroom upstairs."

"What is Brax doing at work this time of night," Andrews mumbled in puzzlement, taking the phone headpiece out of Jonathan's hand without responding to his offer of alternate locations.

"I think I'll take these two out in the yard for a romp," Genna whispered to her husband.

Genna managed to coax Blacky to follow her and Sky out of the study and through the great room into the side entrance to the yard. The larger dog's tail was tucked between her legs and she kept as far away from the two men as possible on her way out of the room, but she followed Genna and Sky to the freedom and soft coolness of the Virginia night.

Genna let the two dogs explore the fenced yard for some time before she softly called to Sky to "Come." Despite his obvious enjoyment at romping with his exciting, new friend, the tiny dog responded instantly. In testimonial to the truth of the CD and CDX titles he'd earned, he instantly stopped his romping and came to sit quietly in front of and facing his standing mistress. At a signal from Genna to "Heel", he circled her body and returned to a sitting position facing forward and adjacent to her left leg. Commands to Sky of "Down" and "Stay" allowed Genna a chance to move away from Sky and observe the behavior of the larger dog when faced with a rigidly, fixed playmate.

Assured that Sky would hold the long "Down" until another command released him, Genna casually flopped down on the grass close to the diminutive champion and waited for Blacky's reactions. Wary of Genna at first, the black dog gradually relaxed when Genna made no move toward her. Genna spoke to her in a softly pitched voice, telling Blacky that she was a smart dog as was Sky. To further accustom Blacky to the sound of her voice, Genna continued to discuss the case with Sky.

"Now that Uncle Kevin knows that Mushie was stolen, he's probably thinking that explains why the Institute personnel want to get these two guys back. Sifting through motives of greed, differences on research methods, ordinary garden-variety adultery, animal rights issues and the like, Uncle Kevin hasn't mentioned the most obvious motive raised by Mushie's situation. And the strongest! Now I find that interesting!"

At first Blacky seemed puzzled by Sky's stillness and Genna's voice, but as time passed the black dog seemed to become accustomed to both. She even forgot her fear enough to stretch her muzzle out and sniff at Genna's hand. Only when the black dog got up and began to explore the yard on her own did Genna get up from the grass, release Sky from his stay-command and call both dogs to follow her. Blacky's reentry into the house was accomplished with little show of reluctance and with tail held high.

Chapter 13

"Do you think this Roalf could be involved with the murder?" Jonathan was saying when Genna and the two dogs reentered the study.

"At the moment, I don't think anything except that it is something else to check." Andrews responded. His voice carried none of the excitement evident in that of his godson. "According to Foster, cleaning crews don't stay around very long. The work is hard, the pay is lousy, the benefits are nonexistent and the average longevity is about three months. The fact that a newly-hired staff didn't show for work on a Friday night would be meaningless at any other time. But he was working in the hallway outside the victim's lab. Langston mentioned seeing him there when he returned to the Institute at 9:45pm. So Roalf could have seen or heard something important last night."

"Did I miss something?" Genna asked as she settled Blacky back into the corner of the study with the bowl of food close by. "Was the phone call from one of the officers assigned to your homicide?"

"No, it was Billy's son, another lieutenant of homicide. Braxton was at the office directing the investigation of a second homicide discovered today, and he was calling me to relay a message from my partner. It seems Sgt. Foster tried to call earlier but the phone was busy for a long period of time, no doubt made so by a certain individual who likes to obstruct murder investigations," Andrews said.

"Oh, stop grousing," Genna chided him. "He could have left a message for you. Besides, you're as happy as Jonathan and I are about finding Mushie's owners and you know it! So what did Sgt. Foster or Lt. Brown have to say? Who's Roalf?"

"Foster went back to the institute to question the cleaning crew. One of them, Drew Roalf, didn't show up for work tonight, and he couldn't be reached at his home number," Jonathan injected before Andrews could respond.

Taking Sky's bowl of food from the bookcase, Genna placed the container on the floor a small distance from Blacky so that Sky could enjoy his meal or share it with Blacky as he chose. Finally, she asked, "And this Roalf is the cleaning person who was newly-hired last night, the night of the murder?"

"Yes. Roalf started work as a member of the cleaning crew only last night, seemed a fair if slow worker according to all my partner can determine from the other members of the cleaning crew with whom he talked. Roalf didn't show up for work tonight when Foster went to question the group. He was supposed to but he didn't. Foster got Roalf's home number and tried to reach him at home, but got a recording," Andrews explained.

"Could he have had something else to do with the murder?" Genna asked.

"There's no way to tell at this point," Andrews cautioned, "but a lot of possibilities exist. Roalf was an inexperienced and slow worker, according to Foster's sources. He was assigned to clean and wax the ground lobby area which included the area outside Porter's office suite. He might have seen something and been frightened at learning it related to a murder. He might have had something in his background he didn't want police investigating. Porter might have admitted him to clean since the victim was in his office to monitor things. But if he did see the victim last night or see something strange, I'd think he would have mentioned it to someone else in the cleaning crew. Unless he didn't realize it was strange until he learned of the murder." It was obvious

111

that the portly sleuth was worried about this latest line of thought.

Softly, almost as though he'd forgotten the presence of two other humans in the room, Andrews continued, "Maybe he saw something he wasn't supposed to see. Or heard something he shouldn't have. I should have asked Braxton to describe the second homicide victim found this morning."

Andrews was out of his chair and reaching for the phone before he really finished vocalizing his thoughts. Remembering his manners, he belatedly mumbled, "Hope you don't mind", almost simultaneous with giving his charge card number to the operator.

Several barks into the phone later Andrews had asked for Braxton Brown and then a description of the other murder victim. Some of the tension seemed to go out of his body as he listened. If possible, he slouched even more and the thickening around his middle was more pronounced, causing an even wider gap in his shirt front where the button was missing.

"Well, short and thin does not describe this Roalf, so your victim can't be my missing cleaning crew. Thanks. If Foster calls again, tell him I'm staying in Williamsburg tonight, but I'll call him tomorrow when I return to Richmond." Andrews smiled and nodded at the phone at something Braxton Brown was saying, then ended his conversation with another relieved, "Thanks."

Turning to Genna and Jonathan, Andrews said, "Well, the description Braxton gives of another homicide victim found this morning doesn't match Roalf's description."

During the phone conversation, Sky had taken advantage of the vacated chair to stake a claim on the warmed cushion. When pushed by his beefy guest, the tiny fur-ball crowded against the arm of the chair but did not vacate the padded comfort as Andrews reseated himself in the portion of the chair left to him by Sky.

"Damn, Sky, how can you take up so much space at your size!"

Andrews' grumbling at Sky's presence prompted a hand signal from Genna to the dog to get down. The motion was obeyed with some reluctance by Sky, who slowly removed himself from Andrews' chair and returned to the floor to lie by Blacky's side.

"So we're back to the same number of suspects with the possibility now that this Roalf might have witnessed something that was significant," Genna mused. "What did you make out of the poem you read?" she injected, following another line of thought.

"The sender was opposed to Porter's use of animals in research," Andrews answered, wondering where Genna was leading. "The victim's wife indicated Porter suspected Langston or Raines might be behind the angry mail. Neither Foster nor I have talked to Raines, but Langston was certainly angry about one incident involving an animal."

His eyes gravitated to the black dog lying quietly in the far corner of the room. Andrew's nemesis Sky was curled in a ball next to his new found friend. Silky white and unkempt black fur rhythmically rose and fell together with the steady breathing of the resting animals. He tried not to think about the future in store for the black dog which was the property of the Institute and destined for experimentation.

Genna noticed the redirection of Andrews' attention to Blacky and responded as though she could read his thoughts.

"I know. Her coat needs a good brushing, but that might frighten her too much right now. She'll need a few days of getting to know us and Sky. Then maybe she won't panic when I try to groom her."

Andrews nodded but gave no verbal indication that he'd heard Genna's comment. His attention and dialogue returned to the murder under investigation.

"Mrs. Porter seemed to indicate her husband was suspicious that someone on the institute's staff sent the letter, the notes and that poem. It seems the letter didn't mention the gender of the child, but the notes did. So the victim surmised that the same person sent them all.

113

Besides which he seemed to have been suspicious that someone was messing around his research notes. Mrs. Porter didn't think her husband had discovered who it was, but had determined it was an insider to the institute," Andrews admitted.

"Do you think Porter found out who was sending him the notes and drawings after he left his wife last night? And that the sender killed him to keep him quiet?" Genna asked.

"It might explain the when. But it doesn't explain the method of killing. Why such a brutal manner?" the bulky man argued. "Sending the letter and drawings might be considered unethical in his circles, but nothing I've heard so far would have been considered illegal, as least nothing that would have justified anything more than a public nuisance. Nothing was a direct threat. To Porter or to his work. He interrupted the correspondence that way, but nothing described to Foster and me so far would have constituted a threat in the legal sense of the word," Andrews reasoned aloud.

Jonathan picked up the line of reasoning. "So even if he had identified the sender and confronted him or her, why would that person resort to violence against Porter? And why kill the victim in such a brutal and painful fashion?"

"Right," Genna chimed. "Someone went to a lot of trouble, sending a letter, a poem and then drawings to annoy the victim. Each thing less direct, more symbolic. And then Porter is killed violently. Almost an abrupt about-face!"

"If various witnesses are right, Porter believed the individual who sent the mail was a member of the institute's staff. If so, then that individual could have observed Porter's responses to each receipt of mail and known that less and less was required to get him upset," Genna reasoned. "Why send Porter vague warnings such as a letter, a poem to reinforce the letter, and then drawings to remind him of the poem in order to work on his conscious, and then suddenly and violently kill him? Did he do something last evening or the last day of his life that made the killing seem necessary? Or are we dealing with a deranged individual?"

Andrews picked up the line of Genna's reasoning and continued. "He went to dinner with his wife to try to allay her concerns over his absences from home at night. Then he went back to the lab to work. The wife was suspicious of more than professional involvement with the secretary. But the secretary appears to have gone home early and to have an alibi for last evening. In any case there's no indication she returned to work also. At the moment I can't see that leads anywhere at all," Andrews summarized. "Earlier in the day he was pushing his partner to finish the experiments on this drug research project. So Berkley could have predicted that the victim would return to his lab the night he was killed. Berkley says he was home all evening with his wife."

Genna and Jonathan nodded in agreement. The conversation drifted into discussions of Jonathan's latest book and finally into Andrews' proposed redecoration of his apartment in Richmond. Time passed quickly as it does between people who enjoy a warm and close relationship. Finally, Genna excused herself to check on Mushie, and ordered Sky not to follow her. The two men settled themselves down to watch an old movie on TV.

Sometime during the shuffling and settling, Andrews discovered that Sky had joined him in the chair again. Blacky's head was up and her eyes followed the movements of the smaller animal with mild interest, but she made no move to rise or to leave her comfortable corner. Andrews found himself crowded to the side of the chair in which he was attempting to relax. From previous experience he knew it would do no good to try to put Sky back on the floor. As long as Genna was unavailable, Sky would make himself comfortable against the human of his choice, that choice usually being the individual who least wanted him around. It was amazing that such a small mass of fur could take up so much space, and it didn't take the portly man long to decide that the movie wasn't worth the effort of unsuccessfully seeking a comfortable position.

"It always feels as though this dog has six legs," Andrews grumbled. "The only way I'm going to get any rest is to go to bed and shut this little pest out of the bedroom." Suiting his actions to his words, Andrews relinquished the chair to the dog.

"Wish that worked for me," Jonathan chuckled in fake sympathy. "Sometime I think he picks locks the way he gets into places that he shouldn't. Want some help with your bag?" Jonathan asked, as he too uncurled his lanky frame from his chair.

Andrews was just heaving his bulk into a vertical position when Genna reappeared from the kitchen, a smile softening the determined set of her chin.

"Mushie is doing better. He even took a little water on his own and ate a few pieces of food out of my hand," Genna announced before Andrews could voice the question.

"Wonderful," Andrews responded, contriving not to let his relief and exaltation show too much.

Sky had awakened when his warming block arose. Now he leaped off the chair and jumped up and down in front of Genna to get her attention. He continued his rendition of a yo-yo until her arms caught him on one of his upward bounds and drew the little dog to her.

"Uncle Kevin has decided that the guest bedroom is the only safe haven from Sky tonight," Jonathan explained, coming over to stand beside Andrews. "How about your bag?" he asked a second time.

"I can get it myself. After all, I'm not exactly a guest." Andrews assured his godson. "The usual room?" he asked cryptically and, receiving an affirmative nod, wished his host and hostess goodnight.

"You must say hello to Amber and meet her little son before you go to bed," Genna injected.

So a tired but patient detective paid due respects to the youngest life in the house before retiring to the guest quarters for a much needed rest. Later, when Andrews was settled in bed with the lights out, he tried to review the events of the day for missed points, but the soft

116

chirps of tree frogs and the softness of the down pillows thwarted his efforts.

For all the swiftness with which sleep claimed the tired man, his rest was troubled by disjointed dreams. Barking dogs and strange voices saying things he didn't exactly catch flitted through his dreams. Liquid brown eyes in a black skull seemed to plead with him for help in unrolling a scroll. Another dog's face with dirty, wolf-grey fur faced him, one ear flopped over and oozing blood and moisture. It seemed a long time before his troubled dreams ceased and he relaxed in restful sleep.

Bright sunshine and gay chirpings from the bird community gradually penetrated his oblivion. Relaxed and drifting between sleep and full awakening, a persistent tickling of his ear demanded action. Finally the urge to scratch became too powerful to ignore and he reluctantly stirred. The hand which reached slowly to scratch the offending tickle encountered soft fur and a small head. A moist nose rooted beneath the hand, attempting to redirect it to scratch, not the human ear, but a conveniently placed canine one.

"Sky, how did you get in here?" Andrews grumbled, startled to full wakefulness.

Sky's response was to wiggle closer to Andrews' head and cover the human's ear and cheek with wet licks. Squirming to avoid the dog's wet tongue and the confining bed covers at the same time, Andrews managed to bang his head against the headboard before struggling to a sitting position and catching the offending bundle of fur in one arm. By the time the grumbling human had put the tiny dog out of his bedroom and firmly closed the door again, his head was aching and his stomach was complaining that breakfast was long overdue. With two such persuasive prods, it did not take him long to shave and dress. The shirt he chose was roomier than yesterday's and he turned toward the door in anticipation of breakfast.

Sky was waiting just outside his door when Andrews emerged.

"Might have known," the hungry man grumbled at seeing the small animal waiting expectantly.

Sky seemed to take that as a cheery greeting and wagged his tail so hard his entire body bent back and forth with each swing of his tail. Despite the much longer legs of the man, dog and man reached the bottom of the stairs and the great room together.

To Andrews' surprise the downstairs appeared to be empty. He looked in the study for some signs of his host and hostess or for the black dog, but the study was quiet and dark. Even more ominous was the absence of the grey dog from the kitchen. His spirits lifted slightly when Sky bounced to the door leading from the kitchen to the yard and looked back expectantly toward Andrews, waiting for the man to reach the door and open it.

Sky was through the door and outside into the fenced area at the first crack in the opening. It took Andrews a little longer to open the door fully and discern that Genna and Jonathan were outside watching Blacky frolic about the yard. Sky breezed by his mistress, giving her ankle a lick on the way, and went to touch noses with Blacky before Andrews could get his bulk through the door. Andrews' relief at seeing the black dog was offset by his rising anxiety at Mushie's absence.

His concern growing with each step, Andrews quickly closed the distance between the house and the yard where Genna and Jonathan were standing. Skipping over the usual morning greetings, he blurted, "What happened to Mushie? Did he take a turn for the worse overnight? Why didn't you wake me?"

Genna's startled look was followed by a soft laugh.

"Mushie is better......" she started, but was interrupted by Andrews.

"Then where is he?"

"If you must know immediately if not sooner, he's upstairs in Genna's study," Jonathan chuckled. "I'm glad to see you objective and unemotional about this," he teased.

"Mushie's owners arrived a little after two this morning. They hugged him and cried and we talked till after three. Jonathan pulled out the sofa bed in the library and we put the three of them up there to get some rest," Genna explained before Andrews could explode.

The bulky figure relaxed at this news, and Genna continued in a more leisurely fashion, "Mushie was recovering nicely by the time Cathy and Paul Massey arrived. After an hour of being held and cuddled by one or both of them, Mushie was fine. He ate a little, drank enough water to get him up early this morning, and was carried upstairs to bed by his adoring owners. He even exchanged a few barks with Sky in the upstairs hall. I'm surprised all the noise didn't wake you this morning."

"Oh,...." Andrews stammered, at a loss for words for once. "Well, that's fine then."

Jonathan looked at Genna and they both laughed aloud. Their delight at Andrew's concerns for Mushie was obvious.

"Mushie's fine. Now how about you? Did you sleep well? Are you ready for some breakfast?" Genna asked.

"Fine, fair and yes. Definitely 'yes' to breakfast," Andrews answered. Now that his anxiety over Mushie was quieted, awareness of the complaints from head and stomach resurfaced. "And something for my headache would be welcomed. Sky managed to get into my bedroom and provide a face wash before I was fully awake. In trying to dodge his wet tongue, I banged my head against the headboard of the bed so hard my ears are ringing."

If Andrews hoped for sympathy he was disappointed.

"So that's where Sky went," Jonathan noted. "I warned you he was a magician at getting into rooms where he wasn't wanted! Genna wouldn't let him into the nursery when she went in to care for Amber and little Rusty, so he ran off looking for sympathy from you."

"Next time, I'll frisk him for a lock pick before going to bed!" Andrews replied drolly. "Have you two eaten already?"

119

"Jonathan and I had some toast and juice about an hour ago. Your partner, Sergeant Bart Foster, called. He said it wasn't urgent, to let you sleep but to ask you to call him sometime this morning at his home," Genna responded.

This bit of news dampened Andrews' eager anticipation of breakfast. Genna's next words depressed his spirits even more.

"What can you eat for breakfast that is on your diet? Will fruit, a piece of wheat toast and two poached eggs be appropriate?"

Andrews cursed the indiscretion which had prompted him to mention his latest diet to Jonathan. Might have know, he thought, that Jonathan would have relayed the information to Genna. And Genna would, of course, make certain the overweight man was constantly reminded of this latest constraint to his enjoyment of living.

"Since it is so late, I was thinking of combining lunch and breakfast," Andrews temporized.

Genna shook her head. "You'll feel much better if you space your meals out into three or four small ones. Fruit, eggs and toast will be just what you need. Lucky for you that you've always liked your coffee black. Jonathan and I have a terrible time when we diet, just making certain we have a substitute for sugar around."

Short of leaving abruptly and stopping on his way back to Richmond to eat, Andrews knew there was no way to get pancakes, butter and maple syrup for breakfast. A successful police detective knew when to bluff and when to give in gracefully. So he capitulated. Besides, this third day of his diet wasn't half as bad as the second day had been. He was hungry but not edgy as he'd been the previous afternoon and evening.

"Sounds fine," he said insincerely. "Maybe I'd better call Foster now and see what he wants."

Despite his divided attentions between breakfast and the homicide case, Andrews had to smile at the antics of the two dogs. Sky had found a ball and was racing across the yard with it in his mouth. Blacky was in pursuit of the smaller dog and ball. Both were enjoying the crisp spring morning, long coats streaming behind them as they ran, tails wagging briefly every now and then. Sky took advantage of a shorter back and legs to make a sharp turn. Blacky's attempt at replicating the same turn tumbled the taller dog tail over ears, but she was back on her feet and scrambling after Sky in the next second.

"That dog will forget all about the lab and the murderer after a few days around here," Andrews thought to himself. "I bet neither of those two have ever dieted!"

Grumbling to himself, Andrews left Jonathan and Genna in the yard with the two frolicking canines and went into the kitchen to call Foster and get an update on the murder investigation.

By the time Genna and Jonathan came inside with Blacky and Sky, Andrews was finishing his phone conversation with Foster. "Ketterholt and Berkley are likely to be even madder when I have to tell them the smaller animal is claimed by a couple who plan to take him with them."

He listened to the conversation on the other end of the phone for a time with an impatient expression on his face before continuing. "I don't know how this might tie in with Berkley's anxiety to recover the dogs. I'll try to talk with Genna and with the people who claim to own the smaller dog." Catching Genna's eye, Andrews continued, "I'm sure Genna will have some ideas about it. Anyway, I'll let you know."

Andrews hung up the phone and turned to face his hostess. Genna busied herself with getting a breakfast together for Andrews, but the mixture of amusement and determination on her face was not related to the housekeeping. Andrews correctly identified the twinkle in her eyes as part mischief and all spunk. The square jaw was set but slight tilts at each corner of Genna's mouth promised a spirited but tolerant discussion. It didn't take twenty years of police experience to tell the chunky house guest the score. All the talking in the world wasn't going to regain him control of the little grey dog sleeping upstairs with his owners.

Blacky's future was bleaker. Foster had just relayed to him the demands of Berkley and Ketterholt for the return of the dogs to the lab.

Chapter 14

The talk with Genna went about as Andrews has expected it would. Genna reminded him that the hospital had violated the law in accepting a tattooed animal without written consent of the owner. Andrews pressed to let him settle it with Ketterholt. Genna offered to have her lawyer contact Ketterholt instead. The offer was delivered with a sickeningly sweet smile. If a spider smiled, Andrews decided, it would do so in the same manner. He was briefly tempted to take Mushie and let Genna square off with Ketterholt. He did not doubt that she would take legal action for the fun of it. But this homicide investigation was tricky enough already with all the high powered personalities involved without adding another dimension. Besides, he needed her help to utilize Blacky's natural responses in identifying the killer.

Jonathan sat at the breakfast table and chuckled at their verbal tussles. "You know she won't budge," the younger man commented. "I think you both love these verbal bouts as a means of getting your adrenaline flowing."

Andrews conceded the issue with Mushie's ownership. "OK. Mushie wasn't much use as a witness anyway, since he'd willed himself to die according to Langston. But will you please give some thought to how I can utilize Blacky's reactions to the various parties in this case to suggest whom the dog might have observed killing Porter," he groused.

Then realizing how desperate he sounded, he continued on a calmer note. "And the sooner the better, because the Institute is pressing for the return of the dogs."

After finishing a satisfying breakfast, he was pleased to note that the gnawing hunger of the previous day was gone and his new diet was causing him less grief.

During the verbal exchange between Andrews and Genna, Sky pushed the door open between the kitchen and great room, a sable-and-white stuffed animal in his mouth. The toy resembled a bull complete with one tiny, black felt horn. Sky looked expectantly from human to human in the apparent hope that one might be willing to play tug-the-toy with him but was ignored. The very end of a black nose in the doorway revealed Blacky's interest in the happenings in the kitchen if not her complete trust in taking an active part. Seemingly resigned to the humans' disinterest, the lively red-and-white dog left the stuffed toy in the middle of the kitchen floor and returned to the great room.

Despite his arguments, Andrews secretly agreed with Genna regarding the best way to deal with Mushie's situation. He was, in fact, looking forward to his conversation with Ketterholt and Berkley. He wasn't sure if he wanted to tell the two on the phone about the smaller dog, or whether he'd like to see the faces of the two when he revealed what he'd learned about the stolen animal. He insisted on the Masseys' full names, address and phone number be provided for his files as well as the number tattooed on Mushie's belly.

He was sorry that the murder investigation drew him back to Richmond this beautiful Saturday morning. It would have been nice to enjoy the weather and the spring scenery. He had not realized how long he had dragged out his second coffee until he rose to go upstairs and pack. In addition to the little sable bull, a small yellow rubber toy remotely resembling a frog, a small brown toy dog and a stuffed grey bunny dotted the kitchen floor, mute testimony to Sky's persistent bids for attention.

Genna insisted on a brief visit by Andrews to the nursery. Amber was anxious but not aggressive when Genna lifted the tiny puppy in her hand to show him off to his great-godfather. Even the jealous barks from Genna's ever present shadow Sky did not seem to disturb the new mother.

Andrews personally thought little Rusty looked like nothing so much as a large, fat rat, but he knew better than to say that around Genna. "He's very....well, pink, isn't he?" he managed instead. "Is his nose going to be pink?"

"Don't be silly, Uncle Kevin. Haven't you ever seen a newborn puppy before? They all have pink noses at birth. It'll turn black. Look," the doting human said, as she pointed to a tiny dot on the edge of the puppy's nose. "See this little pigmentation. More dots will appear until his nose and his little paw pads are completely black."

Andrews managed to appear properly appreciative of the newest love in Genna's life, as he took his leave of the Kingsley household.

Sky was in Andrews' thoughts on his drive back to Richmond. Recalling Sky's attempts to secure a playmate made Andrews almost wish he'd taken the time for one tug-the-toy with the hyperactive fur ball. Almost!

By noon he had driven back to the city, reviewed the reports waiting on his desk, and was impatiently awaiting Foster's arrival at his office.

Andrews' desk had been cluttered with phone messages. He was sorry but not surprised to see that none were from Pepper. Andrews separated the phone messages by individuals. Names he knew to be connected with the press he put aside. He had nothing official to report, and his captain would prefer to do any speculative announcements himself. Names of callers he didn't recognize went into a second pile, unless the note contained a message that it was connected with the Porter case. In a third pile, Andrews put messages from people he knew to be connected with his latest homicide case. In this last pile were two messages indicating one call from Berkley and one from Ketterholt. He was still trying to decide whether he wanted to talk to these last two by phone or face-to-face when a deep, baritone voice interrupted his thought processes.

"Dad said you'd be in this morning. He left this message for you."

The slender figure confronting Andrews across his littered desk extended a long-fingered, coffee-colored hand toward Andrews containing a folded piece of white paper. The smile which Andrews gave Lieutenant Braxton Brown was warm and sincere. The black eyes and smoothly arched eyebrows looked like his father Billy's. But the nose and mouth were finer, the face thinner and lighter, a legacy of his petite, elegant mother.

"What are you doing here? I didn't realize you were on duty this weekend," Andrews greeted him warmly.

"Same as you. Seeing what I can quickly put together on my latest case. Fortunately, mine isn't as touchy as yours, thank goodness. That stack of phone messages you have is depressing." The slender figure pushed a stack of papers back from the front of Andrews's desk and propped his lean frame on the edge. Andrews appreciated the move. Looking up at Braxton's six-foot, seven-inch frame from a desk chair was likely to cause anyone's neck to hurt.

"I hope your investigation is going better than mine," Andrews extemporized.

"Not exactly," Braxton said with a forced smile. "The usual situation, unclear motive, no witnesses and at the moment, no suspects. In fact, all I have at the moment is a death under suspicious circumstances. The department thinks we should treat it as a possible homicide, so we're going through all the usual motions to determine the cause of death by person or persons unknown. But my case hasn't generated the amount of phone calls yours has, and I hope it stays this way."

Understanding Andrews' interest in the note he now held, Braxton continued, "I'm afraid this doesn't do much to help eliminate a possibility. Raines seems to have been with peers for the conference banquet, but left around 7:30 pm to go to his room. As far as Dad has been able to determine, Raines wasn't seen after that until the morning session. Hotel housekeeping said his bed had been slept in Thursday night, but the conference hotel is only a little over two-hours driving time from here. He could have left on Thursday night a little after 7:30 pm, driven here, and been at the crime scene by 10:15 pm."

During Braxton's summation, Andrews had read the cryptic message contained in Billy's note. In its economic verbal sketches, it told him what Braxton was reviewing with more grammatical structure but no more content.

Picking up yet another phone message, Andrews grimaced. "I have to be careful I'm not the next homicide victim," Andrews remarked with more than a little element of truth, as he assigned yet another phone message to its proper pile. "According to these phone messages, two of the individuals connected with the victim would like my head. Politely, of course, but definitely after my head."

"Dad said you removed two dogs from the murder site. Is that what stirred up the two irate citizens?" Braxton was as well informed as any of the personnel working on the Porter homicide of details relating to the case, thanks to his healthy interest in any homicide case and the shared interests of father and son. "Why did you take the dogs anyway?"

Andrews favored the immaculately dressed youngster with a long look before answering. Finally a grin softened his dour look and he answered truthfully, "Because Berkley seemed so keen on getting the dogs or the victim's papers or both. Frankly, I'm not sure the dogs were as important as the papers to him, but I couldn't take the chance."

The admission brought a laugh from Braxton in turn. Andrews continued softly, almost as though he was talking to himself. "Instinct, I guess. Maybe all wrong, but there just the same. I'm sure both Berkley and Ketterholt are hiding something. What, or even that, the points they're trying to conceal have anything to do with the murder, I don't know. Berkley was very interested in getting the dogs. So—I wouldn't leave them for him to get until I know how they're connected with the homicide."

"So you'll stall until you know why," Braxton acknowledged.

"I already know one why. Or at least a possible why on the smaller dog. It was stolen and had a tattoo. It is illegal for the lab to have had it in the first place. They can say they didn't know about the tattoo, and I can't prove they did. At least, not yet. If either Berkley or Ketterholt knew about the tattoo, it might explain why the two of them want to get the smaller dog. They'd have to include both dogs or risk focusing my attention on the tattooed animal."

"Makes sense. Does the captain agree?" Braxton could always be counted on to find the bottom line of any discussion.

"I don't know. I haven't talked with him. On the other hand, I don't have any urgent message from him to join him in his office. So I guess he plans to let me play this one my way, at least for now."

"Careful this doesn't fit under the label of *being given enough rope to hang yourself.*" Braxton smiled knowingly, having been in a similar position more than once. "I'm going after coffee. Would you like a cup?"

"No. I'm trying another diet and caffeine just makes me hungry."

Braxton removed his frame from the front of Andrews desk, unfurled his lean height and straightened his grey plaid suit jacket. "Oh, yes. Dad said you were trying to diet yesterday. I guess the murder was good for something after all. It probably took your mind off food."

"It most certainly did not," Andrews retorted, sounding gruff for the first time during their conversation. But his humor returned and he added, "At least today I have on a shirt that fits. On top of all the homicide related problems yesterday, I was fighting a shirt all day that was too tight. Not a comfortable or relaxing way to spend a day, let me tell you." He didn't bother to add that his stomach felt a lot less hollow than it had yesterday.

"I'm sure it wasn't," Braxton agreed. His lean frame and perfect fitting clothes argued his lack of any personal experience with the discomfort of overly snug clothing.

The ringing of Andrews' phone interrupted any further small talk. Andrews answered and listened for a short time without comment. Pulling a writing pad out of his pocket, he carefully checked a string of numbers recorded on the pad against information provided by the caller. Finally he nodded and said, "No. That's what I needed to know. Thanks."

"Bart?" Braxton inquired.

"No, a confirmation from a motor vehicles check," Andrews said. "I asked for a check on a Pennsylvania plate. The owner's name and address is identical with the name Genna gave me for the people who came to claim one of the dogs."

"What?" The question came out before Braxton thought about it.

"My godson's wife found the tattoo in the smaller of the two dogs. She also called a national registry to get information on the dog. That's how I knew it was stolen. Unfortunately, she also left her name and information on the dog's location. The owners called back, and Genna invited them down to retrieve the dog. All without asking. Now, I've got two people staying in Williamsburg claiming the dog and my godson's wife determined to give them the animal."

"And you're trying hard to get around her." Braxton tried to look sympathetic, but the upward tilt at the corners of his mouth looked suspiciously like he was enjoying the situation instead.

"Well, not exactly. The couple immediately drove from Pennsylvania after learning last evening that he was in Williamsburg. I don't want to think about how many speed limits they broke on the way to arrive in Williamsburg sometime early this morning. The number tattooed on the dog matches the social security number of the owner of that Pennsylvania vehicle. I was certain it would when I let Genna talk me out of discussing the situation with the couple. I don't know how I'm going to handle Berkley and Ketterholt however."

Andrews tried to look worried, if not downright annoyed. His lack of success at hiding his amused indulgence was evidenced by Braxton's next question.

"You can't wait to see Berkley's and Ketterholt's reaction to the news, you mean."

"What news?" Foster's footsteps had been so soft that neither Andrews nor Braxton had been aware of his presence until his question was injected into the conversation.

"Genna found the smaller dog's owners and they've come to Williamsburg to claim him," Andrews summarized.

"I wonder how Berkley will explain that. I expect you'll be delighted to watch him try," Foster observed. Amusement and enjoyment shown in his dark eyes at the thought. "Hi, Braxton. You helping out on this one, too?"

"Nope, got another of my own," Braxton countered. "Just delivering a message from Dad. But I wish you both well with all the egos and self-important complainers associated with yours. I'd better get back to my office and my own cases. Good hunting!"

With that, Braxton excused himself and left Foster and Andrews to continue their conversation undisturbed.

"Well, are you ready for an interesting development?" He drew a chair up close to Andrew's desk and sat waiting for the attention of the senior officer to focus on what he had to relay.

"No, I just came down here on a Saturday morning to have something different to do," Andrews retorted. "Give!"

"After our phone conversation this morning I drove to the address given by Drew Roalf as his residence. I got no answer, so I hunted up the apartment manager and asked when she'd last seen Roalf. She informed me it had been some time, that he'd been in a hospital for awhile and had died about two weeks ago."

"Died," Andrews exclaimed.

130

"Yep. It seems the real Drew Roalf had been in and out of the hospital here at the Institute for the last few months. He finally died about two weeks ago," Foster said, "and get this, at the Commonwealth Cancer Institute, no less."

"He's dead? Roalf, I mean? Then who the hell was working on the cleaning crew the night of the murder?"

"That's the question!" Foster concurred.

"Surely the Institute checks references or previous employers before hiring someone," Andrews deliberated aloud. "If the place is so concerned with security that access is limited to guarded points of entry after six in the evening and staff are required to have security badges visible during the day, it just doesn't make sense not to do some form of personnel screening."

"Died! What did the Institute check when they hired Roalf or whoever was using the name?" Andrews continued, his brow furrowed with his mental endeavors to tabulate all the possible ramifications of this new development to the homicide. "Ketterholt was so worried about animal rights activists getting into the lab despite all the security measures. Didn't the Institute check on backgrounds of persons hired to work on the cleaning crew?"

"I called Ketterholt and asked him the same thing this morning," Foster said. "He told me his personnel office always validate staff hired, that they check with past employers and/or references. He suggested I talk with the personnel officer and gave me her name and home number."

"And," Andrews prompted impatiently.

"And I talked to a Mrs. Nancy Prichard. She was very defensive, insisting that all procedures would have been followed and that Roalf, or whoever he was, wouldn't have been hired without satisfactory references. After a great deal of talking I finally persuaded her to go back down to the office and get me a copy of the employment application."

"Well, did personnel manage to check references and miss that this individual just happen to be deceased?" Andrews blurted.

"The personnel director says she checked and confirmed a satisfactory employment record. Her initials appear on the application form, as you can see here, indicating she talked with a previous employer about Roalf, but..." Foster offered a copy of a job application to his superior.

Andrews took the offered piece of paper and scanned it carefully as Foster continued his report.

"..but, Mrs. Prichard would have to say that now that police are scrutinizing the hire."

"The application supposedly completed by Drew Roalf lists a Mrs. Amy Parrish as the most recent employer. According to that application Roalf worked for Parrish's little landscaping business for the last five years, at least up till about six months ago when his illness became too serious to allow him to continue. The personnel director had spoken to Ms. Parrish and been given a satisfactory recommendation. I spoke with Ms. Parrish and she confirms the conversation."

"Did this Parrish woman bother to mention why Roalf left to the personnel director?" Andrews smirked in disbelief.

"I asked her that," Foster replied, "and she said she didn't want to get sued by anyone, such as Roalf's relatives if he had any, and didn't want to say anything negative about him."

"Unbelievable," Andrews said. "Did anyone from the Institute's personnel office ever interview Roalf?"

"No. The Institute was in a tight spot and desperate for help, according to the personnel director. One of the cleaning crew left suddenly giving only one day's notice. And Chambles had orders to strip the floors, wax, and spruce up that first floor by today because of some big open house for high stake peer reviewers. That meeting should have been going on today but is now postponed because of the homicide. Chambles could have asked for help from other crews assigned elsewhere around the

Institute, and was going to. But this big, beefy guy approached him on Wednesday with an application in hand, saying he'd heard about the sudden vacancy while standing in line in the grocery store or some such and was very anxious for the job. Chambles took the application and told the guy the Institute's personnel office would get back to him. Then after he thought if over, Chambles apparently decided to take a chance with the guy since he seemed so eager for work. So Chambles took the application to Prichard, asked her to check ASAP and to notify Roalf to report for work Thursday evening if possible. Prichard did and a Roalf did and that turns out to be the night of Porter's murder."

"And just how did personnel notify Roalf to report to work?"

"By phone."

"So," Andrews looked a little impatient. "Whose phone number did they really call to reach the fake Roalf."

"The real Roalf's." Foster replied.

"What?"

Foster's dark head nodded up and down. "Personnel called the phone number listed for Roalf. It was his real number. It hadn't been disconnected. Now Mrs. Prichard doesn't remember whether she spoke to a real person or left a message. A Drew Roalf, or someone claiming to be he, called her back."

For once, Andrews seemed to be speechless.

Foster continued, "I got the landlady to let me into Roalf's apartment to check for signs of tampering, a phone tape or whatever. I didn't find anything out of the ordinary. There wasn't any physical phone answering machine there. I checked again with the phone company and he had—well, still has—Voice Mail on his phone."

Before Andrews could interrupt again, his junior partner continued. "I had to go down to the phone company and talk with one or two experts to determine this...."

"Young and female, no doubt," Andrews interjected.

"Young and female," Foster admitted. "Anyway, to continue if certain senior partners will let me.... the voice mail on Roalf's home phone was accessed on Thursday around noon from a pay phone located in the lobby of the Farmers Bank on Main Street and the message from Prichard saved."

"Technological clap trap!" Andrews grumbled. "You're telling me someone retrieved Prichard's message to Roalf from a pay phone and we can't trace it?"

"Exactly."

"But to do that, the person would have to know....", Andrews struggled to remember how a phone's voice mail worked. He still relied on his old answering machine at home.

"Three things," Foster prompted. "Roalf's home phone number, his voice mail box number and his security access code."

Andrews sat quietly absorbing this new twist to the investigation.

"Prichard's notes show a "Roalf" returned her call at 2:16 pm on Thursday, the day of Porter's murder", Foster continued. "He was told to report for work at 7:30 pm to the maintenance staging area in Building 16 and to bring his social security card for identification and tax records. He did. Chambles made a copy of his social security card and sent it along on Friday to personnel and payroll."

"And the number matches that for Drew Roalf in the Social Security Administration data files," Andrews completed.

"You guessed it!" Foster acknowledged.

"Doesn't take a rocket scientist to figure that someone who thought up this scheme would also be certain the guy's social security number would pass inspection."

"But this guy couldn't expect to continue this fake for long. Once the report of Roalf's death works it way through the computers, the number would be purged from their files," Andrews mused almost to himself.

"You're thinking the person behind this scheme didn't intend to carry on this deception for long?"

"Person or persons," Andrews amended. "Maybe Ketterholt was right to suspect an animal-rights group. Maybe a few nights to photograph or video tape the labs were all they wanted. But something happened on Thursday night they didn't plan. Or, what happened was planned all along by the person or persons who staged the employment of the fake Roalf. Genna said that poem sent to Porter was connected with the animal protection movement."

The two men were silent for a space of time, each digesting and assessing the implications of this latest turn of events. Finally Foster mused aloud, "How could the person be sure Porter would be in his office that night?"

"Good question," Andrews categorized but offered no answer.

More silence followed, punctuated finally by a low sigh from Andrews. "Langston suspects a specific individual of sending the letter, pictures and the notes, but he didn't want to talk. Ketterholt and Parrish are going to hide behind regulations and insist they know nothing. It seems to me that what we need may be an old fashion gossip session."

"And I'll bet you have an idea of whom to ask," Foster nodded.

"Well, I don't much see how the bedside manners of the victim are relevant, but I've never known an old lady that didn't have her ear to the keyhole—figuratively speaking—when it came to a possible amorous connection between a married man and his secretary. And if she's been both a patient and a volunteer here at the Institute, she may know something about the real Roalf or the child that was mentioned in the letter and notes that upset the victim."

Laugh lines tightened around the dark eyes of the younger detective. "Shall we arrange a little talk with Mrs. Weir this afternoon?"

"Yes. While you're doing that, I'll try to reach Twill and see if the good doctor has any further information for us."

Chapter 15

Andrews' call to Twill gained him little more information than he knew already. Fiber and tissue samples showed traces of the same cleaning powder retrieved from the victim's lab and from the trash collected from the Institute the night of the murder. The solution forced down the victim's throat was identical with that used by the cleaning crew to clean out drains in the building.

The weapon used to render the victim unconscious had not been found. There were fibers in the abrasion resulting from the blow to the head, but no matching fibers were found in anything removed from the Institute or recovered from the crime scene.

Andrews was even more concerned with what Roalf might have witnessed during the critical hours prior to the victim's death at 10:20 to 10:30 pm.

Foster's call to Elizabeth Weir had been greeted with delight and an invitation to call on her immediately. Andrews insisted on a quick lunch before driving to the address in the Fan area of Richmond given to Foster by the gregarious woman.

Parking took a little more effort, but Foster managed to squeeze their car into a tight space near the restored three-story to which Weir had directed them and they arrived only four minutes late for a 1:30 pm appointment.

The door bell was answered by a large roll of flesh masquerading as a man in his mid-forties. His height rivaled that of Braxton Brown, but more than three hundred pounds of muscle and fat covered his 6' 5" height and resulted in a ponderous but hardly athletic picture. Close-set brown eyes, which made his large nose and flared nostrils more noticeable, fixed on the two visitors. At Andrews introduction, the blocky doorman's expression softened and the man introduced himself as Irvin Elktins, Mrs. Weir's son-in-law.

"Come this way," Elktins instructed, moving his bulk back and out of the doorway to allow room for the two detectives to enter. "My wife Kay is out doing some shopping, but Mother Weir is in the living room. She's expecting you."

Shutting the door with a quiet touch at odds with his bulk, Elktins led the way into a large, over-furnished room to the left of the entrance hall. Among the numerous sofas, chairs, tables and a piano whose surface strained to support an extensive collection of framed photographs, Elizabeth Weir was seated in her wheelchair.

"What fun to see you two again," the friendly woman said.

"I hope we're not imposing on your afternoon too much," Foster greeted the elderly woman graciously.

"I'm always delighted to have interruptions like this. There's not much for an old lady in a wheelchair to do for entertainment, you know."

The mulberry linen fabric of her formless dress gave her sallow complexion color. She looked more rested today. She wore the same honey-brown wig as she had at her first meeting with Andrews and Foster. The lines around her eyes were less prominent today and the line between wig and face did not appear as harsh. The sparkle in her eyes spoke clearly of her delight at this further involvement in the murder.

"Do sit wherever you find comfortable," their elderly hostess directed.

She smiled sweetly at each man in turn. Andrews chose an overstuffed gold chair at her left and Foster settled onto a sofa at her right. Uninvited by either his mother-in-law or the two detectives, Elktins settled his bulk into the remaining surface of the print sofa.

Before either detective had an opportunity to introduce his questions, Elizabeth Weir began a rapid chatter.

"Sgt. Foster said you were interested in information about Drew Roalf. Such a dear man and so brave. He never gave up, you know, never admitted that there wasn't any hope."

Ignoring Andrews' half-hearted attempt to take charge of the conversation, the stooped woman rattled on, "He's dead now, of course. Died just recently. But why do you want to know about him? Porter wasn't his doctor, you know?"

Having flatly refused to recognize Andrews' attempts at questions, she continued to ignore the senior detective's presence and turned her face coyly toward the handsome younger officer.

"Well, the lieutenant has his reasons," Foster responded tactfully, and glanced at Andrews for the senior officer to pick up the conversation.

Deciding the direct approach might be the only way to keep control of the conversation, but not wanting to give away too much information at once, Andrews began. "The Institute received an application for employment from a Drew Roalf for a position with the cleaning crew. Did you know about such an application?"

"Oh, yes. I knew he filled one out. I told you he never would admit that his illness was hopeless." The mulberry-colored figure maneuvered the wheelchair slightly to make facing Andrews a little easier before continuing. "About a month before he died, he went through a period when he felt a little stronger. He started to talk about needing to get a little job to keep him occupied when he left the hospital. He said he didn't want outside work, that the landscaping work he'd done before would be too much for him. Then we'd laugh together about the sloppy way the halls looked and he said maybe he'd help out with the cleaning. I don't think he really believed it himself; he just liked to sound hopeful."

Giving Andrews her sweetest smile, Mrs. Weir inquired, "Surely applying for a job you aren't able to perform isn't a matter for the police. He never improved enough to leave the hospital."

"No," Andrews acknowledged, regrouping his thoughts to make the situation clearer. "The problem is that someone using Roalf's name presented the application to one of the cleaning crew supervisors the evening before Porter was murdered and was offered a job the next day. He was working on the cleaning crew and was outside Porter's office the night of the murder. And now he's missing."

"Oh, dear. Do you think something has happened to him too, something like what happened to Dr. Porter?"

"We have no reason to think so. We'd just like to talk with him and determine if he might have seen or heard anything that might help us with our investigation," Andrews explained.

"Do you think this person might have had anything to do with the murder?" Elizabeth Weir's eyes twinkled more brightly.

Andrews was amused that she should find so much pleasure at being involved with a homicide. He often encountered such reactions and never failed to wonder at the attraction. For him, a homicide was grueling work: sifting through mountains of information, most of it irrelevant, trying to make sense out of any of it, trying to find the thread of reason among all the false trails, and being criticized from all directions that solutions were not immediately found.

"We just need to get a better idea about the involvement of this individual before we form any opinions," Andrews said. "The personnel officer, Mrs. Prichard, claims that she called Mr. Roalf at his home on Thursday morning to offer him immediate work with the cleaning crew that is responsible for the building in which Porter's body was found. She left a message on his voice mail. And someone claiming to be Drew Roalf returned her call at 2:17 pm the afternoon before Porter's murder."

"I don't understand. Who could have gotten the message to Mr. Roalf. He's dead." The elderly woman wrinkled her brow in concentration before turning once again to look at Foster for help.

"We were hoping you could tell us," the younger officer prompted. "Did he have family or a friend who might have had a key to his apartment?"

"Oh, no!" The aging face turned back toward Andrews to include him in the discussion. "At our age, many of our family and friends are gone, you know. Mr. Roalf had a sister, but she died years ago, or so he said. At any rate, he never seemed to have family visitors, just friends he'd met when he was in and out of the hospital...." She paused and then added on a fainter note, "...like me. And once, I think, the preacher from the church he used to attend. Roalf didn't like him much..."

"Who might have access to his apartment now?" Andrews asked.

"Oh, I can't think of anyone." Then in contradiction to her words, continued "except, I suppose, his lawyer who's got to settle Mr. Roalf's affairs if he ever returns from Japan. That's where he's gone on vacation, but when he gets back he'll have to handle the hospital bills and the funeral. Everything else goes to a little charity Mr. Roalf was fond of. For the children with cancer, you know."

Andrews hadn't known, but the knowing brought him no closer to determining who might have accessed Roalf's phone mail log. He shifted abruptly in his chair, which brought a soft creak from the furniture and a worried look from his hostess.

"Anyone who knew this Roalf's phone mail number and access code could have gotten the message, you know, Lieutenant." Irvin Elktins' abrupt entrance into the conversation drew a startled look from both detectives and a flash of annoyance from his mother-in-law. "We've got voice mail on the home phone here and at the shop.

It's a great system and we can phone in and get messages from anywhere."

The man had been quiet and still since settling into the sofa beside Foster, and the two detectives had almost forgotten he was there.

"That's our difficulty," Andrews jumped upon this turn of the conversation toward his direction of interest. "Who would know the voice mail box number and access code for Roalf."

Elizabeth Weir's immediate response was, "Oh, that's easy. Anyone in the hospital, probably." Her smug glance at Irvin Elktins spoke volumes of her intention to remain the center of attention. "Mr. Roalf kept a string of numbers written down on a sheet of paper in the night stand beside his bed. He enjoyed 'checking in at home' as he called it. He liked calling up his home or getting someone else to do it. I suppose he was always hoping to hear from some friend or such."

Andrews squirmed in his chair, the chair complained softly at the stress of the beefy detective's weight, and Foster hid a quickly suppressed smile with the top of his notepad. The one thing more frustrating to an investigation than finding no one with knowledge of an important piece of information is finding that a mob of people had access to that same information.

"Would you remember when you last saw the employment application that Roalf completed?" Andrews continued, trying to look unbothered by the news regarding open knowledge of access to Roalf's home phone messages.

The brown eyes Elizabeth Weir turned on Andrews fairly twinkled. "Well, I can't say that I do. I hardly thought when dear Mr. Roalf was doing all of this that it would be of interest to anyone. Let me see, when did Mr. Roalf die?" the old voice asked, more as a rhetorical question than anything else.

Irvin Elktins supplied the information to her question anyway. "Kay and I took you to his funeral the Tuesday before we left for Florida, Mother Weir. Don't you remember?"

Without seeming to register this latest interruption by her son-in-law, Elizabeth Weir continued to think aloud. "Oh, yes, Mr. Roalf died two weeks ago yesterday. The funeral was a little delayed because of needing to reach his executor who was in Japan. I believe I was at the hospital to visit with him a few days before that. We got to talking about animals and he wanted to show me a picture of his cat. I'd seen it a hundred times, but he wanted to show it to me again, and I humored him, you know. Well, anyway, I opened the drawer in his night stand to get out that picture, and I think I saw that job application then. It was in the envelope with some of his other papers and the picture of the cat. So that would have been about three or four weeks ago."

"But I'm afraid I can't give you date and time," she continued brightly, smiling first at Andrews and then at Foster. Elktins, she continued to ignore.

Andrews smile was lazy but not his brain. "What other things would Mr. Roalf have had in this envelope?"

"Oh, I couldn't say, I'm afraid. I just saw the top of the application sticking out of that envelope when I got his cat's picture out for him," she said.

Andrews interrupted the old woman's memories of her lost friend. "What would have happened to Roalf's things after his death?"

For a moment, Andrews feared the aging woman might give way to tears, but after a slight struggle, the lined face managed to reflect some of its earlier excitement, and Weir responded, "I guess, you know, someone at the hospital would have collected his things and sent them along to his lawyer. If they're important, I suppose the hospital will have a record of the address and name of Mr. Roalf's lawyer, and they can tell you how to find him. I don't even remember his name, just that he had gone to Japan on vacation and the hospital had to communicate with him for burial instructions." Almost as an afterthought, she continued, "I wouldn't mind having that picture of his cat to remember him by."

"We'll see what we can do about that," Foster promised, with a slight, conspiratorial nod at Andrews.

Andrews nodded indulgently. Hoping to gain some feel for hospital gossip concerning the threatening letter, notes and poem received by Porter, he attempted to inject some small talk into the conversation first.

Turning his attention in Elktins' direction he observed with interest, "So you and your wife have been enjoying the beauties of Florida. Guess you didn't expect to find your Mother Weir involved with a homicide when you returned."

Startled by this invitation to participate, Elktins sputtered, looked at Elizabeth Weir, who looked none too pleased, and finally managed to find his voice. "Well, yes...er...no...but we were sort of surprised when Mother Weir told us about the happenen' this morning when we got in."

Foster translated that in his notebook to read a bit clearer than relayed by the speaker.

"It's about time you two came home," grumbled the bloated figure in the chair. "Running off to do Disney things just like two children and leaving me to fend for myself."

"Now, Mother Weir, you know we invited you to go with us, but you said you'd rather stay here," the mound of a man responded defensively.

"I know you and Kay needed a vacation and I don't blame you for leaving me alone to take care of myself," the old lady responded with just enough martyrdom to prick Elktins' pride. "The neighbor down the street was kind enough to look in on me now and then."

"You're not exactly helpless." Elktins' face was starting to get a little flushed with annoyance at the implied accusations.

Andrews quickly injected another question before the exchange between son-in-law and mother-in-law could get any more heated.

"Did your neighbor drive you to the hospital yesterday morning?"

"Yes. But we didn't stay long. My neighbor would stop by or call each morning around ten or so. She works nights, from four till midnight, so she didn't have a lot of time, but she was very good to look out for me."

Elktins appeared to take this last as another criticism directed at him and was quick to defend himself. "Kay and I wanted to get a live-in companion for you while we were away, but you wouldn't hear of it."

"Well, I'm sure these officers don't care about any of that," Mrs. Weir responded.

Andrews adroitly turned the conversation to, he hoped, less combative topics. "You've been very patient to take the time this afternoon to clarify some puzzling points about Mr. Roalf. I wonder if you might have some information on one or two other little things that concern us about this case?"

Elizabeth Weir's face brightened at the prospect of hearing more about the case. Elktins slumped against the back of the sofa, his face still tensed and defensive.

"The victim received a letter several months before his death which seems to have been the beginning of a series of communications designed to intimidate him." Checking Elktins face briefly, Andrews was relieved to see him less tense and more inclined to stay out of the conversation.

"The only identification of the sender so far is information in the original letter. That seemed to be from an aggrieved parent who lost a child who was a patient at Commonwealth. The original letter complained at the excessive cost for treatments the doctors ordering them knew would be unsuccessful. Another note referred to the child as male," Andrews summarized before introducing his question. "In your visits to your former fellow-patients, did you encounter a parent who would fit such a description?"

Before the elderly woman could answer, Elktins responded. "Sure. That frail little man with the wire rimmed glasses!"

Turning his attention to Elizabeth Weir, Elktins continued excitedly. "You remember, Mother Weir. The first day you went back for out-patient treatments. The guy was almost crying and that little blond-headed volunteer was trying to calm him. He asked you if you really thought all those treatments would do anything besides make the doctors and the hospital richer."

Whether or not Elizabeth Weir would have remembered such an incident without Elktins' interruption, it was clear from the look of disgust she gave her son-in-law that she did not appreciate his displacing her as the focus of conversation. "I remember some man getting upset in the waiting room of the radiation treatment lab, but I certainly don't remember his name nor do I know if he was upset about a child," she snapped.

"Do you know the name of the volunteer to whom Mr. Elktins referred?" Andrews queried before the two family members could exchange any more words.

Mrs. Weir seemed reluctant to support her son-in-law's statements by even that much, but finally admitted that Elktins was talking about a volunteer named Pam Hudson.

Andrews noted the signs of strain in the face of his hostess, and exchanged a quick glance with his partner. Foster's brief nod acknowledged his belief in the futility of further questioning, at least for the present.

"Well, I believe that covers our questions, for now," Andrews said. He stood, walked over to his hostess and extended his hand. "Thank you for seeing us this afternoon, and for the helpful information."

Foster rose from the sofa and took his leave of Mrs. Weir also.

"I'll see you to the door," Elktins offered.

On the way out, the two officers again passed the piano with its load of photographs. Andrews paused briefly to view one large color photo of two laughing women with their heads resting on the shoulder of a man in the center. Despite the difference in hair style, Elizabeth Weir was easily recognized in the picture. The second woman was a younger version of the figure currently occupying the wheelchair, which Andrews took to be Kay Elktins, Weir's daughter and Elktins' wife.

A large dog resembling a golden retriever appeared in several of the pictures. In one, Elktins and the dog wore similar party hats and were grouped around a birthday cake. In another, a gold and white cat was stretched out on his back in Elizabeth Weir's lap, feet sprawled in all directions.

Noticing Andrews' interest in the photographs, Elktins explained, "Ginger and I shared the same birthday. I fear Mother Weir enjoyed our joint birthday parties more than either of us." Pointing to the picture of him and the dog in matching hats grouped around a birthday cake, Elktins explained, "That year, Mother Weir was especially excited about her gifts of a collar and a watch band with the symbols of Aries on each. I mean, have you ever?"

"Well, now that Ginger's dead, you won't have to share your birthday with her," Elizabeth Weir snapped. "You aren't bothered by her anymore, and soon, you won't have to be bothered with me, and you can go on all the trips you wish."

"Now, we don't know that she's dead," Elktins began, but shrugged his shoulders and said resignedly, "What's the use!"

Andrews and Foster nodded in farewell to Elizabeth Weir and quickly made their way through the front door. They paused briefly on the front porch to take their leave of their huge host, who seemed to feel a necessity to defend his actions.

"Everything she needs is on the first floor and chair-accessible. And her doctors say she'll have a few more months of stability," he contended. "We'd never have left her otherwise. She's just stubborn. Wouldn't go with us to Florida, but didn't want us to go without her."

Andrews tried to give a noncommittal reply but Elktins continued as though he didn't hear. "Just like this insisting Ginger is dead. The dog just ran off one day and didn't come back."

Foster nodded sympathetically, which Elktins seemed to take as encouragement and continued his plea for understanding. "She drove us crazy for weeks after the dog ran off, calling the pound and the veterinary hospitals. And then just when we think she's forgotten about it, she suddenly decided the dog was dead. Right after the doctors told her she could get about more, Kay and I came home one night to find she'd dug up a little spot in the side yard over there and put in flowers for what she said was a memorial to Ginger. She insisted we have a plaque engraved for the grave with the dog's name, date of birth and the like. Now does that make sense to you?"

Andrews opened his mouth to speak, but before any sound exited, Elktins continued his complaint. "And how can a comfortable flight to Florida be that tiring?"

Taking advantage of Elktins' need to breathe, Andrews shut off any further rehashing of family differences with a quick and firm farewell. The short, but brisk, walk to their car left Andrews a little out of breath, and all he could manage for a few minutes was gasping for air. Foster, meanwhile, was laughing quietly.

"Maybe what you need to keep you in shape is a mother-in-law like that."

"Thank god I have no such," Andrews gasped between rough breathing. "You know she really enjoyed stirring up the poor jerk. I don't know what he spent on the trip, but he's just begun to pay."

Foster chuckled before returning to the business of their investigation. "Well, where to now? Want to try to find this Pam Hudson?"

"No. It's late and tomorrow is Easter Sunday. Why don't you take me back to the office and you call it a day. You were up late last night and early this morning. I've got to call Ketterholt anyway about the smaller dog. I can find out what he knows about this Hudson woman at the same time."

Foster didn't wait for the offer to be made twice. "Great. Megan wants to go shopping for shoes for the kids this afternoon," he acknowledged and then added, "if you're certain you don't mind. Good luck with keeping the other dog out of Ketterholt's clutches."

Chapter 16

Back in Williamsburg, Genna and Jonathan said goodbye to the Masseys and to Mushie. Genna's glee at seeing the little grey dog leave with his doting and relieved owners was tempered by her belated concern at the impact her rashness might have had on Andrews.

She wrapped her arm around her husband's waist, and they walked in step back into the house, Sky the ever present shadow following Genna's feet. "Uncle Kevin hasn't called. Do you suppose this will really cause him trouble?"

"Nothing he can't handle," Jonathan assured her.

"Well, it's done, and I'm not really sorry,", Genna admitted. "Think I'll go check on Amber and little Rusty. Want to come?"

Blacky greeted the three with a hint of a tail-wag as humans and dog reentered the house. The sight of the bigger dog brought a frown of worry to Jonathan's face.

"How do you plan to utilize Blacky to help Uncle Kevin identify the victim's killer? Do you think she'll settle into trusting us and others, but respond with fear when exposed to one or more of the suspects?"

Genna's face clouded. She removed her arm from around her mate's waist, and reached with both hands to encourage Blacky to come to her. "I don't know," she said. "It seems so unfair to encourage her to trust, to help, and then to reward her with returning her to be hurt and killed."

"Genna," Jonathan said softly. "She belongs to the Institute. You can't change that."

Sky could stand being ignored no longer. He pushed his compact body between Genna's hands and Blacky's head, demanding to be noticed. Blacky backed off in confusion and Genna picked Sky up, burying her face in his silky coat to hid the tears which threatened.

"I know," she whispered.

Andrews returned to his littered desk to find a typed report from Pepper briefly outlining his findings to date. Scrawled across the top of the first page in Pepper's spiky handwriting was a message which meant nothing to Andrews. It said, "I'll check and get back to you, but I think that was the dog that died the night of the murder." Andrews puzzled over the message while he reviewed Pepper's notes.

In his characteristic brevity, Pepper covered the points gleaned from papers he'd removed from the victim's office. Andrews read them through with interest, then started back at the beginning and repeated the process. He was slumped at his desk, staring at the report with focused eyes when Billy Brown walked into his office carrying two large cups of coffee.

"Ya' look beat. What's turned up now?"

Andrews' eyes lost their fixed stare as they focused first on the rugged face and then on the large hand holding the steaming cup.

"Great idea. Thanks." Andrews reached to take the offered coffee. "Have you seen Pepper's report?"

"Nope. Figgered you'd tell me if'n ya wanted me to know. He was grumbling 'bout ya note. Axed me to tell ya that he'd double check the research notes."

"He left me a message in his unreadable scrawl about some dog that died the night of the murder. I'm beginning to see dogs in my sleep. Did he bother to explain what the hell he meant?"

The lined black face cracked into a wide grin. "Just said ya left 'im a note on your desk."

"I never," Andrews began and then focused on the notepad by his phone. On it he had noted two things to do before going to talk to Elizabeth Weir. The first was a reminder, listed under *small, grey dog,* to check on the number tattooed on Mushie's underbelly against driver license number in Pennsylvania and names of the couple who came to the Colts' home to claim the smaller dog. A check mark beside that note signified Andrews' completion of that task. The second note on Andrews' pad said simply, "Ask Pepper."

"Did Pepper say where he was going?" Andrews asked excitedly as the implication of Pepper's scrawled note began to penetrate.

"Home, I think he said."

"How long ago did he leave?" Andrews didn't wait for an answer. He grabbed his phone and began dialing.

Billy Brown pulled a chair closer, lowered his substantial frame into it, and settled down to enjoy his coffee. The cup he'd given Andrews was left to cool on the side of the excited man's desk.

"What did you mean . . . . *the dog that died the night of the murder?* "

Andrews puffed and squirmed while he listened to the response from Pepper. "But how can the victim's notes say the dog died, when I took him—his name is Mushie by the way—alive to Williamsburg for Genna and Jonathan to look after?"

A few more squirms, huffs and head shaking by Andrews and he finally said, "Oh, all right. I know you're tired. But I need to know exactly how the dog was referenced. Both the hospital administrator and the victim's partner are making things hot for me. I'll be delighted to return the favor."

Billy Brown took another long sip of his coffee and waited patiently for Andrews to end his phone conversation.

"Pepper find something important?" he inquired when Andrews finally hung up the phone.

"Interesting anyway," Andrews felt rather than looked for his cup and settled back into his chair. "The research notes made by the victim last night indicated a grey, medium small dog, died last night after being given an injection of an experimental drug."

"Sounds like the same dog ya took home last night?"

"The very same. I wrote a note to myself to run the tag number through Pennsylvania DMV to check owner's name against the name given by the couple who came to Jonathan's to claim the dog. I didn't mean the note for Pepper at all."

"Some days ya get lucky," Billy said.

Andrews moved his coffee cup to his lips but did not drink. He mumbled over the lip of the cup and Billy had to strain to follow the next few sentences.

"Did Foster fill you in on the letters, drawing, and the poem the victim received?"

"Yup!"

"Well, Pepper found them among the victim's papers. No usable prints other than the victims. But he also found some other interesting things."

Billy waited patiently, savoring his coffee. From long experience with Andrews, he knew the detective would tell him the facts in his own way and time.

"According to a partnership agreement between Berkley and the victim, the victim took 65% of all profits on research efforts."

"And Berkley didn't like that split." Billy nodded, having experienced more than his share of life's disparities between pay received and effort expended.

"Something like that. Berkley was unhappy about the arrangements and protested the situation several times in writing to the victim. The victim wasn't very happy with Berkley's speed in fulfilling his part in the experiments, and said so in his responses to Berkley's complaints. Complained about Berkley's failure to meet deadlines."

"So....the victim just wrote up fictitious results," Billy concluded. "His partner knew and tried a little blackmail?"

"Pepper didn't find anything like that."

"Too bad," Billy observed honestly.

"Pepper did find one interesting memo from Ketterholt. It referenced a written challenge to some research Porter presented months ago at a conference. Very low keyed. Just a polite reminder that the victim's research notes had better support his conclusions. And a reminder that in current times of restricted budgets, medical establishments couldn't afford negative publicity."

Billy's response was a soft whistle. "No wonder them two fancy dudes wanted to get the papers before we could review 'em."

Andrews finished his coffee finally, crumpled the cup and tossed it at a trash can in the corner. When the toss missed, Billy retrieved it from the floor and put the crumpled cup into the can along with his own empty one.

Returning to his chair, Billy took a small notebook from his pocket and began to brief Andrews on his findings. "Finished checking on Dr. Raines. Brax tell you?"

"Braxton, and your note. So we can't write him off our list," Andrews said.

He briefly summarized for Billy the conversation he'd had with Foster earlier regarding the discovery that Roalf's identity had been used as a cover and that half the hospital probably had access to both the means to utilize the dead man's voice mail.

Producing a tiny pencil and a notebook from some recess inside his shirt pocket, Billy Brown chuckled and shook his head slowly. "Braxton's gonna love thissen." The large hands all but hid the pencil poised over his notepad. "What da ya want me to do now?

"Well, let's see..." Andrews temporized, thinking aloud. "I need to respond to Ketterholt's calls and pursue the points raised in Pepper's notes I'd rather do that face to face."

Billy waited quietly for Andrews to work out his plan.

"Two people have keys to the victim's lab besides Porter. Piper Morgan, his secretary, is one. She said she was home the night of the murder watching a video with a friend until around 9:00 pm, after which she went to bed. Twill has fixed the time of death somewhere between 10:15 pm and 10:35 pm. Check out Morgan's story. Talk to the neighbors. See if you can get a statement from the friend she supposedly was with. You know the routine."

Billy's pen made brief, economical strokes across the pad.

"Foster has a list of the Institute's personnel somewhere," Andrews said.

"Got a copy myself," Billy acknowledged. "What else?"

"Porter had an assistant, a Markley McBroon. She has a key to the victim's lab. Find out what you can about where she was on Thursday night at the time of the murder. Don't ...."

Andrews' rough attempt to force open the center drawer of his desk resulted in a loud squawk and he had to start his last sentence over. "Don't know if she's listed on the sheet Ketterholt gave us yesterday morning."

"She was," Billy assured him.

"OK, that's all I can think of for now. The crime scene team hasn't reported in yet. Guess Braxton's case and mine are competing for lab time. But I saw no evidence that the locks had been forced anywhere in the victim's suite. I think we'll go on the assumption that whoever killed Porter had a key or was admitted by the victim."

Another loud squeak resulted as Andrews closed his desk's center drawer and tried to open a smaller one on the side of his desk. Andrews seemed unaware of the commotion he was creating.

"We're no closer to identifying the individual who sent the letters, drawings and the poem." Andrews continued. "Mrs. Weir mentioned a volunteer at the hospital named Pam Hudson."

Billy quietly wrote the name in his notebook, a slight upturn of his lips betraying his amusement as Andrews continued to search his desk drawers.

"Looken' for anything in particular?" the black officer finally interjected.

"What? Oh,....well, yes. I thought I had a pack of crackers in here."

"Getting hungry?"

"You're damn right," the cranky dieter admitted. "But I can't have anything else 'till dinner. Now where was I? Oh, yes. The volunteer. See if you can contact someone at the hospital and find an address and phone number for this Pam Hudson."

"Want me to call you at home if I get anything?" Billy inquired.

"Yes. If I'm out, just keep calling. I'll try to see Ketterholt tonight."

"And eat," Billy teased as his long legs carried him out of hearing of Andrews' retort.

Andrews gave a grumpy "Hump!" and returned to his search for crackers.

Billy's face reappeared at the doorway briefly. As Andrews' looked up, the grinning rascal said, "Oh, by the way. Foster and I removed all the forbidden foods from your desk so you wouldn't be tempted."

The face disappeared before Andrews could throw a paper clip at it.

Chapter 17

Sunday morning was dreary. Torrential rain hitting the bedroom window muffled the sounds of the city and gave Andrews little incentive to drag himself out of bed. He drifted in and out of a light sleep, gradually pulling himself closer to consciousness by thoughts of food. He was just finalizing his menu when the phone beside his bed interrupted his pleasant musing.

The third jangling ring was rewarded with a gruff "Yeah?"

"My, don't we sound happy this morning," Genna's cheerful voice countered. "Do you have plans for the day?"

"That depends," Andrews acknowledged, instantly alert and cautious at committing himself. It would be just like Genna to get it into her head that a nice walk in the rain would be fun.

"You asked me to check up on activities of animal rights groups. I thought you might like to hear what I've found and share a relaxing Sunday afternoon with Jonathan and me."

"I did not ask you to check anything. Just what do you think I have an entire police department to do?" the grump said. "You just want to hear what I've been doing since yesterday morning."

"Of course," Genna admitted readily.

"Did the Masseys leave with Mushie?"

"Late yesterday afternoon. When we didn't hear from you, I assumed there would be no problems with the Institute," Genna responded.

"A likely story," Andrews challenged, allowing her to hear his chuckle. "More like you took the phone off the hook to keep me from calling. But considering some other things I confronted the Institute administrator with last night, Mushie was the least of his worries."

"That wouldn't work, Smarty," Genna teased back, "taking the phone off the hook. We have voice mail that just takes the message no matter what we're doing with the phone."

At the mention of voice mail, Andrews gleefully related the events of yesterday in which he and Foster had discovered how to leave phone messages for a dead man.

"I can't wait to hear all about it. Can you be here by one for lunch?"

Glancing at this watch, Andrews saw that it was almost nine. He realized that he'd have to get Genna off the phone if he planned to enjoy his breakfast and the Sunday paper before leaving for Williamsburg.

"Well, I guess I can deal with Sky. Besides, I'd like to see Blacky. I'll see you two sometime around one," Andrews agreed and, almost as an afterthought, remembered manners enough to add, "Thanks for the invitation. See you later."

A hot shower dispatched the last vestiges of drowsiness. A short time later, bare-footed but otherwise snugly wrapped in an old brown bathrobe that was two sizes too small, the hungry man pattered about his tiny kitchen as he set a large slice of ham on the stove to fry and deftly greased a smaller pan destined to hold his fried eggs. Any guilt feelings about his diet was rationalized away by the thought that he'd never get any meat at Genna's so it was all right to eat copious quantities of grease and calories now.

He collected the paper and alternated cooking and nibbling with brief glances at the headlines. By the time he finally had breakfast on the table, all he really wanted was another cup of coffee.

Twin worries occupied his thoughts as his breakfast cooled on the table before him. His suspicions that the quality of the victim's research might be a clue to his death had been heightened by Pepper's report and his talk the previous evening with Ketterholt.

Genna's reference to animal rights activities reminded him of the puzzle surrounding the cleaning crew member hired under a dead man's identity. He carefully avoided—or tried to—any thoughts of what Genna might have been doing with her computer.

His meeting with Ketterholt the previous evening had opened new avenues of investigation that required further thought. He considered and rejected calling Foster, rationalizing that today was Sunday and Foster deserved some time with his wife and family. Things could wait till tomorrow.

Ketterholt had softened his complaints regarding the removal of the dogs once Andrews confronted him with the issue of Mushie's tattoo and ownership issue. He'd tried to garner points for a quick agreement that Mushie should be returned to his rightful owners, but appealed to Andrews' for the return of Blacky as soon as the police were satisfied the dog's usefulness to the investigation was at an end. Genna wouldn't be happy about that. Andrews shied away from admitting his own distress.

The situation surrounding the cleaning crew member gave Andrews a mild headache at the very least. Motive unclear, identity of individual unknown, but given the input obtained from Elizabeth Weir yesterday, a large field of candidates who might have hatched the scheme and obtained access to the necessary information regarding Roalf. All of them would have had close connections to the Institute, however. Just how that fit with an animal rights group, Andrews was at a loss to figure.

Thoughts of Genna brought another tightness to his stomach. Just what had she been doing with her computer to glean information on animal rights activities? Andrews was never completely comfortable with her talk regarding computers. He wasn't sure of her talents as a 'hacker' but he didn't want to find out that she could and

158

had broken into some national computer system either. On the other hand, he was sure she wouldn't be too careful about bending a few laws if she set her mind to helping an animal. Bending, be damned! She'd outright break the damn law if something threatened Sky. He could visualize the news headline: "Hacker Introduces Computer Virus into U.S. Biomedical Computer Networks at Instigation of Richmond Police."

He consoled himself with the reassurance that Sky wasn't threatened. This was followed quickly by the disturbing thought that Blacky was. And you couldn't trust Genna to act according to anyone's law but her own when animals were involved. Just look how quickly she reacted to finding a tattoo on Mushie. It was enough to drive a dieting man to eat.

He remembered Genna's framed copy of the poem, Brown Eyes, and wrapped it in plastic to return to her. Then he realized he had 90 more minutes to kill before leaving for Williamsburg.

Returning to his desk, he began a list of tasks relating to the investigation. Under 'Key to murder scene', he listed the victim, McBroon, Morgan and put a question mark by cleaning crew. He noted that Billy Brown has been asked to investigate and report on this.

Under 'Gifts to secretary and others' he listed 1) Danielle Porter's testimony, 2) secretary, 3) another woman. He gleefully assigned that to Foster.

He was interrupted by the phone.

The call was from Foster. Andrews reviewed the information from Piper's notes, the crossed signals that led to revealing the false entries regarding Mushie and the results of his meeting with Ketterholt.

"Yeh, I know. How bizarre can you get," he nodded uselessly into the phone. "We've got a 'dead dog' that isn't and a live worker who is. It's enough to drive a man to drink...or in my case, eat. Which reminds me! What's the idea. Stealing a man's only package of crackers out of his desk!"

The pudgy face faked a scowl in spite of the lack of any audience while he listened to the reply from

Foster. "Well if that's what you call help, I have some help for you. Put Megan on and I'll tell her about a big sale on children's shoes I'm sure she won't want to miss."

Whatever his partner made of that threat brought an appreciative laugh from Andrews. "Anyway, I'm leaving in a bit, going back down to Williamsburg to spend the afternoon with Jonathan and Genna. I've got a nice assignment that's just perfect for your talents with the ladies, but I think it should wait until we see the rest of Pepper's report tomorrow."

Andrews listened briefly to Foster's reply, then said goodby.

Andrews checked his watch and returned to his list. Under "Berkley" he listed 1) 'bit-of-fluff' with a question mark, 2) mean-spirited attitude toward Langston, 3) check alibi, 4) financial arrangements with victim, and 5) reason for wanting to get dogs or papers. He left this avenue of investigation unassigned for now.

Under "Langston" he wrote 1) in building at time of murder, 2) reason for termination of position with CCI 3) source of anger at victim, 4) weapons/lab and 5) wanted incriminating papers found. After consideration, Andrews added his name as responsible for pursuing this line of investigating.

Under "Roalf" (?) he listed 1) timing, 2) reason for false identity, 3) connection with animal rights groups, 4) innocent coincidence, 5) saw/heard something dangerous to killer. Without hesitation he made a one word notation for responsibility in this area: team.

Under "murder weapon" he entered only one question; if acquired from cleaning crew supplies, how and when.

He was interrupted by the phone again, this time by Genna asking if he was through with her framed copy of the poem, Brown Eyes. He assured her he'd remembered it and was bringing it with him. She suggested he pack a bag and stay the night, since she'd bought so much food suitable for dieters in anticipation of his three-day weekend visit which had been disrupted by this homicide investigation. This raised conflicting feelings for Andrews. Staying would be nice; facing Genna's ideas of food suitable for dieters was less appealing. But he allowed himself to be convinced.

He went back to his list and added two more names.

Under "Ketterholt" he listed 1)relationship with victim's wife, 2) nervousness at mention of same, 3) special access available as head of Institute, 4) peculiar comment about answering machine, 5) exceedingly early bedtime on night of murder. Reluctantly, he charged himself with the responsibility of dealing with Ketterholt.

The last name he added was "Raines". Under Raines' name he listed 1) method of travel to conference, 2) alibi for night of murder, 3) dislike for victim, 4) research grant conflicts with victim. He assigned Foster to work with Billy on finishing this segment, then realized he'd not gotten a description of Dr. Raines. So he went back and penciled in a thin item number five which simply said "description of suspect."

Checking his watch, he realized he'd have to rush if he planned to repack the bag he'd never unpacked from the day before and still leave in time for 1:00 pm lunch, so he abandoned his notes and went to redo his overnight bag and collect his windbreaker and Genna's poem.

By the time he walked the short distance to his car, the rain had soaked both his windbreaker and his feet, but the hour's drive to Williamsburg dried his person and relaxed his body. He arrived at Heron's Rest, the Colts' home, to find the rain had stopped.

Jonathan opened the door before he had to knock. Blacky's head came into view from the direction of the study and disappeared as quickly.

"Hello, Blacky," Andrews called cheerfully before he troubled to say hello to his host. "Got a little wet in Richmond. I'm glad it's not raining here."

"It has been. Washes the air, or so Genna says," Jonathan acknowledged. "Lunch is almost ready. Let me

161

have your jacket and we can go sit in the kitchen if you like."

For once, Andrews was not really hungry, but things always tasted better when he didn't eat alone or cook it himself. In minutes his jacket and package were in the closet, his bag was on the steps to take up later, and he was seated with Jonathan at the circular table in the kitchen looking out over the freshly washed back yard of the house.

Genna and Sky were walking around the yard inspecting what appeared to be early Iris blooms in the flower bed. Or rather Genna was walking and Sky was leaping up and down. At one point mistress and dog seemed to be carrying on a discussion over Sky's attempts to taste rather than look at one of the blooms.

"Genna said you worked things out with the Institute about Mushie."

Turning his attention back to his godson, Andrews acknowledged the successful handling of that problem. "Some other interesting things turned up about the dog which I'll share with you later. Genna will want to hear this and I don't want to have to repeat myself. But yes, Dr. Ketterholt was only too glad to agree to the suggestion that Mushie's owners carry him home."

The sound of a door being opened was followed almost instantaneously by a blur of red-and-white fur which circled the table, sniffed at Andrews' ankle and leaped unasked into Jonathan's lap.

"Hello, Sky," Andrews acknowledged with a laugh.

"Well, we can't be feeling too stressed if we're talking cordially to Sky," Genna chortled, following Sky into the kitchen. She brushed at the mark of a muddy paw print on the bright, yellow-and-white stripes of her knit shirt.

"Not now, but who knows what I'll be like sharing a couple of meals with him," Andrews countered. Genna's strong jaw was relaxed today, and soft dark hair brushed Andrews' ear as Genna paused to kiss him lightly on the side of his cheek.

"Glad you could come. Friday night wasn't much of a visit for any of us," she admitted. "Where's Blacky?"

The latter comment was directed at her husband, who was trying to hold the squirming Sky in his lap. "In the den. She recognized Uncle Kevin's car and voice and has no intentions of returning with him to Richmond."

"Smart dog. Sky, get out of here and go play with Blacky. We're going to eat lunch." The tone was conversational, but the slight accent on the 'out' was enough to cue the bright, little dog. With a final lick of Jonathan's hand, Sky jumped down and danced out of the kitchen, apparently looking for Blacky who was still hiding in the den.

Genna opened the refrigerator and began removing a fruit platter and a tray of sandwiches and transferring them to the table. Jonathan went off to wash his hands. By the time he returned, Genna had added a glass of water and a second container holding some thick, pink liquid to each placemat. Andrews was more than interested in the contents of the second glass.

"A health shake," Genna offered without waiting for Andrews' spoken query. "Honey, wheat germ, strawberries and yogurt."

"I hate yogurt," Andrews barked.

"Try it. You'll find you like it." Genna barked back. "Besides, it's good for you."

Andrews sipped the pink liquid cautiously, then decided it was very good and he was hungry after all. Jonathan picked up the tray of sandwiches, holding them just out of reach as he teased, "Now are you going to tell us about your meeting with Ketterholt?"

Genna slipped into her chair and turned an expectant face to Andrews.

"Only when I get my sandwiches," Andrews countered. When Jonathan passed him the tray with a chuckle, he continued.

"Well, before I tell you about my conversation with Ketterholt, you need to know about something else." He told the two eager young people the reference to

163

Mushie's death which Pepper found in the victim's research notes.

"You mean, he falsified the research notes," Jonathan summarized bluntly.

"Well, Ketterholt waltzed around that one last night when I confronted him with the evidence, but yes. The victim left his office early, took his wife to dinner, then returned around 9:45 pm to his office. He died possibly 30 minutes after he signed in at the security desk. Although the research notes show a small, grey dog died that night, there was no time for him to do the experiment, no time to dispose of the body of the dog, and no dog's body found at the crime scene."

Andrews had a smug look that resulted from more than his enjoyment of the cream cheese sandwich he was munching. "I went out to Ketterholt's home to talk with him. Even before I knew about the falsified research results, I'd wanted to see him face-to-face about the Institute having a tattooed and stolen animal."

"What was his explanation?" Jonathan mumbled, his mouth full of cantaloupe. "Genna and I decided he would try to argue that the tattoo was overlooked."

"He did try that argument. I didn't tell him about the entry in the research notes until after I raised the issue of a tattooed animal. At first he said the tattoo must have been overlooked. Then he just said he didn't know but that Porter must have thought he had the permission of the owner." Andrews was pleased enough with himself to justify another couple of tea sandwiches, and he reached for them before continuing. "Then I sprang the questionable entry in the victim's research notes and asked him about his letter to the victim referencing a challenge to a research paper published by Porter."

"Something else your friend Pepper found in the victim's papers?" Genna's sandwiches remained untouched on her plate as she listened attentively to her portly guest.

"Yes. Ketterholt shrugged it off as a routine hazard of the profession. When I asked him about his letter of caution to Porter, he said it was nothing. But he was rattled when I linked the falsified research findings on Mushie with the earlier charge. When I asked to see the earlier complaint that his letter referenced, he tried to dodge the request. Said he didn't know if he still had the complaint."

"You can get it, can't you?"

"If he hasn't destroyed it. For now, I'll wait and see whether Ketterholt responds to the request voluntarily and whether I really need a copy."

Andrews took another finger sandwich from the tray and began to munch on a corner while he explained Pepper's other discoveries, the results of Foster's investigation about Roalf, and outlined his and Foster's discussions with Elizabeth Weir and her son-in-law.

"So you think this volunteer might be able to identify the sender of the poem and notes," Genna injected excitedly.

"Well, at least it's a lead. The first one we've really had on the victim's peculiar communications. Which reminds me....." Andrews abruptly put his half-eaten sandwich on his plate, pushed back his chair and hurried out into the entrance way. He returned a moment later with Genna's framed version of the poem, "Brown Eyes".

"Didn't want to forget to return this to you. Pepper found the copy in the victim's notes, but I made a copy of yours also. Thanks for the loan."

Genna took the framed poem and rose from the table to put it safely on the top of the refrigerator. Turning back toward the table, she started to phrase a question to Andrews, but Jonathan beat her to it.

"Did you get anything else out of Ketterholt?"

"Well, he says he was home alone and in bed by 7:30 pm the night of the murder. Twill fixed the time of death as the interval between 10:15 pm and 10:35 pm Thursday night. So Ketterholt doesn't have an alibi for the time of the murder."

"Think he'd have a motive for killing Porter?" Genna got her question in quickly. Jonathan was left with an open mouth which he finally filled with a sandwich.

Andrews tried not to laugh at their eagerness, as he focused on Genna's question.

"Well, he still insists that the homicide was the work of animal rights terrorists. He certainly didn't want to continue discussions of research fraud and any linkage it might have to motives for Porter's death."

"I'll just bet he didn't." Genna's head nodded up and down in agreement. "His charge that the murder was related in any way to activities of animal rights groups is illogical for several reasons. First, illegal entries are generally made by such groups...but none to date in Virginia by the way... to rescue animals; no animals were taken. Second, any animal rights group worth its name would never have left the little guinea pig in pain. More importantly, no group would have deliberately hurt a human. It would be against their compassionate feelings for all living things on the one hand and reflect negatively on the movement besides," Genna rattled on assuredly. "But,...."

"Hold it," Andrews injected, punctuating his words with a thrust of a firmly clutched sandwich. "Just because such groups haven't broken into labs before in Virginia doesn't mean they didn't start on Thursday night."

"Then why did they leave the little animal to suffer?" Genna countered.

"Maybe the intruders were interrupted before they could take the animals."

"By whom? No one raised an alarm until the next morning?"

"Well, I don't know," Andrews admitted, momentarily at a loss for a response.

"While you're thinking about that one, let me give you something else to think about. Do you know what the term 'indirect cost' means?"

Andrews paused briefly trying to collect his thoughts, and Genna rushed along without giving him a chance to respond. "Facilities such as the Institute collect what is called overhead costs from grants. These costs about equal the amount of the grant itself. These so called 'indirect costs' can be used in any way the institution wishes: to help pay staff salaries, to add to the physical plant. The Institute relies heavily on such funds. And these indirect costs almost certainly pay a good portion of Ketterholt's salary.

Andrews tried to appear unconcerned by Genna's latest line of interest. It was an avenue of investigation that had not occurred to him, but he wasn't about to let her know that. "So where does this information get us?"

"So Ketterholt had more than a passing interest in the quality of Porter's work and the credibility of it. More than one facility has been crippled when research performed by individuals affiliated with the establishment proved to be invalid. Governmental agencies tend to be leery about pouring more research dollars into places that have gained bad publicity for faulty research."

Jonathan interrupted. "That's a new line of investigation, isn't it, Uncle Kevin?"

Before Andrews could answer, Genna picked up her arguments regarding indirect cost benefits.

"Moreover, during the past three years, the Institute has collected close to two million dollars in overhead costs to offset extra security precautions to deal with threats to their research efforts by animal rights groups. But I can't find any incidents where the school has been threatened," Genna concluded smugly.

"Maybe you weren't looking in the right places," Andrews responded.

He'd have to check these latest ideas out when he returned to the office on Monday, but he didn't want to encourage Genna to do much more exploring. Knowing little about computers, he was always suspicious at what she could unearth with hers.

"Just because you can't find references to attacks in newspaper files doesn't mean they haven't happened," Andrews said.

"Oh, I think you'll find my sources are adequate," Genna countered brightly. "Why don't you two adjourn to the den and spend some time with Blacky and Sky while I clear things away in here. And then I'll show you some computer printouts that should interest you."

167

As the two men rose to follow her suggestion, she added, "And we'll all go for a walk a little later in the afternoon. It'll give Uncle Kevin a chance to enjoy the country and Blacky's company."

In the den, Andrews settled into an easy chair and found Sky on his lap instantly. Just like the little imp, Andrews thought, to pick the person who didn't want his attention. Before he could protest, Blacky ambled over to touch noses with her small friend and appeared not to notice when Andrews' hand stroked her head.

"I guess you're good for something, Sky." Andrews made the observation grudgingly but softly. Blacky looked up at the sound of the rotund man's voice, but held her cautious stance near his chair.

Jonathan settled himself into a similar chair and smiled indulgently at Andrews. "I think you've been putting us on these past three years about not liking our dogs. You really like Blacky, don't you?"

"She's a dog. These other things are just doglettes," Andrews insisted.

Jonathan switched the conversation to the latest development in his manuscript. Andrews continued to stroke the black head of the larger dog while he gave non-committal responses at suitable intervals to his godson. A higher pitched question refocused his attention from dog to godson.

"So, you'd like to take a four-mile walk and then read my book!" Jonathan said with a laugh. "Uncle Kevin, you're not paying any attention to me."

"I am! I mean, no I don't!" Andrews stammered. He looked sternly at his host and then down at the bigger dog. Blacky drew away from his hand and retreated to the corner of the den at the sound of harsh tones.

"Did I hear you admit that Sky was good for something?" Genna injected into the conversation. At the appearance of his mistress, Sky deserted the abundant lap upon which he'd been sitting and went to jump up and down in front of Genna until she caught him and hugged him close.

"I think Uncle Kevin is taken with Blacky and tuning out my conversation," Jonathan summarized correctly.

The subject of their teasing did not bother to deny the accusation. He just changed the subject. "So what is it you've found that you're so anxious to tell me?"

Genna responded with a chuckle. "Don't think Jonathan and I don't know you're trying to change the subject to avoid admitting how much you're getting to like Blacky."

Genna crossed in front of Andrews and over to the floor-to ceiling bookcases which lined the end of the den. At Genna's approach, Blacky's tail fanned the air from the corner to which she'd retreated at the change in Andrews' tone. The tail accelerated its orbital motion when Genna spoke softly to the bigger dog. Retrieving a stack of computer sheets from one shelf of the bookcase, Genna returned to Andrews' chair and settled comfortably on the floor beside his legs, putting Sky on the floor beside her.

"Now, this is a count of the number of reports of lab break-ins ascribed to animal rights groups by state," Genna explained, selecting a specific computer sheet to extend upward for Andrews' attention. "You'll note the goose-egg ascribed to Virginia."

"Data source?" Andrews injected. Then his eyes noted a footnote at the bottom of the page indicating the information was taken from a publication of the FBI dated some two months previously. "Never mind."

"Footnoted at the bottom," Genna responded unnecessarily. She gave Andrews a look that was both smug and amused before continuing. "So, as late as six months ago, national data indicated no occurrence of illegal activities by animal rights groups in Virginia. It should be an easy matter to determine data for the most recent six months from your police computers. However," she added smugly, "there weren't any."

Andrews decided against inquiring how she knew that. She might tell and he might then have to do something about it. "And just what makes Ketterholt bring up the subject every time I talk with him?"

"I'm sure you can think of many reasons," Genna reasoned sweetly. "I can think of two immediately." She paused to pat Sky and Blacky, who had once again left the security of her corner to join Sky by Andrews' chair.

When the silence continued, Andrews resorted to a prod. "Well, what two?"

"One, he's paranoid. Two, he's using this as an excuse to justify the excessive overhead for security his facility has been charging federal agencies on grants. Three, he wants to direct your attention away from himself as a suspect. Four, he wants to direct your attention away from someone else associated with the Institute as a suspect. Five,....."

"Never mind," Andrews injected. "You said two. That's an entire laundry list."

"I said two immediately. I could come up with a lengthy list if I tried."

"Seems to me you already did!" Checkmated for the time being, Andrews changed the subject. "Well, are we going for a walk or not? Show me some of this beautiful spring scenery you're always bragging about."

Jonathan and Genna both smiled, but Genna agreeably put aside the papers she'd been sharing with Andrews. Scrambling to her feet with an agility that her fat guest viewed with envy, she headed off toward the laundry room. "I'll get two leads," she said.

Blacky and Sky followed closely at her heels.

"Your wife has a devious mind," Andrews observed, appreciatively.

"Yes," Jonathan admitted with a chuckle. "But which one of those scenarios are you most concerned about being true."

It was Andrews turn to smile. "All of them."

"Despite Genna's denial of any linkage with animal rights activities, the poem certainly suggests the involvement of someone deeply concerned with animal welfare," Jonathan observed.

Andrews nodded in agreement. "The attempt to insert a group member into the ranks of staff, as may have happened with the Roalf impersonation, is standard practice for such groups. They want to collect photographic evidence of animal usage in experiments."

Any further discussion of the murder was interrupted by Genna's return. Leads attached to each dog's collar were held firmly in her left hand. Jonathan and Andrews rose from their respective chairs, the latter more slowly than his younger godson, and the three humans and two canines went outside into the cool spring afternoon. A brisk wind had partially cleared the overcast skies, and the scent of azaleas was pleasant in the fresh air.

Ambling along a well mulched path that led from the rear of the house toward the banks of the James River, Andrews admired the display of color from white dogwoods that shaded the long hedges of colorful azaleas. Blacky seemed to find one large pink and white variety of azalea very attractive and strained against her lead to touch her nose to a blossom.

"Here," Genna said to Andrews, handing him the end of the black dog's lead. "You walk your witness. She knows how to behave on a lead but she forgets sometime."

"You've trained her this quickly?" Andrews' query was a mixture of admiration and astonishment.

"No. She was trained already. Just a little rusty on how to act."

For the next hour, the five walked and enjoyed the cool breezes off the river and the bright splendor of the spring foliage. Andrews forgot about homicides as well as hunger, and ate lightly of the dinner Genna served later in the afternoon. He had showered and settled in pajamas and his robe to read a bit before turning out the lights when he remembered that he'd failed to ask Genna about ideas for utilizing Blacky's knowledge to advance the investigation. Reluctant as he was to discuss the subject, he decided to address the issue before retiring for the night. Putting aside his book, he went to find Genna and settle the fate of the black dog that slept quietly and trustingly now in the den downstairs.

He found her sitting on the floor of the nursery, an anxious Amber watching at her knee. Genna held the tiny puppy on his back in one hand while she talked softly to him and pressed his tiny paws with the two fingers of her other hand.

"Got a minute?" he said by way of greeting.

"Sure. Didn't know you were still up." Genna smiled a welcome but continued to gently pull on the nails of the puppy.

"Well, yes. I thought of something I wanted to settle tonight." Andrews frowned, perplexed by Genna's behavior with the puppy. "What are you doing?"

Genna raised her head briefly, then chuckled. "Oh. Getting Rusty familiar with having his nails touched. I've already had to trim them once."

"He's only three days old," Andrews admonished.

"Puppies' nails grow very fast, and little briar scratches aren't much fun for mother dogs," Genna explained. "What did you want to settle?"

"Just how do we go about exposing Blacky to the suspects in this homicide and utilizing her fear reaction— I guess that is what you'd call it—to furthering this investigation?"

Frown lines around Genna's mouth assured Andrews that the subject was as painful to her as it was uncomfortable to him. She sighed but did not answer until she had redeposited little Rusty in his sleeping box and helped his dam Amber to settle back around the tiny puppy.

"She's settled in here nicely, as you saw on the walk this afternoon and at dinner. I suppose you could take her back to your office, call your suspects in one at the time, and have someone record her reactions." Genna's carefully chosen words were cooperative as far as they went. The stubborn set of the chin promised an argument if Andrews tried to take her up on the suggestion.

When he did not respond, the younger woman turned her attention to the hesitant dog that stood in the doorway holding an empty metal dish in his mouth.

"You can come in, Sky. What's the matter, Baby? Do you want another snack?"

Sky bounded into the room in response to Genna's welcome, jumping into her lap and dropping the dish so that he could rain doggie kisses on her face. Amber grumbled once from her sleeping box, but went back to cleaning her puppy.

Andrews concluded that he did not have a firm list of suspects at this point, and needed to collect a bit more information before testing Genna's suggestion. So he decided to postpone setting a date for Blacky to encounter the suspects until he could learn the identity of the sender of the notes, letter and poem.

"I'm not ready just yet to finalize my list of suspects, so we'll decide what to do when I am," he said.

It was obviously what Genna wanted to hear. Her face brightened. Andrews was prompted to admire the development of little Rusty [he didn't see any change], Rusty's wonderful weight gain [Andrews thought he still looked like a fat rat], and Amber's abilities as a mother [Andrew's found her chief credit to be the calm acceptance of so much confusion around her puppy]. His sleep that night in the guest room at Heron's Rest was dreamless and undisturbed even by the black dog who pushed open his door in the middle of the night and joined him on the queen-size bed.

Chapter 18

Heavy traffic along the fifty-two mile drive between Heron's Rest and his office put Andrews about ten minutes behind schedule. Foster and Pepper were camped out in his office when he arrived, passing the time over cups of coffee. Any smart remarks the fat dieter might have been tempted to make were stifled by the cup of steaming liquid which Pepper handed him.

"Billy explained about the dog," Pepper said between gulps from his own coffee. Like Andrews, he took it black and the liquid was much hotter than the milk-cooled mixture Foster was sipping comfortably. "Sorry for the mixup, but I thought your note about the dog was for me."

"Well I'm not sorry. It brought some things to light that might have never emerged otherwise," Andrews noted agreeably, his mouth warmed by the fresh coffee. He was comfortably full from the breakfast of grain waffles and fruit which Genna had fed him, but the extra coffee tasted good after fighting the traffic on Route 5 for an hour. He settled into his desk chair and briefly reviewed for the two his interview with Ketterholt and Genna's inputs regarding animal rights activities.

"Damn! This coffee is too hot to drink," Pepper grumbled after burning his tongue. "Well, let me bring you two up to date on my review of the victim's papers."

He got no protest from the two investigating officers. Pulling a small notebook from the inside pocket of his navy blazer, he flipped a few pages and began his recitation in a dry, bored voice. "I found an unlabeled folder containing hand-written notes regarding property disposition in various divorce situations." Pepper looked very disgusted, as he added, "But I didn't find any reference to a name or a phone number showing who the victim might have consulted in compiling the notes. Or any date of reference."

When neither detective responded, Pepper continued, "The team that went to the victim's home found nothing of interest in the desk of his study or anywhere else at his residence. Just brochures and magazines with notices of upcoming medical conferences. Unless it's of interest to you that the victim seemed to concentrate on conferences where golf, riding and hiking were amenities available at the conference hotel."

"Let's go back to the papers in his office," Andrews prompted impatiently. "Where were his personal papers, and would they have been accessible to his killer?"

"He kept his personal papers in two locked drawers of his desk. The crime scene found the key to these drawers on the key ring found in the victim's pocket."

"So the killer could have gotten the key, inspected the papers and returned the key?" Foster injected.

"I suppose so," Pepper acknowledged, "depending on how much time he spent at the crime scene."

Pepper waited expectantly for more questions from Andrews or Foster. When neither spoke, he continued. "The victim has two charge accounts listing his office address only. One is an exclusive ladies store; the other, a jeweler. Over the last two months he's bought several pricy things, but the bills were paid promptly." Pulling more papers from another pocket, Pepper handed Andrews a sheet containing some hand written notes in Pepper's scrawl.

Andrews recognized the names of the two stores although he'd never dared to buy his few presents for Genna and Jonathan's sister from either. Prices at the two were way too rich for his income. Passing the sheet to Foster, Andrews observed, "It'll be interesting to see if these costly trinkets went to his wife, his secretary, or someone else entirely. Ask Billy to check with the stores and get descriptions to go with these purchases if possible. Then we'll have to run them down."

Foster made a few notes in his own notebook before putting his nearly empty cup down on Andrews' desk and strolling out of the senior detective's office to find Billy Brown.

"What else?" Andrews prodded impatiently.

"An entire folder on the victim's partnership arrangements was in that locked drawer of his desk. The folder contained....let's see," Pepper paused to pull yet another sheet of paper from the recesses of his navy jacket. "Ah! ...contained a copy of the agreement by which he got 65% of all grant monies, a number of letters from Thomas Berkley indicating dissatisfaction with the split, concerns that results the victim was presenting couldn't be substantiated by research data, complaints that the victim presented too many of their jointly authored papers and reaped most of the benefits of the travel. Copies of the victim's letters back to Berkley indicated Porter wasn't willing to let Berkley out of the contract, mild ridicule about Berkley's naivete regarding research publications," Pepper droned on and on. His tone was sleep-inducing. Andrews was about to interrupt him when the freckled-faced sleuth continued with a slight increase in pitch, "and, an interesting charge by the victim, a carefully worded complaint that Berkley paid too much attention to Mrs. Porter."

"What?" Andrews interrupted.

"That's what the victim said in his memo back to Berkley."

"They saw each other all day long. Why wouldn't he just confront Berkley face to face?" Andrews' full face was twisted into a scowl. "Or take him out in the alley?"

"This crowd seems to record everything, fortunately for us."

Foster returned so quietly the other two men were unaware of his presence until he interjected, "Guess that's reason number two for Berkley's interests in getting to the victim's papers."

"Yes, so it would seem," Andrews acknowledged. Then turning his attention once again to Pepper, he continued. "Anything from Ketterholt about complaints on the victim's research efforts?"

"Nothing I found on that," Pepper acknowledged with a slight shake of his head. "But I did find one thing that was a little queer."

Andrews' brief look of disappointment was immediately replaced with an eagle-sharp, alert stance. "What?"

"Well, it probably has nothing to do with the murder, and I probably shouldn't have even bothered to list it...."

"What? Just spell it out and let us decide whether it means anything." Andrews' tone was sharp and demanding.

"The top folder on the victim's desk was marked with a location and date: San Francisco, June 2. In the folder I found a brochure on a meeting of the International Society of Oncology, a plane ticket, confirmation of reservations for two at the Marquise Hotel, notes concerning experiment results, and a marked-up copy of a paper published fifteen years ago by someone named Earnest Soho."

Andrews squirmed in his chair, impatient for Pepper to get to the meat of his explanation. Foster had pulled out his notepad again and was making brief notes of Pepper's explanation.

"The death of the dog you took to Williamsburg was included in the experiment results."

Andrews' impatience finally got the better of him. "Is that all? We've been over this before!"

Pepper was not ruffled by the impatience. Or hurried. "No, we haven't gotten to the part I found strange."

"Well, get to it, then!" Andrews grumbled and squirmed while Pepper took his time at continuing his report.

"Someone, and the handwriting seems consistent with the victim's, had crossed through a few words here and there on the old report, changing the title slightly and

<paril>
177

changing the author to Porter and Berkley. Throughout the text, slight changes had been made. But overall it was the same publication."

Foster didn't wait for Andrews to respond first. "You mean the victim was plagiarizing an earlier work for presentation at a meeting later this year."

"He seemed to be repeating the experiment and saying that he was confirming the earlier research," Pepper amended.

"And using falsified data in the reconfirmed research," Andrews said disgustedly.

"Well, either his notes about the experiment on the grey dog were false or there were two grey dogs in the lab the same night and the body of one of the two was moved from the lab where the victim was found the next morning."

"In a pig's eye!" Andrews jeered.

For a brief space of minutes, the three men were silent as the importance of Pepper's revelation was absorbed. Andrews was the first to vocalize his thoughts aloud.

"Langston made some negative comments about the quality of the victim's research, but I can't see where exposure of the victim's useless work would hurt Langston. It would have been very detrimental to Berkley. It would have been a financial blow to Ketterholt if questions came up about the credibility and usefulness of the victim's work."

Foster quickly picked up on Andrews' thinking and continued the analysis. "So either Ketterholt or Berkley could have felt threatened by the victim's careless and foolhardy disregard for credible work. But if either one killed Porter, why wouldn't they have made certain to find and destroy the victim's papers?"

"They knew about them and were anxious enough the day after the murder to get to them," Andrews nodded in agreement. "Berkley made numerous attempts to acquire the victim's papers after the body was discovered. And he seemed anxious to get his hands on the dogs also."

Foster picked up the thread of logic, "So if either one of them killed the victim, they were interrupted before they could get to the papers and destroy them. How? And by whom?"

Andrews leaned back in his chair and looked sleepy. Foster made some more cryptic symbols in his notebook. Pepper looked from one to other, a pleased look on his face, then switched to a new point.

From yet another pocket in his blazer, Pepper pulled a group of folded sheets and extended them toward Andrews. "These are copies of the letter you asked about, the poem called "Brown Eyes" and the five drawings Bart asked me to find. Oh, the drawings have the eye portion colored brown to remind the victim of the poem I guess. Sorry but the Xerox only does things in black and white."

"Did the victim make these notes?" Andrews stubby fingers pointed at a sheet of paper on which three names were written. Two of the names were followed by the notation, "no match". The third name, by the notation, "portable in lab".

"No. Those notes were made by one of the guys in the police lab." Pepper removed his wire rimmed glasses and rubbed a none-too-clean looking tissue over the lenses while his near-sighted eyes focused on nothing. "The victim had included typed memos from Langston, Berkley and Raines in the folder with the letter, the poem and the drawings. My assumption was that he suspected one of the three and was trying to compare the type on the letter, notes and poem with the typeface of the memos from each of the three. So I gave all the samples to the lab boys to do their stuff. And our guys agree that the poem was typed on a portable typewriter they found in Langston's lab."

Pepper gave a smug look to first Andrews and then Foster. If he was hoping for a word of praise for his ingenuity he was disappointed. Foster contemplated his notebook before making a few more entries in it.

Andrews sat. And chewed the rim of his empty coffee cup. When he finally spoke, it was to himself.

179

"He was in the building at the time of the murder, signed in at the same time as the victim. Could have walked back to victim's lab with him, had an argument and killed him, removed whatever he used to clobber him over the head.....taken it to his own office suite and given it to the cleaning crew for disposal....no reason for them to suspect it wasn't normal lab trash. And Langston would have left the victim's papers to be found, would have wanted them found."

Turning to Foster, Andrews directed, "Talk to that cleaning crew again. See if someone remembers what was removed from Langston's office."

Foster nodded in agreement and made more notes in his notebook.

Andrews calmly thanked Pepper for a fine bit of work and dismissed the near-sighted man. For a long time, he and Foster sat without speaking, each busy with his own thoughts. Finally, he inquired, "Has Billy gotten anywhere with locating this volunteer, Pam Hudson? Maybe we can find out who sent the damn letter and see if that person is connected to Langston in any way." And then as an afterthought, the frustrated crank added, "Damn, why didn't I ask her who his doctor was?"

"What?" Foster exclaimed. Despite his experience in working with Andrews and his moods, Foster failed to follow this last twist in his partner's thinking.

"Elizabeth Weir. She said Porter wasn't Roalf's doctor. But I didn't ask her who was," Andrews explained. "Anyway, we'd better find out."

Foster made another note before returning to Andrews' question about Pam Hudson.

"Billy's determined that Ms. Hudson will be on duty at the hospital beginning at 1:00 pm today. We can wait and catch her then, if you like. Billy thought you might not want to wait, however. He arranged for us to talk to her at her home this morning at ten if that suits your schedule."

"This morning sounds fine. Maybe she can identify this patient for us." Andrews' face brightened at the prospect of closure on something about the case.

It was a twenty minute drive to Pam Hudson's home. The temperature had turned hot for the season and Andrews was profoundly thankful for air-conditioning. In spite of the temperature control in the police cruiser, his suit jacket was damp along the back and his trousers were damp and sprung at the knees by the time they arrived at their destination. Foster eased the vehicle into a parking space at the curb in front of a neat, white-famed house. The younger detective looked crisp and fresh as usual, his navy suit unrumpled and his powder blue shirt and crisp print tie seemingly chosen to match the blue shutters and trim of the house.

The neat walkway was made of old brick, sunken in places and cracked, but free of grass and weeds. Along the sides of the walk and flanking the house on either side of the front porch, beds of pansies provided a colorful foreground for the yellow spotted leaves of the gold dust acubas nearest the house. Like the walk, the flower beds were carefully mulched and weeded and testified to the occupant's interest in gardening.

Foster's finger pressure on the doorbell was rewarded by a distant peal and shortly by a friendly face with large, sympathetic eyes. The petite woman who greeted them was in her early sixties, or so Andrews guessed. The tiny lines of ageing around eyes and mouth only softened and added to the sense of caring and compassion she radiated. Andrews introduced himself and Foster, flashing his badge through the screen.

"Oh, yes. Do come in," a soft, musical voice instructed. Small hands with short, unpolished nails unfastened the screen and held it open for the two to enter. The loose outfit of a hospital volunteer was kind to the figure of the little woman, softening the pounds added with her years. The pink jumper and pink striped shirt accented a soft, fair complexion.

"Thank you, Ms. Hudson." Andrews acknowledged softly. "We appreciate your seeing us this morning."

"I'm only too glad to help, though I'm sure I can't imagine how I might be of service to the police." The old hands directed the two men toward the comfortable looking sofa and chairs in the living room, closing the door behind them. It was a small room to begin with, and the heavy cherry furniture and two tall policemen seen to crowd it to excess. "Do sit down where you will," the diminutive hostess directed. "May I get you a cup of coffee?"

Both men refused the offer of coffee politely and positioned themselves to sit.

"Please sit here if you will, Ms. Hudson," Andrews directed their hostess toward the near end of her sofa so that she would be between him and Foster.

"I hope you don't mind my dress," she said self-consciously as she took the seat Andrews directed. Andrews and Foster settled into their chosen seats and the room immediately looked a little less crowded. "I didn't know how long this might take, and I thought I'd save time. I need to report to the hospital by twelve-thirty, or I could call them and tell them I'll be late. I want to help anyway I can."

"This shouldn't take very long," Andrews reassured her. "We think you might be able to help us with a few stray issues relating to a case we're investigating."

"Dr. Porter's murder?" The voice was musical, consoling, the issue at hand not withstanding. The fair face with its soft, brown eyes turned first to one and then the other of the officers, thin eyebrows drawn together in concern.

"Yes." Andrews found himself studying the small nose. It lent a perky look to the soft face but wrinkled slightly at the reminder of the recent tragedy at the Institute.

"Oh, I'm not certain I could help you with anything. I've seen Dr. Porter around the Institute, of course, but I didn't know him at all, just to speak to in the halls when he'd pass. And I'd not want to say anything ill of the dead."

"Actually we were hoping you could help us identify a patient of Dr. Porter's. Several months ago you tried to help the distraught father of a little boy who'd come in for

182

radiation treatments. This father was raving loudly in the waiting area about the treatments not helping and berating the hospital for prescribing the treatments to make money rather than to help his little son."

"Well, you know, I can't see where something like that would have anything to do with Dr. Porter's death. I mean, people, especially parents, do get terribly distressed about their helplessness." Ms. Hudson responded.

Before she could digress any further, Andrews injected, "We just need to clear away some peripheral matters so we can keep our investigation on track. Do you remember a situation occurring such as I've just described?"

"Well, this man became very upset in the treatment waiting room a few months ago. He was crying so hard his glasses got all steamed up. His child had just been taken into the treatment room and I remember, I kept hoping he was out of hearing range. The child, I mean. I tried to comfort the father, get him to take coffee from me or something, but he continued to complain about the hospital only being interested in soaking him when it knew it couldn't cure his child. But I don't know if the child was a boy or a girl. They all look the same, you know. It's the chemotherapy. Causes them to lose all their hair. But it'll grow back, once they're done with the treatments. And, you know, after the first shock of seeing themselves bald, the little children adjust to the situation better than their parents, you see."

Andrews, who didn't see, pressed the tiny woman for an identification. "Did you know the man? Could you give us his name?"

"Well, I wouldn't want to get him in any kind of trouble," Mrs. Hudson explained. "It isn't often that a parent loses control as he did. Well, not in public anyway. I find mothers in the rest room some times crying uncontrollably. But I wouldn't want to make his life more difficult. His child died you see. Several months ago I think it was. Another of the volunteers told me. I missed seeing Mr. Graft around and I asked Martha about him. That's one of my fellow volunteers. She said the child died."

She turned to Andrews and then to Foster, her kind face troubled. "I wouldn't want to get Mr. Graft in trouble. He's had so much already."

"We just need to clear up a few things with him, Mrs. Hudson." Foster added his own assurances to his superior's. "Do you remember Mr. Graft's first name?"

"Paul, I think. You're certain I'm not getting him into trouble?" Troubled eyes in the pink and white face turned back to Andrews, and continued. "He was worried about his child and about the cost I suppose. People say a lot of things they don't mean. I just don't see why you two are interested in this. Was Dr. Porter his doctor?"

Andrews was tempted to ignore this last question, but the gentle face and voice touched him deeply. "We just want to clear up some things about patient relations. Might we impose on you a bit more and ask to use your phone book?"

Redirecting Pam Hudson's attention to a need for help was a perfect ploy. "Oh, do stay seated, gentlemen!" she directed in response to their bobbing up and down as she rose from her own seat to search for the requested phone book. She excused herself, returning very shortly to place the big directory of white pages in Andrew's lap.

"Thank you, very much," Andrews responded with a smile. "Here, your eyes are better than mine," he said to Foster, passing the phone book over to his partner.

"Do you need more light?" Ms. Hudson inquired solicitously.

"No, I'm fine," Foster reassured her as he opened the book to the appropriate page and consulted the listings for "Graft". "Here it is."

"Would you like to call on my phone?"

The detectives declined and expressed their thanks for her time and help. After a few gracious words of good-bye on both sides, she escorted them to her door and waved the two to their waiting car.

Chapter 19

Graft's address was in the inner city, part of a sad series of streets containing run-down three-storied wooden structures built in the twenties. The front yards were brief strips of dirt between sagging porches and cracked sidewalks. Here and there, boards replaced the window areas of some of the structures. A few residents attempted to brighten their area with flowers, but the occasional basket of bright blooms only intensified the seedy appearance of the structure it adorned. Two-one-seven had once been white with green trim. Peeling paint on shutters and house produced a spotted brown pattern on both. Unlike some places, the yard was clean if bare of all but the most stubborn patches of grass.

Foster parked the car against the cracked curb in front and the two officers walked across the shallow front yard to the sagging porch. Andrews found no bell to ring, so he knocked loudly on the paint-chipped door. He had raised his hand to repeat the knock after a long stretch of silence, when the door was opened by a thin, stoop-shouldered man.

Deep-set brown eyes behind thick glasses met Andrews' with resignation. Approximately one-hundred-and-sixty pounds were stretched sparsely over a frame that would have reached six feet had it stood erect. Thick brown hair heavily streaked with grey was carefully brushed, if poorly cut, and framed a long face with sunken cheeks and dark circles beneath the eyes. Faded blue denim pants, the right knee area carefully mended, and a plaid, open-collared shirt covered the thin body.

"Good morning. We're looking for a Mr. Paul Graft." Andrews studied the effect of his words on the listless figure in the doorway.

"You're with the police, I suppose. I heard about the murder of Dr. Porter on the radio. I've been expecting you."

The dull eyes confronted Andrews, but the man did not reply directly to the question of identity.

"I'm Lieutenant Kevin Andrews and this is Sergeant Bart Foster. We're with the homicide division of the Richmond Police."

Andrews pulled his identifying badge from his pocket and opened the leather case to allow Graft, if he was Graft, to see. The man waved the presented badge away with a bony hand.

"You might as well come in and talk inside."

"You are Mr. Paul Graft." Andrews voice was soft, non-threatening, more a statement than a question. No avoiding of questions was acceptable, though the sight of this defeated example of humanity was not what Andrews had expected as the source of the threatening letters.

"Yes," the pallid figure finally acknowledged. He stepped back and sideways to allow the two police officers to enter into the fifteen-foot square room which seemed to serve as the principal living area for the apartment. A small bedroom and dinky, ill-equipped kitchen were visible off the main room. Unlike the outside of the house which was sad and neglected, the apartment radiated a worn but gentle sense of caring. Two oval woven rugs divided the large living area into seating and dining areas.

Graft closed the door and led the way around worn but lovingly tended furniture, directing with hands and nods the seating of the two investigators. "Excuse the mess. I've just gotten back from the laundry and haven't had a chance to put things away."

At Graft's direction, Andrews and Foster took seats on the sofa with their backs to the sun. Graft followed behind them, taking a chair close to the sofa.

The soft, sage-green walls were bare except for one large poster of a country scene which had been hung on the interior wall between the chair and sofa. Inexpensive though it was, it tied the colors of the wall and simple furnishings together with the faded afghan which was carefully folded and draped over the back of the sofa.

"Why were you expecting us?" Andrews asked.

"Why else? The letter I sent him of course. That doctor that the papers say was killed last Thursday night. I figured he kept it and the police would find it and come looking for me. That's why you're here, isn't it?"

Foster had so far remained silent, but had extracted his trusty notebook from the recesses of his suit on sitting down. Discreetly, he began to record the conversation with Graft. The principal subject appeared not to notice.

"Why don't you tell us about it," Andrews prompted. He weighed the need for reminding Graft of his rights and decided against it. As long as the conversation was about a letter and nothing further, it seemed an unnecessary deterrent to a promising conversation.

"There's not much to tell. I was devastated over the loss of our Danny. My wife tried to stop me sending the letter, she said it would just make more trouble for us, but I wouldn't listen."

Tired eyes confronted Andrews, silently asking to be spared remembering.

"Danny?" Andrews kept any compassion from his glance.

"Our son, Leslie's and mine. He died this past February." The tired-sounding voice broke at the memory.

Andrews waited patiently to allow the frail man to recover his composure. Finally he prompted the grieving father softly.

"You blamed Dr. Porter for your son's death?"

187

"Yes. I did. I still do."

Another long pause followed. Andrews finally opened his mouth to voice another prompt, but it proved unnecessary. Graft continued on his own.

"Danny had cancer. At first Leslie and I were grateful for the care the Institute gave him. But Porter continued to put him through repeated cycles of chemotherapy and radiation treatments long after he knew it was hopeless. It did no good and it made Danny miserable. He would cling to my wife and me and beg us to let him be. But Porter wouldn't quit. At his prompting, the Institute threatened to take us to court if we refused to bring Danny in for treatment. Porter knew it was hopeless, but he just kept putting Danny through the pain and misery." Tears stood in the brown eyes, but the tired voice continued in a steady tone.

Andrews steeled himself to prod deeper into painful memories but was spared the effort. Grant's poise held, but tears overflowed his eyes and traced shiny streaks down his thin cheeks. His voice was steady if throaty with suppressed emotions as he continued. "Our insurance ran out. The hospital wanted money we couldn't pay. The hospital garnisheed my pay for the bills, and I lost my job. We tried again to bring Danny home. Porter admitted the treatments were hopeless, but he wouldn't let us bring Danny home and let him die in peace."

The tears flowed more freely, but the throaty voice ceased. The thin man seemed lost in memories, unaware of the passage of time and the presence of the two officers.

Finally, Andrews queried softly, "You hold Porter responsible for Danny's death, then?"

"Not his death," the slight man rasped, "just the manner of it. We might at least have brought him home to die in peace. It would have made losing him a little easier, if we could have had a few days with him to say goodbye."

Before Andrews or Foster could respond, the grieving father went on with his recollections. "Not that the people at the Institute weren't kind. The other patients, young and old, spent a lot of time talking with Danny, trying to cheer him. I went to pieces one day when Danny was taken down to radiology for more treatments, and everyone was most patient and kind to me. The other patients at the hospital and the staff arranged a birthday party for him his last birthday. One of the nurses even brought Danny a dog collar she'd gotten from somewhere, a lovely affair decorated with antelope heads. She suggested he might like it for his next dog."

The slight voice chocked back a sob. "Danny had lost his old dog several months before. He loved the old fellow and took his death very hard. The nurse meant to be kind. She meant to take Danny's mind off his illness, but it just brought back painful memories. He took a turn for the worse just after that and never recovered. He died not long afterwards."

For long moments the three men sat in silence, each seeking to deal with his own sense of futility at the premature extinction of a young life. Andrews was the first to speak.

"What prompted you to write the letters?"

"I saw Porter quoted in the newspaper. Something about all the wonderful things that medicine was doing for young cancer victims today. He seemed so smug, so pleased with himself. I just had to correct that smugness, needed to make him understand how much his arrogance and lack of compassion had cost my wife and me." As though realizing for the first time that Andrews' question contained a plural, Graft clarified, "But it was just the one letter. I don't know anything about other letters if he got more than one."

Foster glanced at Andrews for approval. Andrews' acquiescence was a slow lowering of the eye-lids but sufficient. "And you're certain you only sent one letter to Dr. Porter?"

Graft re-adjusted his point of focus to the younger officer's face, squinting at the increased distance. Andrews shifted into a more comfortable position on the sofa after extracting the papers from his pocket that Pepper had provided earlier.

Graft still looked blankly at Foster. When he did not reply, Andrews extended the packet containing copies of the letters, drawings and the poem to the seemingly puzzled man. "What about all these items, Mr. Graft? Didn't you send these to the victim as well?"

The slight figure seemed confused at first with the material handed to him by Andrews. But he slowly collected himself and studied the pages carefully. "This one," he said finally, "is a copy of my letter to Porter. I don't know anything about any of the rest."

The lack of either caution or cunning in the eyes dashed Andrews' short-lived expectations of an easy solution to this current investigation. "Can you think of anyone else who might have written the letter to Porter?"

"Anyone," Graft responded bitterly, "but no one that I know."

"Not your wife, perhaps?"

Graft shook his head slowly. "No, she tried her best to keep me from writing. Leslie's too busy trying to work and keep house to spend time blaming others." The downtrodden figure continued apologetically, "I don't make enough at my night job to keep us afloat in even these shabby quarters. Leslie has to work to help with expenses."

"Were you working the night Dr. Porter was killed?" Andrews injected smoothly.

"No, I wasn't. I was home sick the night he was killed." The tired eyes met Andrews' frankly. "I'm afraid I have no alibi, Lieutenant. My wife had a chance for some overtime and didn't come home until midnight." The words came out in a rush, as though the frail body faced the worst and wanted to get it in the open.

"I don't remember the papers giving a time of his death, but Leslie was out all evening, so I'm afraid I can't prove that I was here."

The two detectives asked and were given the places of employment of both the Grafts. Andrews would follow procedures and check out the information given by this beaten man, but his instincts argued that he and Foster had heard the truth from Paul Graft.

"Well, I think that's all for now," Andrews said. "We know where to find you should we have further questions."

Surprise and relief were equally mingled on Graft's face as the three rose and shook hands. The two detectives thanked the sad, stooped figure for his time before leaving the apartment.

Chapter 20

"I don't know about you," Foster said, turning the ignition key in the police cruiser, "but I believe the man."

"So do I. Check it out all the same." Andrews squirmed and fought with the problem of securing a normal-length seat belt around his more-than-normal bulk. "This damn thing reached the catch on the way over," he grumbled.

"He could have padded his weight I suppose," Andrews continued, "Got it. He's about the right height for the man Chambles described as the cleaning helper using Roalf's name." Another audible groan was heard. Then Andrews continued, "But he can't see without those glasses, and the fake Roalf didn't wear glasses."

Foster laughed. "It's a good thing I'm accustomed to screening out irrelevant verbiage."

He eased the car out into traffic, while Andrews got his seat belt fastened, adjusted and himself settled.

"Shall we pay another visit to Langston and see what he has to say about the typewriter in his lab?"

"Not now." Andrews' response was decisive.

Foster drove almost a block in silence before the older man picked up the conversation. When he did, it was to argue with himself. "The dogs weren't afraid of him. The little one was petrified of Berkley, but neither dog seemed to fear Langston overly much. The typewriter was found in his lab, but it doesn't have to be his. On the other hand, the notes and the poem would fit with what we know about Langston. What's wrong with my logic here?"

Foster broke into his partner's monologue with a chuckle. "I'd like to be around when you try that argument on the Captain. On second thought, I'd think I'd like to be as far away as possible!"

"You're right," Andrews acknowledged, grinning at his driver. "Which leaves us with the problem of who sent the poem and drawings. If Graft didn't, then someone else did. Langston danced around, hinting at knowing who sent them, but refusing to say who. Maybe his dancing was a cover for sending them himself. I want to review my notes from yesterday and Pepper's full report before deciding what we're going to ask the good doctor."

Looking at his watch, Andrews realized there was a reason for the empty feeling inside his chest. "It's about time to eat, don't you think. How about picking up some burgers on our way back to headquarters?"

Foster was unsupportive of this devious move. "I'd sort of like to swing by a Ukrop's salad bar and pick up something. Think you could go for that instead?"

Andrews' answer was a grunt. "I suppose I could live with that," he conceded.

By 2:00 pm, the two officers were back at their office and settled behind their respective desks. Andrews mood was cranky and slipping into sour. Rabbit food and dressing always left him that way. He'd considered and rejected finding something nasty to assign to Foster to get even for the sergeant's cajoling him into eating within his diet. But he reasoned that he'd just end up sharing another high-fiber, low-enjoyment meal with the slender bastard if he didn't crack this case.

So he sent Foster away to explore the 'female attachments,' as Andrews chose to reference the possible romantic complications between victim, secretary and wife. And to deal with the interview of Dr. Walter Raines.

Andrews tackled a report Billy Brown had left for him.

In his cryptic style, Billy reported the results of his investigations of the two individuals having keys to the victim's lab.

Beside the name of Mark McBroon, Billy had noted his lack of success thus far in interviewing her.

"Great!" Andrews muttered aloud. "A dead dog that isn't. A working stiff that goes around using a dead man's name. And a female named Mark. What can happen with this case next?"

He was interrupted by Braxton Brown, who wandered in looking neat and fresh as usual. "What do you want to happen?"

Andrews gave the younger man a nasty look. "To forget diets and homicides for the rest of my life," he barked.

Braxton chuckled, "Dad and I wondered if you'd like to come out to the house Saturday night for some beer and cards?"

The mention of beer lightened Andrews' expression a bit. "Well, that sounds like fun. Thanks. I think that could be arranged. Poker again?"

"Sounds fine to me," Braxton nodded agreeably. He turned in the doorway and added, "Think Foster will be interested?"

"As long as he doesn't bring his 'diet-police' badge with him to the game," Andrews snapped.

"I'll tell him you said so." Braxton chuckled as he returned to his own office.

Andrews returned to Billy's report. His old friend's thoroughness was recorded in economically worded notes. Billy's interviews with neighbors at Miss McBroon's apartment complex revealed only one witness, and that one very unreliable. An elderly busybody reported that Miss McBroon had never come home at all the night of the murder. Billy's assessment indicated this witness was eighty-one, lived around the corner of the building nearly a block from McBroon's apartment, and went to bed around eight at night. Another neighbor of McBroon seemed to offer more reliable information. According to the bachelor who lived in the next apartment, Ms. McBroon's car was parked outside the neighbor's apartment—in the parking space he viewed as his—from mid-afternoon on the day of the murder until after he went to work the next day. It was gone when he came home on Friday evening.

Billy's report on Piper Morgan made Andrews chuckle despite the serious nature of the content. His old friend had attempted to interview one of Morgan's neighbors, only to pick the neighborhood snoop. Billy ended up hearing about everyone in the surrounding two block area before he could get the woman focused on Ms. Morgan. Andrews was immediately grateful for at least two things. First that he'd not been involved in the interview which seemed to have lasted about three hours. Secondly, the fat-fighting crank was grateful for Billy's abbreviated manner of communication; it made skipping to the important parts much easier.

With some editing, Andrews determined that the local consensus regarding Piper Morgan was that she was carrying on with the doctor for whom she worked. She seemed to spend too much on clothes and didn't return invitations to neighbors, often bragged about expensive presents she'd received from 'her doctor friend' and commented that his wife didn't understand the importance of his work. There was more, but Andrews' eyes were focused on the most important point in the interview. The neighbor had gone over to Morgan's house at 10:20 pm the night of the murder to borrow a light bulb. The one in her reading lamp had gone out. She'd gotten no answer to her knock at Morgan's door.

Andrews forgot his dignity to the point of laughing aloud at Billy's final comment. Foster took that precise moment to wander back into his superior's office and catch him.

"Billy's report is all that amusing?"

"Billy's interviews with one of Miss Morgan's neighbors indicates that her alibi isn't all that tight. She didn't answer a neighbor's attempt to call at her door at 10:20 pm the night of the murder. But Billy was sent to determine the whereabouts of the people Berkley said

195

had keys to the lab." Andrews still had a hard time suppressing his amusement. He summarized his old's friend's report for his partner. "Billy concluded that he couldn't confirm where she was at 10:20 pm the night of the murder, but he didn't know where her key was at any time during that night. She certainly could have given it to anyone and retrieved it in time to open the lab and discover the body on Friday morning."

Foster smiled also. "He's doing better than I am. I've been trying to set up an interview with Miss Morgan but haven't been able to contact her."

"She's probably at work at this hour," Andrews offered, putting aside the report he'd been holding.

"It would seem so," Foster agreed, "but we've still got the crime scene sealed, and I've had no luck with finding where she's temporarily working. I called Berkley to see if he knew, but he hasn't returned my call either."

"Have a seat and let's talk." Andrews waved Foster toward a chair as the phone rang, interrupting the two.

Andrews barked an acknowledgment of his name into the instrument, then listened with only nods of his head to a brief conversation on the other end. "OK, thanks for the confirmation."

He returned the phone handset to its cradle. "Twill says there's nothing new to tell us. He's sticking to his previous analysis that death probably occurred four to five minutes after the acid was poured down his throat. No evidence that he was secured much longer than a few minutes prior to that."

"So whoever killed him got to him almost immediately after his return."

"It would appear so. Langston returned at the same time according to the security logs for that evening. And Langston was very critical of Porter's callous nature with lab animals. Might that explain the brutal manner of the killing."

"He signed in at the same time as the victim, was overheard on at least two occasions to wish the victim a violent death, and would have been happy to have

Porter's papers found." Foster looked expectantly at his partner.

"I think a little talk with Dr. Langston is next on our agenda." This time Andrews did not resist the idea of confronting the feisty Dr. Langston again. "Do you want to go with me?"

"That depends," Foster admitted. "I wouldn't want you going to his home alone. On the other hand, I'd like to talk to Hogge and Chambles again, make certain Roalf didn't say something to one of them that we've overlooked. And you wanted me to recheck with the crew about materials removed from Langston's office the night of the murder."

The partners' conversation was interrupted once again, this time by a call from the Captain who requested a briefing on the case.

"I'll be right down," Andrews promised his superior.

To Foster, he said, "Tell you what. Call Langston. Tell him I'd like to meet with him at the Institute tomorrow morning. You arrange a meeting with Hogge and Chambles for the same time. That way you'll be nearby if I need you."

Foster nodded his agreement and walked briskly out toward his own office. He paused in the doorway. "I think I'll look up Dr. Walter Raines this afternoon and interview him further about the night of the murder. According to Billy, he should be back at work today."

"Fine," Andrews concurred. "Call me tonight if you get anything interesting."

Andrews was dozing in front of a boring television when Foster called shortly after dinner.

"Well, Dr. Raines would seem to be a viable suspect."

That awakened Andrews from his lethargy. "You're sure?"

"Yes. He drove his own car to the conference. He admits checking it out of the hotel's parking garage on Thursday night, the night of the murder. He says he told

197

other colleagues at the conference that he was going to bed because he didn't want to eat with a group that kept asking him to go to dinner, that he'd been out with them for an early dinner and a round of bars the day he arrived at the conference. That would be Wednesday, the night before the murder."

Foster paused for breath, but continued before Andrews could comment or query. "According to hotel records, the car registered to Raines left the hotel parking garage at 7:24 pm, returned at 12:47 am on Friday morning. Raines says he drove to Georgetown, ate alone in a trendy restaurant he picked at random, had a few drinks, relaxed, and started back to the hotel around 10:30 pm. He doesn't remember the name of the restaurant. He paid in cash so there's no charge slip. He got lost on the way back to the hotel and drove around and around Washington trying to find his way back to his hotel."

Foster paused to give Andrews a chance to digest his input.

Andrews interrupted. "Who carries around enough cash to pay for a meal and drinks in Georgetown?"

"Just telling you what the man said," Foster chuckled. "Very convenient, though. He was alone, he can't remember the exact restaurant, he admits to a 'few' drinks which could cover the supposed confusion at finding his hotel in a timely manner."

The sound from Andrews' end of the phone sounded more like the grinding of teeth. "His statement about Wednesday night is interesting too. These colleagues will support his claims, and what would you like to bet that they were touring Georgetown on Wednesday night. So if we circulate pictures, people may remember seeing Raines but not know if it was Wednesday or Thursday nights. Another fine mess! Anything else?"

"No, that's about it. Except that I called Ms. Weir back and asked who Roalf's doctor at the Institute was."

"For what?" Andrews responded, bewildered by this last bit of conversation.

"Don't you remember? When we left Ms. Weir's, you said that you forgot to follow up on her comment that Porter wasn't Roalf's doctor. And you asked,'Who was?'"

"Oh, yes. I do remember," Andrews responded. "And.....?"

"Raines was Roalf's doctor.

The silence extended for some time before Andrews finally and dejectedly admitted, "Don't know where that gets us either."

"Nor I. See you tomorrow morning."

Chapter 21

Two pairs of hazel eyes stared at each other across the littered desk of Dr. Mathew Langston. Andrews' were larger and had a little more grey around the rim of the irises. Langston's were focused, angry, and enlarged by his thick glasses.

Andrews pressed his point. "It isn't often these days that we can match type fonts. More and more, people utilize computers and computer printers. But we know for certain that the poem and one of the notes received by Porter were typed on the old portable typewriter we found in your lab."

Langston exhaled harshly before replying to the policeman confronting him across his littered desk. "We keep the small typewriter in the lab, to type labels for the samples. Almost anyone could have wandered in and used it, you know."

"Well, that wouldn't be exactly accurate, Dr. Langston." Andrews being his most reasonable was no more comfort than someone slowly peeling the skin away from the cuticle. "This is a secured building after 6:00 pm. During the day, only staff with a key-card can get in without signing in with security. Someone in this office would surely have seen and queried a person sitting in your lab and using your typewriter."

Langston didn't bother to respond.

"Now, you signed in the night of the murder at the same time as the victim...."

He was interrupted by an agitated Langston. "I told you before that I didn't see Michael when I came in. Just one of the cleaning crew in the hallway downstairs."

"So you said," Andrews acknowledged. "But there's the problem with your heated exchanges with the victim in which you wished him a long and painful death. And you yourself said that his death seemed to have replicated one of his experiments with Porter as the experimental animal."

Both men were so interested in the verbal exchange between them they failed to notice the door to Langston's lab which had opened quietly to admit a slightly-built young woman with long, red hair. What more either man might have said was arrested by the light, breathy voice which injected itself into their conversation.

"Maybe I can settle things, Lt. Andrews."

"Mark, you were to stay out of this." Langston's face softened as he rose from behind his desk and walked to stand beside the slender figure which had entered the office. "There's no need for you to be involved."

Before either of the younger people could say more, Andrews quickly analyzed the situation. "Miss Markley McBroon, I presume?"

The long, oval face turned from its examination of Langston's face to confront the seated detective. "Yes, I'm Markley McBroon, but most everyone just calls me Mark."

Looking at the two together, Andrews began to understand a good many things all at once. "We've been looking for you to interview you on your relationship with the victim. Unsuccessfully, up to now, I might add."

"Mark," Langston began protectively.

"Oh, sit down Matt. You know I can't hide from the police forever." The slender figure in a white lab coat efficiently cleared another chair of books and folders, repositioned it with Langston's help, and faced Andrews and the chair behind the desk.

"You were Porter's lab assistant and you had a key to his office and lab." Andrews' statements managed to sound accusatory even to him despite his intentions to merely summarize the situation.

"Yes to both." Blue eyes in a clear, slightly freckled face, turned defiantly to confront the accusations. "But I didn't go near his lab the night of the murder. I was here with Matt all evening."

"She certainly was, Lieutenant. I can vouch for that." Langston had resettled himself in the chair behind his desk, but his body leaned slightly toward the red-headed woman as if wanting to shelter or support her wherever possible.

Andrews ignored the younger man and continued to address his questions to Markley. "Dr. Langston wasn't here all evening. However, we'll get to that later. You sent the poem and the drawings to Porter?"

"Yes," Markley McBroon admitted. "And I typed the poem on Matt's typewriter in the lab."

"Did you write the poem yourself?" Andrews asked.

Langston opened his mouth to inject something, but Andrews' raised hand silenced the doctor.

"No," McBroon responded. "I found a copy of the poem in a packet of handouts obtained when attending legislative hearings on a pet protection bill. Lt. Andrews..." The slender figure leaned forward toward the listening detective, "I was very bothered by Dr. Porter's callous behavior toward lab animals. And by his repeating useless experiments over and over. I know, I'm not a doctor and maybe you think I don't know useless experiments from useful ones, but I do. I do."

The blue eyes filled with tears and Langston rose from his chair, intending probably to come around to comfort the agitated McBroon.

"Sit still, Dr. Langston." Andrews snapped the command as sharply as Genna training one of her dogs.

"And the drawings?"

"I sent the drawings too. Dr. Porter was upset over a letter he'd gotten from the parent of a little boy that died at the Institute."

"How did you know it was a boy?" Andrews' sharply injected question was intended to keep his emotional witness on edge.

"Oh, well, I recognized the handwriting. I mean, I'd seen Mr. Graft's writing before. When he was trying to help his little son keep up his education, showing him how to do script writing. It was large and distinctive. And I thought at the time that the letter looked just like Mr. Graft's writing." The slender woman seated in front of Andrews seemed to realize what her words might mean, and hastened to retract any intent to blame the supposed letter-writer. "But I don't mean to say that I know the letter came from Mr. Graft. Dr. Porter didn't know who wrote the letter. I just assumed Mr. Graft did. And I hoped I could use it to make Dr. Porter become more sensitive to what he was doing."

Exhausted for the moment, the slight figure slumped back in her chair, turning appealing eyes to her protector.

Langston responded immediately. "Lieutenant, you can't believe that Mark had anything to do with Porter's death. We were together all evening."

"Not exactly, Doctor," Andrews corrected. "You went out a little after eight, returned at the same time as the victim, and left again sometime around midnight."

"When did you leave the building the night of the murder, Miss McBroon?"

Slightly teary blue eyes opened a bit wider as the young woman considered Andrews' latest question. "I didn't," she said finally. "I stayed in Matt's suite here all night, slept on the sofa over there. After things quieted down, Matt checked but the lights were still on in Porter's suite, so we were afraid to try to take the typewriter out. So Matt just left and I locked the doors and slept here"

"You were trying to get the typewriter out of the building?" Andrews jumped on that quickly.

"Now don't get the wrong idea, Lieutenant." Langston jumped to the defense of the two. "Well, yes, we were trying to get it out. But not because we knew you'd be looking for it. We didn't know Porter was dead. Porter had been comparing memos and letters with the type face on the poem. Mark made the foolish mistake of sending the drawings and poem through the Institute's interdepartmental delivery. So Porter was trying to figure who was doing it. I was afraid he'd eventually spot the typewriter up here. Not that he came up to my office all that often. He and I didn't get along."

"I was the one who wanted to get rid of the typewriter," McBroon admitted. "I told Matt what I'd done, and asked him to help me. I knew Porter would blame Matt if he could."

"Where were you around 10:15 pm last Thursday night?" Andrews queried sharply.

"Is that when it happened? I mean, is that when he was killed?" It was difficult to resist the appeal in the innocent, oval face.

"Just answer the question, please."

Langston looked at McBroon, before answering firmly. "I went out to get food for us, Lieutenant. Neither of us had eaten dinner. I brought back hot sandwiches. That was around 9:45 pm. I don't remember exactly what we were doing at 10:15 pm, but probably still eating our late dinner."

"Did you leave your office between the time you returned at 9:45 pm and the time you left for the evening?"

Markley McBroon turned frightened eyes toward Langston, who grimly admitted that he left his office twice. "I went down once around eleven hoping everyone would have left and Mark and I could get the typewriter out without attracting too much attention. But the large guy in the cap was still waxing away at the floor in front of the elevators and the lights were still on in the office of Porter's secretary so I figured he was still in his office."

"Were the lights on in Porter's lab?"

"I don't remember. Probably wouldn't have been able to tell. The labs are meant to be soundproof so the doors fit tightly." It sounded lame even to Langston.

Andrews nodded. "And the second time?"

"When I went down again a little after midnight, there was no sign of the cleaning crew, but the lights were still on in Porter's suite, so I came back up and told Mark I'd go on home and she should just lock up my office and stay for the night."

McBroon and Langston exchanged anxious looks before turning in the pudgy detective's direction.

Andrews thanked them for their candor but expressed a wish that McBroon had come forward initially with the information. He instructed them to keep themselves available and tried not to smile at the looks of obvious relief and affection exchanged by the two.

"Oh, we will," Markley assured him. She apologized for her actions, and then smiled beguilingly at Andrews before adding, "We're caring for the little guinea pigs from Porter's lab, as you can see."

She gestured toward a cleared section of Langston's office where an arrangement of glass walls had extended the cage in which the victim's test subjects had been housed when Andrews first encountered them. Now the five little animals were sleeping peacefully amid cedar shavings, bowls of water and food. Small twigs and brush had been scattered on top of the cedar shavings to provide privacy and cover. Andrews had noted the arrangements when he'd entered Langston's lab earlier, but had not mentioned his pleasure. He did so now. Then he excused himself and went to meet Foster to compare notes.

Chapter 22

Andrews and Foster had agreed to meet for coffee at a local tavern. Despite the unexpected find of McBroon in Langston's office, Andrews had finished his morning interviews first and arrived at the tavern ahead of Foster. He used the time to phone Jonathan and Genna to asked about Blacky, and treated himself to coffee and a Danish before Foster put in an appearance. Andrews managed not to evidence any shame when Foster arrived to find him finishing off the last bite of his forbidden treat.

"Did you talk with Hogge and Chambles?"

"I called and arranged to speak with them later in the afternoon. Chambles talked to the cleaning crew last night, and has some stuff for me to review. I decided to finish off interviews with neighbors of the secretary and the victim's wife this morning and catch up with Chambles later today. How did your morning go?"

Andrews summarized his meeting in Langston's office while Foster waited for the coffee and pastries he'd ordered. Between appreciative bites of his pastry and cautious sips of his steaming coffee, Foster in turn summarized his morning interviews with neighbors of Piper Morgan and Danielle Porter.

"Billy and I divided up Miss Morgan's neighbors, but I got very little from my witnesses. One of them remembers seeing Morgan's car parked in the usual place outside her apartment when he came home from work. But he never went out again after 7:10 pm, so couldn't say whether it was there all evening." A cautious sip interrupted Foster's dialogue.

"Another neighbor says she saw a very expensive purse and a tennis bracelet that Morgan told her were gifts from the victim. I inquired about the other items listed as purchases on accounts addressed to the victim's office. The neighbor confirms seeing those in Morgan's possession."

Foster took another sip of his coffee before continuing. "But neither neighbor admits to having seen anything of the victim or anyone answering to his description calling for Morgan or being seen around her apartment. So either Morgan and the victim met somewhere else, or the neighbors just didn't see him around."

Andrews waved the waitress over for a refill on his own coffee.

Foster waited till the woman was out of hearing before continuing. "As near as Billy or I can tell, she was definitely at home up till about 9:00 pm watching a video with a neighbor. But she didn't answer the door to this same neighbor who returned at 10:20 pm to get a light bulb. Morgan says she went to bed. She could have been at home and asleep, not heard the neighbor's knock. Or she could have been out. The neighbor looking for the bulb didn't pay any attention to whether Morgan's car was gone, just assumed because they'd been together up until 9:00 pm that Miss Morgan was home and asleep."

"Cripes! This stuff is really hot!" Foster grimaced as he tried to take a gulp of his coffee. "But," the dark eyes teased, "Danielle Porter wasn't!"

"Oh." Andrews' cup halted halfway to his mouth. "She went to dinner with her husband and then he took her home. You mean she didn't stay at home?"

"Exactly! You remember the block of a woman with the straw for hair that answered the door the day we went to see Mrs. Porter?" Foster didn't wait for Andrews to reply. "Well, she was very delighted to be interviewed and offered the opinion that her neighbor was doing much better now that she'd gotten some rest. It seems that the Porters went to dinner, then returned, then he left and then Mrs. Porter left. Busy goings-on the night of the murder."

"Do you think this woman's information is accurate?"

"The Porter's garage is next to this woman's bedroom window!" Foster's long-lashed eyes sparkled over the steam of his coffee cup.

"Did madam hair-of-straw, what's her name...." Andrews struggled briefly to remember, "Martha Moss, wasn't it?"

Andrews swallowed another mouthful of coffee before beginning again, "Did Ms. Moss have something important to add?"

Foster nodded. "She said that Danielle left right after her husband on the night of the murder and didn't return till almost midnight."

"Ah!" Andrews said.

"Well, don't get too excited. When I pressed Moss on the return time, she changed it to 'just before the news'. Then she couldn't remember whether it was the ten o'clock or the eleven o'clock news."

"Not very helpful," Andrews complained.

"But we can be certain that Mrs. Porter went out again the night of the murder. She told us she went up to bed when her husband and she returned from dinner."

When Andrews failed to comment further, Foster continued. "Moss was very firm about problems with the victim's relationship with his wife. Mrs. Porter was apparently very suspicious of her husband's relations with the secretary. According to what Moss says that Mrs. Porter told her, the victim's wife had tried on several occasions to get information out of the Institute's administrator and Porter's partner about what was going on."

Foster finished the last of his Danish and pushed the plate away, to Andrews' relief. The younger man continued, "I get the impression that Moss expounds on what is said a great deal, but that still leaves a lot more distrust on the part of the victim's wife than she indicated in our interview last Friday."

"One other interesting bit of gossip, though." Foster drained his cup and placed it beside his empty plate. "Moss says that Mrs. Porter told her that she—Mrs. Porter—called and went by Ketterholt's home the night of the murder. And according to this round-about gossip, Dr. Ketterholt answered neither his phone nor his door that night."

"Ah! But he told us he was home all evening the night of the murder." Andrews nodded. "He said he went to bed very early. Looks like another talk with Dr. Ketterholt and with Mrs. Porter is in order."

The two paid for their snacks, settled on taking separate cars back to the Institute, and agreed to meet outside the office of the Institute's administrator.

Chapter 23

A nervous Ketterholt faced the two detectives across his mammoth desk top. Foster's notebook seemed to be the focus of the man's nervous glances as he continued to press his beliefs that the homicide was the work of animal rights activists and had little to do with individuals personally related to the victim.

"It may very well be as you indicate, Dr. Ketterholt, "Andrews acknowledged in his most agreeable tone, "but we need to clear up this little discrepancy regarding your activities the night of the murder. Now, according to your statements the morning that Dr. Porter's body was discovered, you were home the night of the murder. But Mrs. Porter called and then came to your home that night and received no response."

The nattily dressed executive seemed to shrink with each of Andrews statements.

Andrews waited, offering no help but not hurrying the Institute's director either. Finally Ketterholt responded resignedly, "Mrs. Porter has created some embarrassing scenes over the last several months. She suspected her husband of being romantically involved with his secretary. Anyway, sometimes she'd drink too much at parties and then attempt to come on to me in the hopes that I'd say or do something to help her prove that Dr. Porter was being unfaithful."

He looked very pained and very put upon. "I'm sure you gentlemen can appreciate how uncomfortable that would make me feel."

If Ketterholt hoped for sympathy from the two detectives he didn't get it. Foster discreetly made a few entries in his notebook. Andrews just looked bored. Each stroke of Foster's pen seem to make Ketterholt more uncomfortable.

Ketterholt adjusted the notes holder on his desk for the third time since beginning the conversation with Andrews and continued. " She—Mrs. Porter—wanted to pump me for details about her husband's late night work schedule. I declined to discuss them because I really didn't know that much about them. She assumed my refusal had a sinister motive. She seemed to take my reluctance to interfere in Porter's business as evidence that he was involved with his secretary, and that I was trying to cover up for him. Very disturbing to a man of my position."

"I'm certain that could be a problem." Andrews tried to sound agreeable and understanding. Actually he was getting a little impatient. "So where were you the night of the murder?" Andrews asked.

"Home. I was home, as I told you. Actually I answered her call, but when I realized it was she, I responded like a recording."

"I see," Andrews temporized.

He seemed to remember at one point that Ketterholt had blurted out something about not having an answering machine. This might explain why that statement had gotten into one of their earlier conversations.

"So you picked up the phone on the night of the murder, realized it was Mrs. Porter, and said something about being a machine and she could leave a message."

"Yes. But then she showed up at my front door a short while later," Ketterholt agonized. "Imagine what my neighbor will think. A young woman beating on my front door late at night. And after I've gone to such lengths to politely explain to this neighbor that I'm not interested or able to think of female friendship so soon after my wife's death. Can you imagine what this neighbor thinks if she saw Mrs. Porter knocking and sobbing outside my door late at night?"

The poor man actually looked embarrassed. Having seen Mrs. Porter, Andrews would have been inclined to find being chased by her, even if true, an ego-booster rather than an embarrassment. But it obviously was painful to Ketterholt.

Andrews tried to keep a straight face while he continued. "What time was it when she came to your door?"

"Around 9:30 pm, I think. She seemed to stand out there and knock forever, but it was really only 9:35 or so when she left. Thank goodness. I was afraid she'd awaken the neighbor with her pounding."

Satisfied that they were finished with the embarrassed director of the Institute for the present, the two thanked him for his time and reached the relative privacy of the hallway before Foster began to laugh.

"Well, I don't think he ever played around on his wife. He's blushing as badly as a kid in junior high at the idea of a girl chasing him."

Even Andrews managed a grin. "Yes, but it might be interesting to see what one of his neighbors has to say. If Mrs. Porter was making a spectacle of herself, maybe someone else noticed. I think I'll take a drive out to his neighborhood and ask around."

"Why don't I meet you back at headquarters then. I'll see if I can catch Hogge and Chambles and see what their conversations with the cleaning crew have turned up."

Chapter 24

Colorful flowers sparkled in the spring sunlight on the well manicured lawns of Ketterholt's neighborhood. Andrews didn't appreciate their beauty. He was hungry and the clumps of color reminded him of toppings on a pizza supreme.

His interview with the executive's next-door-neighbor had been productive but long. The empty feeling in the region of his stomach was accompanied by a growing craving for pizza. Suddenly the five-day stint of his present diet seemed measured in pizzas missed. Fortunately for his resolution, he passed no pizza restaurants on his drive back to headquarters.

Foster was on the phone when Andrews passed his desk, so he waved to him as he went by. Andrews was consulting the phone book's yellow pages for the nearest pizza delivery when Foster walked into his office.

"Thought you might be interested in getting pizza sent over, so we can compare our notes and decide on what to do next." Andrews slyly proposed.

Foster settled into a chair before countering the suggestion. "Gosh. I don't think so. It's a little early for dinner and a little late for lunch. Megan is going to have my head if I'm not home tonight to eat with the family." He waited a bit before adding, "Besides I doubt that'll do much for your diet."

Andrews grumbled, but put aside the phone book. "OK, what've you got for me?"

The smile on Foster's face did not fit the seriousness of the information he was relaying to his partner. "Hogge did a great job of interviewing and documenting the activities of the cleaning crew. The five members of the crew plus Chambles took a break between 9:00 pm and 9:15 pm approximately. But they were all together drinking sodas or coffee in the conference room of the administrative wing and talking. Three of them went off to the bath rooms but were back in two to three minutes. Not long enough to have killed Porter. At about 9:20 pm, two of the crew went to the fourth floor to begin cleaning up there and were together till around 11:50 pm."

"Constantly together?" Andrews injected.

"So they said. And according to Hogge that would be routine," Foster assured him.

"Go on," Andrews directed.

"Two others went up to the fifth floor to clean and check things out from there. Same story. Together constantly till about 11:55 pm when they finally finished the first floor offices. Routine is for one pair to do the even floors and one pair the odd floors. Because of the concern for a freshly shined and cleaned floor for the big meeting originally scheduled for last Friday, two of them —Chambles and Roalf—worked on the hallway and Administrative wing on the first floor."

"What about the crew Langston reported seeing?"

"There were two of them, the one that went into Langston's office and the one waiting in the hall. They didn't clean his office, but they remember seeing him. The door to his lab was locked from the hall, closed from his office and he told them not to bother. They don't remember anything unusual being removed from his office. But they only emptied the waste baskets. Their stories check with each other's and with Langston's."

Andrews nodded but didn't say more. He was busily searching his drawers for something.

"Roalf—well, the individual using Roalf's name— and Chambles were responsible for doing the first floor. Chambles says he left—well, Roalf for lack of anything else to call him—with the polishing equipment to take care of the hallway on the first floor, while he went off to clean the administrative suite. Chambles ran out of furniture polish at some point and went back to get some from the supply closet. He noticed two sets of footprints across the main hallway, but didn't see Roalf. But it didn't concern him greatly. He just figured Roalf was off getting something or in the rest room. Chambles returned to the Administrative suite, finished up there and returned to see if Roalf needed help. He estimates that would be about 10:45 pm."

"So Chambles confirms seeing two sets of tracks across the floor, and only two." Andrews' interruption was more a statement than a question.

Foster nodded and continued. "According to Chambles, when he returned around 10:45 pm, Roalf hadn't gotten as far as Chambles thought he should have and Chambles chided Roalf for his lack of progress. Chambles said Roalf complained about the equipment being new to him and heavy to use, and also that he'd had trouble with personnel tracking areas he'd cleaned and having to do them over."

"That would fit with the victim coming in at 9:45 pm and with Langston walking across the area on his way to the elevators."

Andrews had at last given up searching for food in his desk and slumped back in his chair. The part of his brain that was concerned with food did not diminish his sharpness for facts. "What about Hogge? Where was he between 9:45 pm and 10:30 pm ?"

"With one of the guards, around the corner from the hall to the administrative suite. He observed the guard let both Langston and Porter into the South Complex. He confirms Langston's story. Although both signed in at the same time, Hogge says that Langston actually got there first and was probably out of sight before Porter appeared."

Andrews sat for a few minutes digesting the information Foster presented. Then he shared with Foster the results of his own afternoon investigation. "My conversation with Ketterholt's neighbors doesn't help to resolve the situation, either to prove or disprove his claim that he was home the evening of Porter's murder." He sounded disgusted.

"No one can confirm he was home, then."

"He's being chased, it seems. His next door neighbor. Very gushy. Very determined. Lost her husband shortly before Ketterholt's wife died. Now she seems to think Ketterholt is her property to look after. At any rate, she saw a nicely dressed woman drive up around 9:35 pm on Thursday night and observed her standing and knocking on the front door. Said she stayed almost five minutes before driving away in a cream colored car that could have been a Lincoln."

"Ketterholt's neighbor didn't actually see him, then?" Foster asked.

"No. She said Ketterholt's car was still in his garage, but when I pushed her for details, she admitted to watching TV from 8:00 pm until she heard the pounding on her neighbor's door and the woman, probably Mrs. Porter, calling to Ketterholt. So the neighbor really can't be certain that Ketterholt hadn't already gone. The neighbor tried to call him after the woman left, around 9:40 pm and got no answer from Ketterholt's home."

Foster flipped back through his notebook searching for something. "That puts the victim's wife some twenty minutes from the crime scene just thirty-five minutes prior to the time the victim was killed. Ah! Got it," the younger man exclaimed.

"Got what?"

"The car registered to Danielle Porter is a cream Lincoln Town Car." Foster looked uncommonly pleased with himself.

"So. She was at Ketterholt's home. Could they have cooked this up between them, seemingly giving them both alibis? Ketterholt obviously knows his neighbor's obsession for keeping track of his movements."

Foster thought about that briefly before responding. "Aside from the problem of how he'd have gotten from his home to here and back without the neighbor realizing he'd moved the car in and out, there's the problem of getting into Porter's suite. Roalf was waxing and polishing the hallway in front. He mentioned seeing Porter return and Langston track across the area, but not a third person."

"What if Ketterholt let himself in while the crew was taking a break? Before 9:45." Andrews' face brightened, though whether with a thought of finding something to eat or the prospect of pinning this case on Ketterholt, his partner couldn't say.

"He didn't have a key to Porter's lab. Unless he had Morgan's key—the one Billy couldn't alibi," Foster noted with a smile.

"Not likely," Andrews admitted. Both men were silent for a long time, puzzling over the facts determined so far. Finally Andrews grumbled, "We seemed to have so many suspects at the start. After five days of intense investigation we're no closer to catching the killer."

"What about Berkley? Have we eliminated him?"

Andrews look thoughtful. He didn't like the man, but objectively what could he say about Berkley as a suspect? Finally, he responded to his patient partner. "He said he left early the night of the murder. Said he was home with his wife, but we haven't questioned the wife yet. He didn't gain access through the security gates after 6:00 pm, but he could have stayed in his office, gotten into Porter's office in the 15 minutes the cleaning crew were on break, stayed there the rest of the night," Andrews sketched a possible scenario for the two sleuths.

"But it doesn't explain the brutal fashion of killing," Andrews concluded.

"Maybe it does," Foster countered. "If you wanted to mask the closeness of the victim and killer, why not make it look like a madman had done the killing?"

Andrews shook his head slowly. "I still think Berkley would have destroyed any evidence of the shoddy research the two were doing. At least I'd have expected him to get rid of the dogs."

"How? Without letting anyone else in the lab?"

That stopped Andrews. Finally, he nodded. "You're right. He couldn't have gotten rid of the bodies. But why not destroy the dogs, at least the grey one. One of the two, Porter or Berkley, had already shown it as used in an experiment."

Andrews fidgeted a bit, reached for the phone book again, put it back down, and finally returned to the discussion of the case.

Finally Andrews came to a decision of sorts. "Why don't we meet back here at seven in the morning and pay a breakfast call on Berkley. Catch him and his wife together and see how his alibi holds up."

"Fine with me. Want me to stick around tonight for anything?"

"No," Andrews conceded, a little too eagerly. "Why don't you get along home and mend some fences with Megan. I'll see you in the morning."

Foster didn't wait for the offer to be extended twice or for Andrews to change his mind. With a hardy "Night" he walked briskly out of Andrews office and sight. But just outside he paused with a grin on his face and listened expectantly. He heard the eager voice of Andrews on the phone ordering up a medium pizza to be delivered to his home in time to coincide with the end of his twenty-five minute drive back to his apartment.

Chapter 25

Andrews could distinguish little about the exterior of Berkley's home except that it sat back from the street on a beautiful stretch of landscaped turf, was massive in size, and Georgian in design. He and Foster had deliberately arrived at breakfast, unannounced, to question Berkley and his wife.

Edith Berkley had a startled expression in her weak, blue eyes that seemed to be permanent. Her greying hair was short, crisp and curled softly about her small face. She made a pleasant hostess in a long, colorful robe.

Berkley's annoyance at finding the two detectives at his door so early had been quickly concealed. The two officers joined the doctor and his wife around a large circular oak table in a dining alcove with steaming cups of coffee in front of them. The victim's partner had brushed aside their questions regarding the worth of the research efforts and the incorrect entries regarding the tattooed dog Genna had identified as Mushie. He'd explained—in a rather self-important tone—that reaffirming results for a presentation was a routine and common activity of researchers. He was very firm in defending his complaints about the contract arrangements. He seemed a little nervous when the talk swung toward suggestions that the victim was involved with his secretary. He really tried to avoid admitting that Danielle Porter knew or suspected the extra-marital activities of the victim.

He seemed almost relieved when Andrews asked if Berkley and his wife would consent to talking with the two detectives separately, just to establish firmly their whereabouts on the night of the murder. "Of course, Edith and I want to cooperate in any way possible, don't we, Dear. We have nothing to hide. How do you want to do this?"

Foster finished his coffee and nodded at Andrews before suggesting, "Suppose Mrs. Berkley and I go into the living room and talk there. The Lieutenant hasn't finished his coffee, so you guys can finish up in here." Without waiting for an answer he rose and nodded Edith Berkley through the doorway to the hall ahead of him.

She seemed a little nervous as she settled on a large white couch in the beautiful expanse of living room. The decor was as neat and crisp as the hostess Foster faced from the other end of the sofa. "Now, don't be concerned with these routine questions, Mrs. Berkley. We just have to document the whereabouts of persons connected with the death of Dr. Porter. Naturally, since your husband and he were partners, we have to record the facts....just for the records."

Edith Berkley nodded courteously, but said nothing. The shock of finding a homicide detective....two of them, in fact....at her door was obviously not something she found easy to deal with at any time, much less this early in the morning.

Foster continued in his most soothing voice. "Now you and your husband were home last Thursday night, I believe. Is that correct?"

"Oh, well I don't know." The dainty woman squirmed a bit before continuing. "I mean, we went to the Thorntons for dinner last week. That was sometime during the middle of the week, I believe. Marge Thornton isn't the best of cooks, but we had a marvelous game of bridge after dinner and stayed quite late."

"Was that the night Porter was killed?" Foster tried to keep his voice calm and unhurried. Just being questioned seemed enough to push up Edith Berkley's blood pressure.

"No...oh, no. That was the night before. We were due at the Delaney's for dinner the night poor Michael was killed. But I just couldn't make it. My stomach had been complaining all day. Marge's new recipes often affect me that way. Anyway, Tom came home early but I wasn't able to go. He was so sweet. He arranged everything, called the Delaneys' with our apologies, fixed me soup, and then gave me something that eased my stomach and I slept though most of the night."

"So the night the victim was killed....last Thursday ...that's the night you were sick?"

"Oh, yes. I'm sure that's right. I remember I slept late the next morning and Tom was gone when I got up. I was just sitting down with a cup of tea in the kitchen when Tom called to tell me Michael had been killed." Small hands with short nails nervously twisted each other. "Such a shock! I remember my stomach almost getting the best of me again."

"When's the last time you remember seeing your husband on Thursday night?" The question produced a shocked expression on Edith Berkley's face despite the soft tone of Foster's query.

"Oh, you're trying to see if he really was here. Now my husband may have had his differences with Michael Porter, but take my word for it, he'd never have killed him. Oh, my goodness, how can you even think such a thing?"

"These are just routine questions," Foster assured the small woman. "Just for my records, when's the last time you remember talking to your husband before you fell asleep on Thursday night?"

At first Foster thought she was too indignant to answer, but his patience was finally rewarded by a reply.

"We watched a TV program together on the bedroom set. That ended at 7:30. Tom kissed me goodnight and turned off the set."

Edith Berkley watched as Andrews recorded the time in his notebook, before continuing. "But Tom came downstairs to watch TV on the set in the den. He was here all night."

"Did you awaken and come down later in the evening?"

"Well, no. But he told me he was here. And I believe him."

"I'm certain of it," Foster replied enigmatically.

Thanking his hostess for her cooperation, the handsome sergeant suggested they return to her husband and Andrews in the kitchen.

After briefly rejoining Andrews and Tom Berkley in the kitchen, and expressing their thanks for the cooperation and coffee, the two detectives retraced their steps to the car through gathering signs of another rain storm.

En route to the victim's home, the two compared notes on their respective interviews with the Berkleys.

"Berkley accused Danielle Porter of coming on to him pretty strong at a party, then acting like a wronged woman when she spotted her husband. He called her a tease, but said he didn't need her kind of trouble so stayed clear of the lady after that."

"What did he say about the letter from Porter accusing him of seeing too much of the wife?"

"Claims he went to him and set him straight....that there was nothing between them. Berkley claims that was the last of it," Andrews summarized. "How about you?"

"The wife was very nervous, but mainly about admitting that she was asleep at the time of the murder."

"Oh," Andrews muttered expectantly.

"Don't get your hopes up! Berkley was with her at 7:30 pm so he couldn't have stayed in his office late."

"Well, we'll see what Danielle Porter has to say for herself," Andrews mumbled.

The rain fell in a driving downpour as the two continued their journey toward the victim's home.

Chapter 26

Danielle Porter answered the door herself and admitted two dripping umbrellas from which emerged two equally drenched men. After disposing of rain gear in the foyer, Danielle again settled Andrews and Foster in the victim's study. The dark green rug barely showed the effect of two pairs of wet shoes.

The slender blond made no attempt at conversation after inviting them to sit in the same chairs Andrews had found so unsuitable to his ample form on their previous visit. The eyes looked greener today, lacking the puffiness and red rims which Andrews had noted before. She turned them on Andrews now, waiting for him to explain this visit. He'd called earlier to say that he had a few more questions. She had not asked and he had not volunteered the nature of those questions.

He decided to try the shock approach. "We've discovered some discrepancies with certain things you told us during our visit the day your husband's body was discovered."

If he'd hoped to fluster the cool, elegantly dressed woman before him, Andrews was disappointed.

"Yes, I was afraid you might," Danielle Porter said. "It was foolish of me to try to deceive you. But I needed time to think about it."

"Would you like to begin again?"

Green eyes flashed briefly in Foster's direction, swiftly taking in his notebook and ready pen. A slender, long-nailed hand betrayed her nervousness as it brushed long strands of blond hair away from her face. "I followed

223

my husband that night, back to the Institute. At least, I intended to."

Andrews waited.

The widow paused overly long before continuing. "I'm not proud of my jealousy, and I was hoping you wouldn't have to know. But since you've found out somehow, I suppose you already know that I followed Mike. I knew I'd never get past the guards, not without them notifying Mike. And I didn't want that. I wanted to see who else was working with him that night."

Andrews settled back in his chair, or as far back as his bulk and the chair's sparse construction would allow. He let Danielle Porter proceed at her own pace.

"I went to a phone booth and tried to call Dr. Ketterholt. I knew he had a separate key to the basement doors and could by-pass the guards. I got a response that sounded like a machine, but I didn't think it was. I thought it was Dr. Ketterholt. He's acted strange toward me since a party some months ago, as though he thought I might be romantically interested in him. I didn't know what to do, so I drove over to his house."

"Why would you go over to his home when he didn't answer the phone?" Foster paused in his note-taking to inject this into the conversation.

Danielle Porter turned slightly in her chair to focus on the younger detective. "I thought he didn't want to talk to me, but that he'd have to if I showed up at his door."

"And did he?" Andrews injected. "Talk to you, I mean?"

"No. I pounded on his front door for a long time, but he never came to the door."

"What time was this?" Foster held his pencil poised above his notebook, ready to record the answer to his question.

"Around 9:30 pm I suppose. Someone next door came to her window. She may have seen me, but I don't know the exact time."

"What did you do then?"

"Gave up and came home." Danielle waited for Andrews to speak. When he did not, she added, "Went upstairs and cried myself to sleep."

"Why did you think Ketterholt didn't want to talk to you?"

The beautiful complexion flushed and briefly marbled with a dark red, but the smooth voice was under control when Danielle answered. "I approached him several months ago at a party given by the Institute to celebrate a very successful year, meaning to ask his help in learning what was going on between Mike and his secretary. We'd both been drinking. I was upset at the way Mike's secretary had been looking at him. I was trying to be discreet in what I said to Dr. Ketterholt, but..." The woman's voice broke, but continued again after a short pause. "Whatever I said gave him the impression I was romantically interested in him, and the poor man has been running from me ever since."

Turning appealing eyes on Andrews, Danielle pleaded, "I just wanted his help in getting into Mike's office after hours to see for myself what was going on. The poor fool misunderstood my motives."

Andrews continued without sympathy. "Ketterholt wasn't the only male at that party to misunderstand your motives that night, was he, Mrs. Porter?"

"Oh, you've been talking to Berkley I suppose!"

"Among others. What happened with Berkley?"

Danielle glanced in Foster's direction, perhaps seeking sympathy, but received only an expectant stare. Shifting uncomfortably in her chair, she reminded Andrews that he was none too comfortable either. His attempts at resettling resulted in a slight protest from the chair frame. But it was covered by Danielle's continuation of her story.

"I went to Berkley to ask if we might return to Mike's lab some night and have him explain the work they were doing. He seemed to think that meant I was interested in him romantically and made a grab for me. As I say, we'd all had a lot to drink." Green eyes appealed to Andrews for permission to end the conversation.

Andrews's only response was, "and what happened after that?"

The slender widow continued with a catch in her voice. "Well, I set Tom straight with a rough push just as Mike came into the room. He...Mike, I mean... didn't say much, just took my arm, gave Tom a harsh look and pushed me out to the buffet table for coffee. Later..when we got home.... he accused me of deliberately trying to make him jealous by starting something with his partner."

For a while the only sound in the room was the rain being blown against the windows by the brisk wind. When Andrews' stern looks produced no further monologue from the victim's wife, he concluded, "Thank you for this further information, Mrs. Porter. Are you certain there's no other information concerning the night your husband was murdered that you think would be useful for us to know?"

"No, there's nothing else I can think of," she replied, very subdued.

The rain had not abated. By the time Andrews and Foster regained their car, rain gear and the bottom halves of each man were wet and cold. Andrews cursed the ever changing weather that was Virginia in the spring. He squirmed and fussed with his seat belt while trying to get the heater going in the car. He complained about needing air conditioning one day and a heater the next. In so doing, another button was lost from his shirt. Andrews grumbled that diets never worked.

Foster hid a smile and suggested they might want to get a light meal at a local dive famous for spicy but low-fat fare.

The raw spring day kept most people away, so Andrews and Foster found a secluded booth in back, ordered up some spicy dishes, beer for Foster and diet cola for Andrews. After ten minutes of stuffing his face, Andrews was in a mellow mood.

"I don't remember hearing anything about the cleaning crew member that Roalf replaced." Andrews paused to stuff another fork full of food into his mouth. "What have you got on him?"

"It was a she named Gladyse Hooke," Foster replied, keeping pace with his boss in the eating department.

Between chews, Foster continued. "We got off on the other suspects last night and I forgot to tell you about this Ms. Hooke. Something funny about the way she left. She was notified she'd won a contest, two-weeks all expenses paid in Duck, North Carolina. She rushed to take advantage of the prize. But then she found that only three-days of expenses were paid, and she had to return home on Sunday evening. She showed up again on Monday wanting her old job back."

The importance of this little piece of information penetrated Andrews' preoccupation with eating. The fork paused half-way to his mouth. "So someone conveniently got her out of the way. Maybe we'd better look more carefully into the timing of this murder."

"I thought we had been," Foster said. "Whoever is behind this....and I think we have to assume a connection....gave themselves three days. So he...or she....or they didn't know exactly how long whatever they planned would take."

"What if murder wasn't in the original plan? What if Porter came back unexpectedly that night. He was supposed to be having dinner with his wife. His secretary knew about the dinner with the wife. And she probably told half the rest of the place." Andrews finally remembered the fork poised just in front of his mouth and continued with stuffing his face. "I can't see where that gets us, though. He was murdered."

"It might argue on the side Ketterholt keeps pushing though, that animal rights activist planned to rescue the animals and destroy his papers. Only when he or they searched his desk and realized the worth of his papers in bad publicity, they left the papers."

"That doesn't make sense," Andrews protested. "The papers weren't out and exposed, they were still locked in the victim's desk. With the key to the desk in his pocket." Another fork of food proceeded his next pronouncement. "And the dogs and guinea pigs weren't rescued, and one of them was in severe pain."

"Maybe they were interrupted," Foster suggested.

"By whom? The lab was secure and no one found the body until the next morning." Andrews chewed angrily, punctuating his point by poking his empty fork in Foster's direction.

Both men consumed their lunch in silence for a brief time. The rain beat heavily on the window of the cafe, but neither man seemed to hear.

Finally Foster remembered a final point he'd not shared with Andrews. "Hogge was thorough. He had copies of Hooke's hotel charges faxed to him with times and signature. Shared them with me, along with a copy of her signature acquired this past Monday night. There's no question in my mind that she was in Florida the night of the murder."

"Of course, she was," Andrews snorted, grabbing for his cola. "Damn, that was a hot pepper!" Two coughs and a sputter later, he continued, "Whoever got her out of the way would have made certain to use the right bait."

More rain beat against the windows. The two detectives finished the last of their lunch wrapped in their own thoughts.

Finally Foster broke the silence. "Any ideas where we go next?"

"No." Andrews was short and honest. "We seem to be at a dead end. I think I'll give it a rest. Drive to Williamsburg and see Jonathan and Genna. Why don't we call it a day?"

"Fine with me," Foster agreed. "Maybe I can pick up the supplies to repair the closet shelf Megan wanted me to fix last weekend."

By the time the two returned to the squad car, Andrews was soaked again. Transferring to his own car back at headquarters, the contented crank stopped by his apartment for dry clothes, a call to the Colts, and an overnight bag.

Chapter 27

It rained on Andrews during most of his drive to Williamsburg. The weather matched his mood. He saw no obvious line of attack to identify the impersonator of Roalf. He was disappointed at the little return on his efforts in the case. The rain moved out shortly after his arrival at Heron's Rest, leaving behind another dramatic shift in temperature and humidity. Bright sunshine and higher humidity made the rain soaked wooded areas and cleared spaces shimmer. Genna and Jonathan insisted on a brisk walk before dinner.

Most of the grounds at Heron's Rest were soggy from the rains, so Genna and Jonathan convinced Andrews that a walk in the restored area of Williamsburg on cobblestones and sidewalks would be just the thing. He was not convinced that walking would help either his hunger or his diet, but allowed the arguments of host and hostess to prevail.

After much discussion, Genna decided that the proposed outing would be good for Amber also. Amber had spent almost every minute of the last five days in the nursery with little Rusty. Amber nervously oversaw the arrangements of heated bottles and lamps set out by Genna to keep Rusty warm during his dam's absence. But once out of the room and on a show lead, the dainty little dog pranced off with her human family.

The two encouraging humans and one protesting visitor piled into Jonathan's station wagon with Blacky, Sky and Amber. Sky, of course, monopolized Genna's lap. Amber thought of Jonathan as her private property and lay plastered against his right leg as he drove, daring anyone including Genna and Sky to remove her. That left Blacky and Andrews the entire back seat to themselves, for the drive into Williamsburg's restored area. There the three humans and three dogs consigned the 20th century vehicle to a conveniently located parking lot in the rear of Rizzoli Book store.

The group unloaded and walked, pulled, huffed and jiggled their way over to Duke of Gloucester Street, affectionately called DOG street by the residents of Williamsburg. The beautiful thoroughfare sparkled in the late afternoon sun, restored to its 18th century glory and washed fresh by the recently-passed 20th century rain storm.

The group turned away from the College and made their way into the restored area, joining the crowds of tourist who ambled along the sidewalks and in the cobble streets which were closed to modern motor traffic.

Amber and Sky walked in perfect step with Jonathan and Genna; Blacky and Andrews renegotiated the direction and speed of their movement every few steps, which was all right with the flabby detective. It gave him an excuse to stop often and rest, on the pretext of untangling Blacky's lead from around his legs.

In deference to Andrews' slow progress, the Colts turned around at the old court house and, to Andrews' secret delight, started back toward the commercial end of DOG street. Genna checked the windows of Casey's Department Store to give Andrews a chance to catch up, but then passed the cut-through to the parking lot and car and continued up toward Richmond Road. As his host and hostess led the way along the grounds of the College of William and Mary, the hungry man began to grumble.

"Just where are you two dragging me?"

"Nowhere, Uncle Kevin," Genna chuckled. "But Blacky seems to be dragging you all over the sidewalk."

His grumbles were suppressed by a promise from Genna of a surprise for dinner, so he and Blacky managed to stumble along to an outdoor cafe across from the college. There the three enjoyed a satisfying treat of fresh salad, hot sandwiches, and drinks at an umbrella-covered table.

The two Papillons curled under the table and were almost invisible. But Blacky had to be convinced not to bark and jump at the entertainment provided by six mallards, which wandered across the street waddling and quacking into the outside sitting area of the deli, looking for their evening handouts.

Between chuckles at the ducks, Genna resumed the discussion of the case. "So Berkley's wife says he was home at least in the early evening hours of the night of the murder. How much credit can you give to a loyal wife's testimony?" It was obvious that she would have been only too pleased to stick Berkley with Porter's murder.

"His wife was asleep at the crucial time," Andrews said. "So she really can't say he was at home at the time Porter died. But she does know for certain he came home. And since he did, that leaves us with a problem of how he could have gotten back into the Institute without being seen."

"So the poems and drawings were related to Porter's experiments and the attempts of his assistant to make him more sensitive to his animal subjects. Too bad she wasn't successful." Jonathan offered the salt to first Genna and then to Andrews, neither of whom accepted.

"What about the man who wrote the letter, Graft? Did you find out any more about his activities the night of the murder?" Genna jumped a little as Sky lunged from underneath the table at a mallard duck that had waddled too close to Genna's leg for Sky's protective nature.

"Billy left a report on my desk which I read before leaving Richmond this afternoon. Mrs. Graft indicated she talked to her husband at 8:00 pm on Thursday night for about ten minutes. Phone records confirm a call between her office and home at that time. Otherwise, we've nothing but his word that he was home that night."

Their conversation was interrupted by the growing congestion of cars along the street beside the outdoor cafe. Looking around, the three spotted a sight deserving of attention. A Williamsburg police officer had stopped the traffic along Richmond Road to allow the six mallards to waddle their way back to the university grounds. One hungry female mallard had stopped in the middle of the road to finish consuming a large piece of bread she'd carried that far in her mouth. The police officer was tapping his night stick on the pavement behind the feathered pedestrian, urging the bird along.

"No horns, no curses, no irate drivers!" Andrews marveled at the patience of police officer and drivers alike. Most of them even had grins on their faces, and one passenger in a car with Delaware tags was trying her best to get a picture of the event.

The marks of ducks' feet wandering back and sideways in the wet pavement of the road, reminded Andrews of the conversation the mallards' street crossing had interrupted.

With one last clatter of his nightstick on the pavement, the police officer finally succeeded at clearing the road of ducks. Traffic resumed along Richmond Road, and Blacky settled herself under Andrews' chair again.

"Too bad, with all this canine help we brought," Andrews joked, "we don't have one decent duck herder in the bunch."

"Please don't insult our two companion dogs, extradinare! They only herd their owners," Jonathan responded with a chuckle. "Their kind have been doing that since the 15th. century so they know their job well."

With a last amused smile at the ducks, Andrews and his godson returned to their discussion of the case. Genna seemed lost in thought, continuing to stare at the road which the ducks had crossed.

"So whoever killed Porter would have had to walk over the floor Roalf—or whoever was impersonating Roalf—was waxing." Genna's voice was low and unnaturally slow.

Then she and Andrews chimed together, minds and words working along the same path, ".....or be Roalf!"

Their duet startled Jonathan briefly, but he was the first to inject the next point of consideration. "Roalf? Would he have had time?"

"Yes, I think so." Andrews tried to remember exactly what Chambles had said about the interval between Porter's arrival and the time of his death. "Chambles left the Roalf impersonator in the hallway and was gone for about an hour, from about 9:25 until 10:35 pm. He returned once for some supply he needed, saw two sets of footprints in the wet hallway, didn't see Roalf. When he finished the Administrative suite and returned again, the Roalf impersonator had not gotten much done on the floor, and made excuses about the newness of the equipment and the two individuals who tracked across the wet floor."

Jonathan picked up the brain-storming. "The individual claiming to be Roalf had just been added to the cleaning crew. The murder may have been planned for any evening that the victim returned and the Roalf character could break away long enough to kill him."

"But the person impersonating Roalf must have known the arrangements at the Institute fairly well to know to seek a job from Chambles, and to know the victim's habits," Genna injected.

"Someone at the Institute or someone who knew the Institute's procedures very well," Andrews acknowledged. "And knew Porter's history of experimentation with animals well enough to replicate the killing."

"What about Langston and McBroon?" Jonathan paused to pass over his spare napkin in response to Andrews' frantic hand motions when the sub sandwich he was eating fell apart. "Could they have been in it together?"

Andrews was momentarily occupied with mopping up his shirt from the spill of tuna, lettuce and tomato. It was Genna who responded to her mate's question. "Not unless Roalf was in it with them. Chambles indicated that

Roalf complained of two sets of tracks on his floor, the victim's and Langston's."

Andrews had finally salvaged his sandwich and his shirt. "I don't know if the two were involved in the killing. Certainly Langston couldn't have impersonated Roalf because the cleaning crew and the security crew saw the two individuals at roughly the same time the night of the murder. And the other suspects we've been considering. They lack alibis for the time of the murder, but do have alibis which preclude them impersonating Roalf. Which means," Andrews sounded very disgusted, "that I've got to start from the beginning and rework everything."

Descending dark brought an end to the outdoor meal but no resolution to the identification of the Roalf impersonator. Still, Andrews had to admit that by the time the six had returned to the car and to Heron's Rest, he was pleasantly full, relaxed and ready for a nice, quiet snooze in front of the television.

Genna left the men in the television room and took the three canines out into the yard for play and necessities despite Amber's eagerness to return to her puppy. Amber waited impatiently by the door to be allowed access to the house and to Rusty. Sky and Blacky ran and romped around the side yard, soaking up dirt and water from the rain-soaked ground until they exhausted their energy and returned to stand at the side door with Genna.

Once inside, the two Paps walked over to the rack of towels beside the washing machine, waiting patiently for Genna to pick them up one at the time and towel them dry. Blacky had to be caught at the door between the laundry room and the kitchen. The black dog submitted apprehensively to being enveloped in the big, fluffy expanse of cloth but seemed to enjoy it after it was over. Then Genna took Blacky and a reluctant Sky to join the two men in front of the television, while she and Amber returned to the nursery.

Little Rusty was sleeping soundly, but roused with the return of his dam. Genna picked up the tiny puppy and kissed his head as she marveled at the growing number of black dots which were quickly turning his pink nose, lips and paw pads from pink to black. "I think he sprouted several more black spots while we were gone, Amber."

Rusty squeaked softly in protest. After more than two hours without his dam, he made it plain that he was hungry and wanted only to eat. So Genna returned him to his dam, and removed water bottles and lamps from the area.

Before returning to her guest and husband, she made certain that the guest suite had fresh towels in case Andrews should choose to spend the night in Williamsburg.

Chapter 28

Thursday morning was beautiful. Andrews arose early and left for Richmond without awakening either Genna or Jonathan. He left a note saying only that he'd arranged an early morning conference with Foster.

Genna sat with eyes fixed on her computer screen. The frown on her face deepened the crease running vertically from the inner corner of her left eyebrow, giving her the look of a hawk about to swoop on prey. It was an appropriate picture, for the pieces she shuffled were summary notes of Kevin Andrew's investigation of the Porter homicide. She was too engrossed in the video screen in front of her to notice, but her growing excitement translated into audible muttering as the output from a complex computer program scrolled across her computer monitor.

She had assembled a reasonably clear picture of the crime and its perpetrator. The low, intense tone of her infrequent mumbles attracted the attention of the two dogs who had been napping quietly on the floor of her study. Sky raised his head, shifted his position, and returned to his nap. Blacky raised her head expectantly and fixed her soft brown eyes on the muttering figure. When the sounds continued at irregular intervals, Blacky stirred from her position on the sunlit rug and crossed to sit by Genna's chair.

"The simplest explanation which covers all the facts....." Genna whispered. Blacky nudged the dangling hand of the dark-haired woman in case an ear scratch might be in the offering, but Genna ignored the black canine. "So that's the when, the where and the who. And if my guess is right about the why...." Genna's verbalizations of her thoughts trailed off. Noticing Blacky's bid for attention finally, Genna gave the animal a brief pat on the head before returning both hands to the computer keyboard.

"I don't know that Uncle Kevin will ever believe the motive, Blacky. He's always saying that either greed or hate are behind most murders. And the murderer sure hates Porter. But will Uncle Kevin ever understand what prompted the hate?"

Blacky's tail wagged lazily at the sound of her name. But the succeeding minutes brought nothing but the click of computer keys, so the black dog returned to lie once more in the spot of sunlight on the study rug.

Genna fine-tuned her analysis program, refining variables and rerunning her intricate delineations on suspects, movements, and descriptive locations concerning the homicide, with no further verbalization of her thoughts. Finally she was satisfied that most of the points regarding Dr. Porter's death were covered and explained. All but one, in fact. Genna's fingers paused on the keyboard as she pondered the best way to obtain an answer to the remaining point.

Ask Uncle Kevin directly, and share with him her ideas about the solution to the case? The more Genna thought about the case, the less she wanted to do that. For starters, she didn't want to return the black dog that now begged for attention at her side.

She told herself that Andrews would never believe her solution without all the facts being explained. He'd find it difficult to understand the strong emotions which had prompted the murder.

Try to determine the answer herself? How much risk would there be?

The frown line splitting Genna's brow relaxed, and a lop-sided smile softened her face as she made up her mind regarding her next step. Her course of action decided, Genna filed her programs and data files before turning off her computer.

"Well, Blacky, shall we go and see for ourselves? Will you come along and protect me from the dragon?"

Blacky abandoned her sunny spot at the sound of Genna's voice, and returned to Genna's side. Genna turned her full attention to caressing the dog's silky ears. Sky quickly abandoned his pretext of sleeping and hurriedly pushed between Blacky and his mistress, insisting on getting his share of attention. Genna laughed at both dogs, briefly endeavoring to do justice impartially to each with her caresses, before rising from her desk chair.

"Come on, gang. Let's go get Mistress dressed. She has to check on a house in Richmond." Patting left hand against thigh, Genna called both dogs to follow her as she made preparations for a drive to the city in search of the final answer.

Genna stopped by the nursery long enough to check on Rusty and Amber, and interrupted Jonathan to tell him that she was taking Blacky out for some air. Her mate was too engrossed in his writing to consider the strangeness that Sky was not included in the outing.

No parking was available in front of the house. Genna finally found a parking space a block away and across the street. Leaving Blacky in a car on even this mild of a day was out of the question. The inquisitive woman arrived in front of the house with the excited and rambunctious canine straining on the lead.

From the sidewalk Genna examined for herself the scene which Kevin Andrews had described. Three steep steps led from the sidewalk to the level of the front and side yard, another four steps from the yard to the porch. A rustic fence defined the limits of a side yard to the left of the house and served as a backdrop for a dense display of iris plants which were not yet in bloom. A narrow gate closed off the remainder of the yard from view. Consistent with many of the houses in Richmond's Fan District, this one was almost touching the adjacent house on the right, leaving no room for yard or passage between the houses on that side. Genna scanned the left side yard and located a small circle of bricks in the corner marked by a small granite stone and brightened by an arrangement of cut azaleas in pinks and whites.

Genna considered her next move. She was very curious as to what, if anything, might be engraved on the granite stone, but could not decide on how best to get close enough to see. Blacky tugged on the leash, anxious to continue exploring along the street. Genna toyed briefly with the thought of boldly entering the property and looking over the grave, then using the excuse that she'd followed the black dog if confronted by any of the house's residents. She was spared the trouble. The front door opened and a large woman in a wheelchair rolled herself onto the porch.

Kevin Andrews had described the round-faced woman occupying the wheelchair several times to Genna, so the clever snoop had no trouble identifying the individual as Elizabeth Weir.

"Do you like flowers, young lady? The azaleas are especially beautiful this year, I think. All the rain we've had, I expect." The elderly woman's voice was light and friendly, but her shrewd gaze examined dog and younger woman carefully.

A tightening around the elderly woman's eyes was enough to convince Genna that Elizabeth Weir recognized Blacky. The animal's tenseness showed that Blacky also recognized the voice from the porch. Genna swiftly abandoned any thoughts of concealing the purpose of her visit. "It is not the flowers which interest me, but the site marked by the floral display which brought me here today," Genna stated frankly.

"It is rather nice. It marks the grave of my dog. Her name was Ginger", Elizabeth Weir responded pleasantly. "What's your dog's name?"

"I don't know what her name was before she ended up in the lab at the Institute. I've called her Blacky since the night my husband's godfather brought her to me. He's Lt. Kevin Andrews and is in charge of the Porter homicide investigation. I believe you've met him several times."

When the formless lump in the wheelchair did not respond, Genna proceeded. "Uncle Kevin has been carefully comparing movement of individuals connected with the case on the night of the murder. Most of them don't have tight alibis for the time of the murder."

"And he sent you to tell me this?" Weir smirked.

"Not exactly." Genna felt somehow that she owed the determined woman an explanation. "Late yesterday afternoon I watched a group of ducks leave tracks across a street in Williamsburg and it occurred to me that the only way the murderer could have left no tracks on the floor outside Porter's office that were not noted, was if the individual called Roalf had also been the murderer. And," Genna paused to add impact to her next statement, "the alibis of the other suspects do preclude them from having impersonated Roalf. Dr. Berkley's alibi the night of the murder was very thin, but he was at a dinner party with several witnesses on Wednesday, the evening you began your Roalf impersonation by handing an application to Chambles."

Elizabeth Weir's expression did not change. Cold eyes focused on the brash younger woman standing on the sidewalk in front of her house.

Genna asked softly, "Your dog isn't buried here, is she?"

The forced smile on the elderly face wavered briefly but remained in place. The smile did not reach the eyes in the bloated face, however. "What else would you expect to find in a grave?"

"A red collar with the symbol of Aries on it," Genna answered bluntly.

Elizabeth Weir laughed harshly and her sharp eyes locked with Genna's. Then she shrugged and dropped all pretense of a smile. Motioning toward her front door, she said, "Maybe you'd like to come inside and talk about this."

"No, I would not," Genna said. "I'm not certain it would be without risk."

The large block of human flesh in the wheelchair laughed disagreeably at that response. "Perhaps you're right. I take it you haven't told Lt. Andrews of your suspicions."

"No," Genna admitted, "but I left him a computer tape of my analysis just in case."

Genna allowed that point to germinate in the rotund woman's brain before continuing, "He mentioned talking with your son-in-law on the porch of this house. He didn't fully describe the house and yard, and until I came today to see I couldn't be certain whether it was accessible by wheelchair. I thought not, but I needed to be sure. Mr. Elkin said you'd created the little burial area yourself. That was weeks before the murder. It proves that you can and did get around without the wheelchair, since you must have done so to get to the area in the side yard."

The bulky figure in the chair wheeled herself close to the edge of the porch menacingly, but made no attempt to rise from her seated position. Nevertheless, Genna glanced nervously up and down the street for signs of activity in case she should need to call for help.

"Even if true, should I understand the significance of that fact?"

"I think we're both very well aware of the significance of that," Genna responded in a smooth tone at odds with the butterflies in her stomach. "You've always appeared in a wheelchair. That, and a healthy person's natural uneasiness at discussing health conditions with cancer victims, contributed to blinding Uncle Kevin to your possibility as a suspect. He's never seen you standing up, but the picture of you with your daughter and son-in-law showed you to be very tall. Uncle Kevin will think of that eventually. But he'll have another problem. He'll have trouble imagining that you had a motive for killing Dr. Porter. He's never owned or been owned by a dog."

Mrs. Weir stared stonily at the younger woman on the sidewalk below her. Then she nodded knowingly, saying, "You're a very brash young woman, and very sure of yourself. Just for amusement, I'd like to know why you think I'd want to kill Michael Porter."

"Kill? More like an execution. An eye for an eye. You killed him in a similar manner to his killing of your dog, Ginger," Genna responded. She watched Elizabeth Weir for a reaction, but the older woman maintained a poker-face.

Genna continued, "The nurse brought a red dog collar to little Danny Graft, meaning to cheer him with the thought of getting another dog. It didn't work as she'd intended. Instead it brought back unhappy memories of the dog that he'd lost and sent him into a crying fit. Everyone was so concerned with the child's emotional response and with the father's, that no one noticed what happened to the red collar."

Genna maintained eye contact with the obese figure seated on the porch above her. Her voice was low but firm as she retraced the critical path of the homicide trail, much as her computer analysis had displayed it on her screen. But Genna's nervousness was transmitted to the black canine, who repeatedly had to be restrained from attempts to drag her human friend away.

Elizabeth Weir neither moved closer nor made further attempts to interrupt. Indeed, her face seemed to soften slightly and one corner of her mouth turned up in a slight smile...or sneer. Genna couldn't decide which, but felt compelled to continue.

"The witnesses mentioned that Danny and his father were visiting with other patients, but no attempt was made to identify them. It didn't seem important after Uncle Kevin identified Paul Graft. But you were present. You recognized the collar as the one you'd given Ginger, the one which matched a watch band given to your son-in-law signifying the birthday the two shared. You slipped the collar into a pocket or your purse while everyone was busy trying to calm Danny Graft. And you brought the collar home and buried it as the only thing left of your beloved Ginger."

The elder woman's eyes seem to lose focus, and she took up the tale without pretense or false protestations of innocence now. "I asked around and found that Porter had used the dog in an experiment.

Markley McBroon was very concerned about Porter's experimentation. Without knowing it, she gave me all the information I needed. I found that he bought dogs from anyone who would bring them to the hospital. He knew many of the dogs were stolen. Several of the people around the Institute, including Markley, complained to him about the practice in fact. He just didn't care. He wanted cheep victims for his research papers, just to promote more grants and more money for himself. He didn't care about the animals' suffering or the owners' grief." As though exhausted by the admission, the blob of flesh slumped deeper into her chair and Elizabeth Weir's voice trailed off into silence.

Genna couldn't help but feel for the woman. Despite knowing what she had done, Genna understood the passionate love for an animal that would fuel such an intense hate. "You were very ingenious in your preparations for revenge on Porter."

"You think so? Yes, I thought it was well planned," the elderly woman brightened visibly at this dubious compliment. "I knew the security setup at the hospital, knew that I'd need a way to get inside in the evenings. The cleaning crew seemed like the best bet."

"It didn't take too much effort," Mrs. Weir continued, "to persuade Roalf to apply for a maintenance position with the hospital. Sort of like whistling when you pass a graveyard. It was a joke between us. We made up a lot of the stuff. Roalf thought it was all in fun. He knew he'd never leave the hospital."

"And I suppose you lifted his social security card after he died?" Genna knew logically that this had to have happened, but could not find such an event supported by any of the information discussed by Kevin Andrews.

"Oh, no," Elizabeth corrected, "right after he filled out the application. He never intended to mail the thing, of course. It was just a joke between us. But I took it, along with his license and social security card. Told him I was putting them back in the drawer of the table beside his hospital bed. He never looked for them. Didn't realize I'd taken the stuff. He died a short time later."

"Didn't someone ask about the missing identifications?" Genna was fairly certain she knew the answer, but she needed to keep the other woman talking if possible.

"Oh, no. Roalf had no family, and the hospital was too busy getting him out and a new patient in to worry about what might or might not have been in the drawer of his nightstand," Elizabeth corrected. "His attorney might try to find them, now that he's returned from his trip, but he won't know where to look."

"Lucky for you, an opening with the cleaning crew occurred during the time your daughter and son-in-law were away," Genna interjected. "Otherwise, you'd have found it difficult to explain your absence from home long enough to establish the Roalf persona and carry out the homicide."

"Luck had nothing to do with it, my dear." The mass of fat in the chair chuckled in self-appreciation before continuing. "It cost me nearly a thousand in savings to set up that phony win for Hooke to get her out of the way at the right time."

Genna nodded appreciatively. She'd suspected as much, but it was satisfying to have another of her points confirmed.

"I'm surprised that you had the strength to carry off the role of Roalf, even for the single night you worked, especially the one night you were there most of the evening," Genna probed lightly hoping for more information from Mrs. Weir.

"I've worked most of my life. I'm not small or weak," Elizabeth Weir responded proudly. "The doctors said I had another six months. A little thing like cancer wasn't going to prevent my doing what I needed to do." The thick figure in the chair seem to gain height slightly as Elizabeth Weir drew herself up straighter in self-appreciation. "But I was busy dealing with Mr. Dog-killer Porter for some of the time that Thursday evening, and

I really didn't care whether that hall got cleaned and waxed," the elder woman admitted.

Genna guessed this last was in reference to the reprimand from Chambles regarding the unsatisfactory waxing job done on the hall floor outside the murder victim's office.

"I'm still curious what you used to subdue Dr. Porter. I mean, after he was trussed up in that animal restraint device, it was relatively easy to pour the drain cleaner down his mouth, but how did you get him quiet and into the device. Uncle Kevin said the lab boys found no sign of a blunt weapon in the lab?"

"Easy as could be, my dear," the block of a woman replied. "Just a lot of dry cleaner in my sock. Works just as good as sand. And of course, as arrogant as Porter was, he'd never dream that a lowly laborer would be a threat, so he turned his back on me after cursing me out for daring to enter his lab. It never occurred to the great man that I hadn't done so by mistake."

Genna nodded understandingly. "So all the crime lab results showed were signs of a blow to the head, traces of cleaning material which were an expected substance to find in the lab."

"And I returned the sock to my foot and wore it out of the lab," Elizabeth Weir gloated, "with no one the wiser." Then her eyes focused on the sleek, black canine who had finally settled into a sitting position in front of Genna. "That one was new to the lab, I guess. Anyway she wasn't as nervous or as troubled by what was happening to Porter as the smaller grey dog. Do you know what happened to her, the little grey dog?"

"She was a he. He was identified by the tattoo on his stomach and his owners located. His name is Mushie and his owners drove down from Pennsylvania and reclaimed him the Saturday morning after Porter's death."

Elizabeth Weir nodded, a look of calm acceptance on her face now. "So I suppose that finishes it. You'll tell your Lt. Andrews, and he can close this investigation. But," the old lady said with a spark of her old bravado, "I'm not sorry about any part of it, except that you found me out. Not that I mind what happens to me. I don't have that much longer to live anyway. But since this case is finished, I suppose that black lovely will be returned to the research institute. Frankly, Porter wasn't worth the life of one dog like my Ginger. Now bringing the law down on me will cost another beautiful animal her life."

"Not in my lifetime," Genna responded, her stubborn jaw set firmly on that promise.

"I'm tired," Elizabeth continued. "You do what you must. I'll be here. I'm not going anywhere," she said as she wheeled her chair and reentered her home.

Genna stared at the empty porch and doorway long after the figure of the obese woman had disappeared inside. Finally, she turned and made her way back to her parked car, a relieved and bouncy Blacky frolicking in front of her as she walked. "She's wrong about that last, Blacky. You'll stay with me until you die of old age, one way or another. I'll make certain of that. If I rearrange the pieces of this puzzle and lay them out for Uncle Kevin, he has only to dig in that sad little monument to find the collar. And then, I suppose, he will think there are no further reasons for me to keep you."

A young woman in walking shoes and an exercise suit, passing Genna's car as Genna was loading Blacky into the front seat, overheard her say to the dog, "And just why should I help Uncle Kevin solve this puzzle. After all, he told me he didn't want any help?"

On the drive back to Williamsburg and home, Genna continued her conversation with Blacky. "He's smart. He didn't get to be a homicide detective by missing much. But don't worry. Blackmail or bribery or just plain dog napping! Whatever it takes, you have a home at Heron's Rest for the remainder of your life.

By the poker game on Saturday night, both Andrews and Braxton Brown were in need of relaxation. Andrews had collected another homicide case without feeling any closer to solving the Porter killing. Braxton had a new double homicide added to his case load along with the frustration of seeing an earlier suspect released on a technicality. Foster and Billy were trying to keep the beer and food flowing.

Andrews paused overly long on deciding on his discard. Braxton injected an innocent query. "Any further progress on that Porter killing?"

"Nothing," Andrews mumbled. He finally decided on his discards and tossed aside two cards, retaining a pair of kings and an ace before continuing with the conversation.

"Haven't turned up a thing in all our questioning and prodding since Wednesday evening. Except for one funny thing." He let that tantalize the three card sharks that sat around the table with him. Foster looked slightly puzzled. Billy was inscrutable as usual.

Braxton allowed a look of curiosity to cross his handsome face as he dealt replacement cards to the other three. "And just what would that be."

"I figure Foster and I have missed the significance of something we've turned up in the past weeks. Genna has stopped asking questions about every little step of the investigation. And when she does that, she's on to something. Can't for the life of me figure what it is though."

And for the moment the chunky detective ceased to worry about it, because Braxton has just dealt him an ace and a king as replacements for his two discards!

Coming in December 1999
Pawprints on My Heart

The following preview is one of the many short stories about Papillons contained in the forthcoming book from Astra Publishers.

The Papillon, or butterfly dog, is noted for its beauty, intelligence, and affectionate companionship. The breed's intelligence goes far beyond learning and following commands. As all who have ever fallen under the spell of these toy dogs know, these little fur people think for themselves. When death or hardship infrequently result in an older Papillon losing its original owner, national and regional rescue groups swing into action to provide a new home. This is the story of one twelve-year-old rescue, the very special lady who adopted her, and the hauntingly beautiful poem written in her memory.

Available at your local bookstore or from the publisher: For information, write to:
Astra Publishers
209 Matoaka Court
Williamsburg, VA 23185-2810   USA

Requiem for a Rescue
by Phyllis Harwood

I didn't start out to adopt an old dog. Certainly, I didn't plan to give my heart to a twelve-year old. Some of life's finest gifts just seem to happen in spite of our planning, however. And so it was when I adopted an elderly Papillon named Miss BeBe just short of her thirteenth birthday. Through our three years together I learned a great deal about Papillons: their assertiveness and courage, the needs and habits of an elderly dog, and the steadfast love that is a part of every canine but especially obvious with this little rescue. Most of all she taught me the meaning of holding fast to a dream.

Our story, BeBe's and mine, began as stories often do, with sad loses in both our lives. Her mistress got a new job, a new apartment, and didn't want BeBe any more. I lost my dearest fuzzy face Doc, the last in a long line of dachshunds.

I'd shared my life with long-haired dachshunds for almost 30 straight years. After Doc's death, I just needed to grieve. My resolve to go without another companion lasted about a month. Then I decided to get a repair kit for the big hole in my heart.

I expanded my search for a new companion to include a Papillon, since I had seen a papillon puppy at a dog show. The tiny face with big ears intrigued me, as did the descriptions of the breed I'd unearthed in my reading. I planned to search for a dachshund puppy, or a papillon puppy or a shelter dog, and start a new relationship with whichever one I located first that seemed to click with me.

I started checking newspaper ads, found a few for doxies, but none for paps. Undeterred, I pursued my quest with calls to vets, and the local kennel club secretary. My persistence was finally rewarded by contact with a Papillon breeder who invited me over for a visit to meet her pack. There was even a young male that was available for adoption.

I was so excited. Meeting a large group of papillons in their own home was a delight. They ranged in age from 10 months to 14 years, and I was especially taken with one 12-year-old female named Fallon. She seemed to be the official hostess of the house. I would swear, if I did such, that Fallon gently climbed on the sofa beside me to inquire if I'd like one lump of sugar or two in my tea. The breeder smiled at my infatuation with the elderly canine hostess, saying that all visitors fell in love with that particular champion. I was distressed to discover that I did not seem to click with Fallon's great-grandson, however, the young male that was looking for a home. He wasn't a puppy and was far more independent than I wanted.

I returned home to think, or more accurately, to brood about the whole matter. I talked to myself, my daughter, my vet and anyone else with ears. I was so unhappy. With the wisdom and straight thinking of youth, my daughter finally advised me, "If you don't click, you don't click. There are other dogs, so call the breeder back and tell her you aren't interested in the young male." So I did. I was grateful that I got a recording. I didn't have to talk to the breeder and just left a message. I was certain the breeder would be upset about a lost sale and I'd never hear from her again. How wrong I was!

In a few days, the breeder called to say she understood and agreed with my assessment that the young male was not right for me. But, she asked, would I consider giving an elderly rescue a home.

She explained that she knew little about the rescue , who she said was called Miss BeBe. The vet who had attended her since puppyhood had refused to euthanize her when requested to do so. At the vet's request, the owner agreed to sign over the old dog and let the vet find her a new home. The vet had placed Miss BeBe in one home, which didn't work out well because of a young child. Next, he'd tried to locate a Papillon rescue group. One of his patients put him in touch with the breeder I'd visited in Williamsburg, and she offered to give Miss BeBe a home for the remainder of her life.

I was cautioned that little was known about the aging little papillon, except that she was in good health for a dog nearing thirteen. When my husband found out how old she was he asked if I wanted him to go ahead and dig a hole for her in our pet cemetery out back of our home. He figured she wouldn't last long. But I had read that Papillons often live to 16 years of age, and my heart ached for this little oldie even though I'd never met her. I thought about it for a full twenty-four hours before calling back to say I'd like to meet Miss BeBe. And on July 5, 1996 I went back to Williamsburg to meet her in person.

I cried when I saw her drooling, sad face. As I held this soft, bony, forlorn little lady dog in my arms, I knew it was a pairing meant to be. I promised her that only death would part us from each other -- no more strange people, although I'm sure she thought us strange, and no other strange new homes.

In the months and years that followed, BeBe allowed me into her life, but only on the edge, never near the preciously guarded center. That center belonged to the one she loved best, the one for whom she always waited and looked for to the end of her days.

I had her about five months before she showed any interest in me. She tolerated my care and affection, but would then sashay off to another room. I kept the phone line busy talking to the breeder who'd placed BeBe in my care. 'What was I doing wrong? What else could I do?" From BeBe there were no kisses, no cuddles, no affection, just tolerance, and not well hidden at that!

By now, the mutual concern for this unhappy little waif had drawn the breeder and me together and cemented a warm and lasting friendship. She had become simply my friend Jean. We spent long hours sharing many things including Papillons. We struggled to try and refocus our way of thinking to view the world through this little lady dog's eyes. I was coming to realize that to BeBe, the vet had simply misplaced her, failing to return her to the owner she loved as he had done all the previous times in her life. And so she tolerated me as her caregiver while waiting, hoping that every hour and visitor to our door would be her beloved mistress, coming to take her to her old home.

In desperation, Jean sent over a young puppy, Princess, as a friend for Miss BeBe, and as competition for food and affection. The new arrival stimulated a little more interest in food, but little jealousy for attention.

However a bit of thaw occurred just before Princess arrived. BeBe scratched me on the ankle with her paw, her first sign in five months that she knew I existed. It was a brief but welcomed sign. I loved her head, and she went off into the other room.

I fixed baskets, blankets, and coats for BeBe, my little old lady, to keep her comfortable and warm and because it just seemed like the thing to do for such a dignified lady. She thought little of the coats, but seemed to realize that they kept her warm, so she put up with them. After Princess came to join our group, the coats were a convenient handle by which Princess attempted to pull BeBe around or entice her to play.

BeBe slept with me almost from the day she came into my home. Sometimes, accidentally I'm sure, she snuggled close, but more often she stayed as far away as it was possible to get in a twin size bed. She let me know her needs. I often got long stares from her when it was time for her to go to bed and I was reading. After a few stares, however, she would give up and go to lie in one of her conveniently placed fancy pink baskets to wait for me to take her into the bedroom and on to the bed.

Val, another of Jean's children, joined us in May of 1997. Val and Princess were the constant shadows and attention-demanding companions for which the breed is famous. Now my progress around the house featured a parade of three papillons, but BeBe always brought up the rear and was never really interested in any of us.

Despite the temporary nature in which BeBe regarded her living arrangements, she nonetheless established her feeding requirements very early in our association. "Commercial dog food is for dogs" was her motto, and she obviously did not consider herself a dog! She loved meat sauce served with mashed spaghetti. Her second choice was raw or cooked, finely chopped beef. Other acceptable food offerings were macaroni & cheese [mashed if you please], finely broken McDonald's cheese burgers [hold the pickle and the bread please], and finely chopped chicken or turkey.

She preferred to sleep late -- and undisturbed! On days when I volunteered or needed to go out before 10 am, she was offered food at 6am which she rarely ate. Her other three daily feedings, at 2pm, 6pm and again at 11pm, were treated with patience, restraint or just ignored depending on the whims of the moment and her ranking of importance of the food offering. After Princess and Val came to live with us, BeBe's dishes had to be carefully protected for the glutinous interest of the two younger paps. But she didn't seem to care whether the two stole her food or not.

For the first few months after BeBe came to live with me, she'd go and come between the house and fenced-in yard by herself, returning from outside to frisk around with her butt in the air, and her front paws stretched out in front as if inviting someone to play. Sometimes she even held her tail up a little, but not for long, and she never curled it over her back.

As the months turned into years, age took it toll. For the last six months or so of her life, her mainstay was baby food, veal and turkey being her favorites. Any tasty treat I could offer, I did, but they were rarely acceptable. I carried her up and down the steps between the house and her small yard for many months before her death. In March of 1999, she went in for her annual immunization and check. I was told that her lungs sounded like a many-year, many-pack-a-day smoker. My vet said little more, except the vague instruction to take her home and love her -- which I did, had been doing and would always do.

If my friend Jean read anything more into my vet's cryptic message, she did not say. She often brought her aging sixteen-year-old Mischief over to visit. We would gossip while Princess and Val jumped around and played, begging to be scratched, petted, noticed. Mischief would sit quietly, on or touching Jean at all times and grumbling whenever the two young Paps came near his mistress. BeBe checked the incoming visitors to see if her long lost owner had come and retreated to one of her baskets and ignored us thereafter.

BeBe waited patiently and quietly through all our months and years together for the old mistress who never came. She whined, a low hoarse noise, only a few times in her life with me, and that when she slipped down the blanket to the floor at the foot of the bed. Mostly BeBe was silent, very silent, waiting and listening.

Then two days before her death, she had two seizures, one each day. She made a rapid, hoarse bark at the beginning of each seizure. I was not overly fearful. Jean's Mischief had been on preventative for seizures for the previous eight months, so I took BeBe to my vet expecting to be given medication to control her seizures.

Instead, my vet gave me the distressing news that BeBe had only a few days at most to live, that she was drowning in her own fluid. Through tears, I chose to let her go as peacefully as possible since there was no hope of recovery, no future except to struggle for breath.

Two weeks after her death, I started writing the poem which follows. I miss BeBe. She was a stately, little lady dog. I always hoped for a breakthrough in our relationship, but our best effort was just friends. BeBe was ever true to her original human. I always hoped somehow she would see her human again. Maybe she will.......over the Rainbow Bridge.

Miss BeBe's Refrain
August 11, 1983 - May 22, 1999

I am confused, so sad, forlorn.
As first I met you on that morn.
With tearfilled eyes, you softly said,
"We'll be together, till one is dead."

253

So it began, our journey strange.
You did your best to ease my pain.
As months and then the years went by
You seemed to know my silent cry.
You're just not HER. Oh, can't you see,
I know she's coming back for me.
She's coming back and I must go.
She is my human, don't you know.
She'll pick me up with eyes aglow,
And scratch behind my ears just so.
And tell me lovingly and great
Just how she kept my dish and plate
For my return to her dear care.
She's coming back, my love to share.
But I'll abide with you awhile,
Just don't expect my eyes to smile.
No happy tail or loving rub
Or playful time in the bubble tub.
I guess I'll let you love my head,
Because I do enjoy your bed.
I even snuggle when it's cold.
I guess it's 'cause I'm getting old.
Those coats you make are hard to take,
But my hair is thin and I do quake.
The food is pretty good as well.
With these three teeth I can't quite tell!
She's coming back and I must go.
I can't relax. I miss HER so.
I search in every room and place,
And yet I can not find a trace.
My eyes are dim, my hearing's bad.
She holds my heart and I'm so sad.
Oh, please come quickly, so I can go
To be with you in a place I know.
The Vet says it is time to go.
I feel so bad; my breathing's slow.
But wait....I must press on you see
I know she's coming back for me.
The end has come and YOU'RE with me.
Oh, where, oh, where, can my lady be?
Your eyes are wet, your voice is soft.
"I love you, BeBe," as I drift off.
The Rainbow Bridge is where I'll be.
I know she's coming there for me.

To BeBe, my little rescue who lived with me and my family for almost 3 years. She was ever loyal to her original owner of approximately 12 years. I truly hope BeBe's human will meet her at the Rainbow Bridge.
Phyllis Harwood, June 6, 1999

Paw Prints Through The Years
by Jean C. Keating
art by Beverly Abbott

When divorce shatters a nineteen year marriage, the author buys a show dog to have a hobby she can enjoy as a single. The resulting lover affair with a bright, active little Papillon leads to more and more papillons. The ensuing years are full and funny as a multitude of papillons are joined by strays and two abandoned kittens to bring entertainment and purpose into her life. In a testament to the power of positive thinking and the strength of belonging that animal companions provide, the author shares the joys of a life enriched by laughter and love. The animal companions ease the hardships of dealing with an Alzheimer stricken parent, as well as the routine bumps of life. Through two decades and six generations of her canine family, the author's adventures take her from the beginning steps of showing her first purebred Papillon to the elegance and prestige of the Westminster Kennel Club show.

Beneath the affectionate story of sharing a life with animals, the philosophy of living one day at the time with hope gives this book an uplifting message of happiness. The author's voice alternates with whimsical holiday letters from the dogs in which the canine perspective on life is presented. The author's months of dieting are reduced to humor as one of the dog's comments in a letter to friends that "it does limit the quality of handouts around here. Are they still making steak, or is chicken the only meat left in the world?"

Hardback: $28.00   **ISBN 0-9674016-3-1**

The following chapter from Paw Prints Through The Years is reprinted here for your review and enjoyment.

Happiness Is A Dog Named Vinnie

I don't know about other women's intuition, but mine was nonexistent on that long-ago morning. I had no hint, no tingle of a notion that the events of that day would bring such a change in my life.

It certainly needed changing. The emotional severance of divorce was bad enough. The daunting task of splitting property and possessions acquired over 19 years of marriage had exceeded my abilities to cope. I was deep in my own private pity party, convinced that I was the only one who'd ever been hurt by such a tragedy. I finally consented to go with my friend to a dog show in Virginia Beach only because she just wouldn't take no for an answer.

Even while I vowed I would never depend on another human being for the rest of my life and never enter into the joint ownership of anything, some appreciation for the importance of a friend remained. So I dragged myself to the show, but stubbornly promised myself I wouldn't enjoy it.

Fate, with perhaps a helping hand from my guardian angel, decreed otherwise. 'Across a crowded room'—in this case the floor of the indoor dog show in Norfolk—I spotted HIM. Soft, expressive brown eyes that held a mixture of intelligence, compassion and bubbling mischief locked with mine. HE didn't seem to mind that I was frowning and stumbling along. He cocked his head and nodded in my direction, seeming to invite me to come closer. Captivated, I stepped on one woman's toes and fell over a gentle mastiff headed for another ring.

Long black-and-brown fringes softened large ears that rotated like radar dishes at the sound of my greeting. A wide white nose band and blaze added dazzling brilliance to his flashing eyes as he lifted first one dainty front foot and then another from the lap of the man who held him, dancing his happiness at life. A long white plume of a tail fanned his human's face and moved the entire rear end of his body with its energetic greeting. I had seen a lot of dogs wag their tails. That was a first for seeing one wag his ears also. And what large beautiful ears they were! I forgot I was mad at the world. All I could see, feel, think about at that moment was the deliriously happy and beautifully expressive bundle of silken fur that charged the space around him with positive energy.

Such was my first meeting with a papillon. In French, the name means butterfly. That morning the large erect ears and trailing fringes of this little charmer fanned the air with all the grace, beauty and lightness of the delicate and colorful insects for which the breed was named.

I managed to learn his name was Vinnie before his amused human excused himself to take the little bundle of happiness into the ring. I grabbed the vacated chair at ringside to watch my newest interest show off.

The indoor dog show was noisy. It wasn't the twelve hundred or so dogs that created the din, it was the more than twelve hundred people there. Vinnie didn't seem to mind the noise in spite of his keen hearing. When his human put him on the floor, he circled and danced on dainty feet, following his human into the exhibition ring. His little white paws seemed to glide effortlessly across the black mat which formed a border and a diagonal pattern on the ring floor. When not moving he would stand with feet planted, tail constantly in motion, and head, ears, and eyes *talking* with his human or the judge. His entire body proclaimed his joy at doing what he was doing and in being alive.

Even in the protected environment of a dog show ring, accidents can happen. And one did that day. As the group of dogs and handlers paraded around the ring, the human behind Vinnie stumbled on the mat. She fell forward and nearly stepped on him. With cat-quick reflexes and strong patellas, the little athlete leaped up and away from the danger. My most enduring and delightful memory of this beautiful dog was that of an airborne aerialist. All four feet and body were in the air, hair fluffed out by the wind currents around him as his trajectory carried him up, over and down again to the mat. He quickly recovered himself and continued the smooth forward gait of his performance.

I was too ignorant of show procedures at that time to know whether he won or not. I know that I would have given him all the ribbons.

By the time Vinnie and his human finished their performance and returned to their ringside chair, I had already decided that I wanted a papillon. I managed to overcome my fascination with that little bundle of energy long enough to obtain a business card that told me how to contact Vinnie's breeders and to learn that his other, longer name was Debonair Calvin Klein.

I didn't give his owner/handler/breeder long enough to return home before I was talking to his wife on the phone about a papillon for my very own.

I left the show in a far different frame of mind. One tiny bundle of flashing white and mahogany showed me the way

258

Happiness Is A Dog Named Vinnie

It was time to let go of an old life and 'reach for the stars.' Suddenly the chore of property settlements was just a job to be assessed and completed. My focus was on a new life and love.

In time Vinnie's half sister, my beloved Maaca, would come to share my life and be my first show dog and champion. Vinnie's daughter Fallon would follow a few years later. Together these two relations of Vinnie would be the foundation of a clan which over the years would come to be known as the butterflies of Astra [Latin for star]. For more than twenty years these two and their descendants have brought warmth, love, laughter and happiness into every moment of my life.

There is a wise axiom that 'happiness is a choice'. Vinnie obviously chose to enjoy life, the scene around him that day, and to warmly draw all about him into his web of excitement.

I think dogs were sent by God to teach us to make the most of each day. I'm glad I took the hint.

Jean C. Keating

Books are available from

Astra Publishers

209 Matoaka Court
Williamsburg, VA 23185
www.Astrapublishers.com

Free shipping and handling is available on all orders totaling more than $25.00. Discounts are available to book stores, animal welfare organizations and clubs. Contact the publisher at info@astrapublishers.com for further information.